Like a Lion He Prowls is a p
exceptional storytelling, meaningful allegory and direct, compelling biblical teaching. You won't be able to put it down and yet much of it deserves, and even requires, time for prayer and reflection. This book is a treasure trove of beautiful language, pithy precise phrases, charming and illuminating allegory, personal reflection and spiritual challenge. I can't wait until I hold my own copy in my hands! There is so much I want to underline and highlight and some notes I want to jot in the margin. It is a book I fully interacted with.
—*Shannon Shearer, MDiv,*
Pastor of Youth and Family Ministry

I *thoroughly* enjoyed this book. It was engaging and well-written and something quite different and unique. I keep thinking about it, so it really had an impact on me.
—*Sara Davison, Author of the romantic*
suspense series The Seven Trilogy

The author's heartfelt desire to please God and encourage the reader is woven consistently from the dedication to the final words. In just one reading, I learned much about myself and how easily I have innocently—and maybe not so innocently—fallen victim to the evil one's ploys. *Like a Lion He Prowls* is the most perfect of perfect titles for this book.
—*Ruth Waring, Author of* Come Find Me,
Then Came a Hush *and* Harvest of Lies

What a delight it has been to read *Like a Lion He Prowls*. The author's mastery of language combined with an incredible story and some surprise inclusions all contribute to its wonderful success. I found myself reading and rereading its instructive offerings. So fascinating! So captivating! So instructive!
—*Garry Schubert, Retired Educator*
and Praise & Worship Leader

This book really got me thinking and evaluating things in my life. The story was gripping, the devotionals thought provoking and the work pages, along with the appendices, helpful. What a privilege it was to read this book.
—*Esther Wyngaarden, Educator*

Like a Lion He Prowls is a book that intrigued me and spoke to the deepest recesses of my heart. It challenged me to persevere along the Christian journey despite the many ups and downs. I could read this book many times over and it would still speak volumes to my heart. I will recommend this book to others.
—*Patricia J. Kimmerly, Avid Reader*

LIKE A LION HE PROWLS
Copyright © 2017 by Katherine J. Le Gresley

All rights reserved. Neither this publication nor any part of this publication may be reproduced or transmitted in any form or by any means, electronic or mechanical, including photocopying, recording or any information storage and retrieval system, without permission in writing from the author.

The allegory contained in this book is, in part, a work of fiction. Names, characters, places and incidents either are the product of the author's imagination or are used fictitiously, and any resemblance to actual persons, living or dead, businesses, companies, events, or locales is entirely coincidental.

Unless otherwise indicated, all Scripture quotations are taken from the Holy Bible, New Living Translation, copyright © 1996, 2004, 2007, 2013 by Tyndale House Foundation. Used by permission of Tyndale House Publishers, Inc., Carol Stream, Illinois 60188. All rights reserved. • Scripture quotations marked (NIV) are taken from the Holy Bible, New International Version®, NIV®. Copyright © 1973, 1978, 1984, 2011 by Biblica, Inc.™ Used by permission of Zondervan. All rights reserved worldwide. www.zondervan.com The "NIV" and "New International Version" are trademarks registered in the United States Patent and Trademark Office by Biblica, Inc.™ • Scripture quotations marked (NRSV) are taken from the New Revised Standard Version Bible, copyright © 1989 the Division of Christian Education of the National Council of the Churches of Christ in the United States of America. Used by permission. All rights reserved. • Scripture quotations marked (KJV) are taken from the King James Version, Public Domain

Printed in Canada

ISBN: 978-1-4866-1420-2

Word Alive Press
131 Cordite Road, Winnipeg, MB R3W 1S1
www.wordalivepress.ca

Library and Archives Canada Cataloguing in Publication

Le Gresley, Katherine J., author
  Like a lion, he prowls : an illuminating look at the battle plan of the adversary / Katherine J. Le Gresley.

Issued in print and electronic formats.
ISBN 978-1-4866-1420-2 (softcover).--ISBN 978-1-4866-1421-9 (eBook)

  1. Christian fiction, Canadian (English). I. Title.
PS8623.E4674L54 2017   C813'.6   C2016-907521-4
                                        C2016-907522-2

LIKE A LION
He Prowls

An Illuminating

Look at the Battle Plan

of the Adversary

GEN. 14:19 b

"Blessed be [you, Dear Doris] by God Most High, Creator of heaven + earth.
And blessed be God Most High who has defeated your enemies for you."

Katherine
aka your not-so-
secret Pal :)
PS. 3:3

Katherine J. Le Gresley

This book is dedicated to all of our Father's children
and to our beloved Emmanuel.
In Him we are victorious.
How great is the love our Father lavishes upon us.

Psalm 124:6-8
"Praise the Lord, who did not let their teeth tear us apart!
We escaped like a bird from a hunter's trap.
The trap is broken, and we are free!
Our help is from the Lord, who made heaven and earth."

The traps laid for us are everywhere; they are an unavoidable part of life in this fallen world. The adversary delights in setting the bait and watching the jaws of his carefully laid snares snap the life out of his prey. He savours the bondage, the pain, the misery, and rejoices in his triumph as the life seeps from those he seeks to destroy. Yet, as the psalmist reminds us, we have escaped his traps. They are broken, and we are free. God Himself has shattered the snares of the evil one and loosed His children for Himself. We need never be ensnared again. Hallelujah!

ACKNOWLEDGEMENTS xi

part i
PRISONERS OF WAR 1

CHAPTER 1: A PEOPLE AT WAR 11
  Is Satan Really at Work in the World Today?

part ii
THE BATTLE PLAN OF THE EVIL ONE 21

CHAPTER 2: LIKE A LION HE PROWLS 26

CHAPTER 3: THE ARSENAL OF THE ADVERSARY 31
  Deception: The Plight of the Fledgling Butterfly
  Seduction: The Folly of the Sleeping Swan
  Fear: The Falcon's Downfall
  Busyness: The Beaver's Obsession
  Reason: The Raven's Debate
  Pride: The Arrogance of the Elk
  Ignorance: The Fish's Folly
  Compromise: The Seagull's Decision
  Accusation: The Curse of the Ravenous Mountain Lion
  Conformity: The Error of the Geese
  Complacency: The Otter's Indifference
  Indulgence: The Insatiable Thirst of the Wolf
  Entitlement: The Petulance of the Selfish Otter
  Self-Sufficiency: The Bane of the Elegant Swan
  Discord: The Puffin's Fury
  Forgetfulness: The Bear's Downfall
  Confrontation: The Dilemma of the Cornered Raccoon
  Distraction: The Confusion of the Loon

CHAPTER 4: ANALYSING THE ATTACK 64

part iii
HE HAS NOT LEFT US DEFENCELESS 93

CHAPTER 5: VICTORY IS ASSURED–GOD *IS* IN CONTROL 99
    Victory is Assured

CHAPTER 6: ARMED FOR BATTLE 107
    The Armour of God

CHAPTER 7: RESTING IN THE PRESENCE OF OUR LORD 112
    The Gift of the Sabbath

CHAPTER 8: RESISTANCE IS NOT FUTILE 115
    Resistance: The Victory of the Lowly Kingfisher

CHAPTER 9: A PLAN OF RESISTANCE 120
    Keys to Resistance

part iv
WE BELONG TO HIM 131

A SONG OF JOY 197

APPENDICES 199
APPENDIX A: PRACTICAL IDEAS FOR CELEBRATING THE SABBATH
APPENDIX B: MEMORY BEADS
APPENDIX C: COME AWAY

ACKNOWLEDGEMENTS

When I dreamt as a child that I would one day write a book, I admit, I never actually believed that my dream would come true. And it wouldn't have. Not without the help and encouragement of so many people along the way. People like my family—my parents, my sisters, my nieces and nephews, my aunt—who bore with my first attempts, applauding my efforts and urging me to press on. You have always been, and will no doubt always be, my most appreciative audience. I would especially like to thank my parents for their amazing support. You were the ones who removed my final excuse for not pursuing my writing dreams by sending me to my first writers' conference just over ten years ago. Without you, my childhood fantasy would never have come to fruition. The book you hold before you is a testament to your faith in me and the best thanks I could possibly offer.

My friends in the writing world have also played a big role in furthering my dreams. Les, while you probably don't remember me, your sound teaching and good advice gave me the tools I needed to write the words entrusted to me. It was in your class that all the strands came together and the vision for this book unfolded. Thank you for taking the time to share your expertise and taking an interest in helping a newbie to find her way. Sara, your tireless editing and attention to detail have done much to help polish this work. I learned so much from working with you and hope to be able to do so again on my next project. When I grow up, I want to be an editor just like you! And Ruth, what words can express my gratitude for your encouragement and aid along the way? Truly, this book would not have been birthed without you. It's been a long journey, but each time I came close to giving up and setting it aside, you were there, encouraging me and prodding me forward. Your listening ears and strong shoulders have buoyed me along and given me courage to follow in your footsteps. I've learned a lot from you. You are a friend beyond compare; I never cease to thank God for bringing us together.

And then there are my friends at Heritage—Esther, Grant, Garry, Milly, Evelyn and so many others across the years whom I couldn't possibly begin to name. You've served as my sounding boards, my guinea pigs, my cheerleaders. Thank you for allowing me the privilege of sharing with you my writing. You were the first people to whom I dared to admit that I am a writer, and you fell for it! Well surprise, surprise folks: I really *was* writing a book!

Finally, and most importantly, I acknowledge the Sower of Stories, the Giver of Words, the Revealer of Truths—my Saviour, my Peace and my Joy. To Him alone does the real credit belong for the book that you hold in your hands. May He bless it and use it to touch the lives of His children as we journey back to the Father who sent Him to carry us home. Truly, He is both King of Life and King of Love. I can hardly wait to see what happens next!

part i

PRISONERS OF WAR

A melancholy smile creased the face of the king as he strode toward the entrance of the great garden paradise his children called home. The afternoon sun beat upon his shoulders and he quickened his pace, mindful of the ever-lengthening shadows stealing across the path. His children would be wondering where he had gotten to.

Resting a work-worn hand upon the carefully laid stones of the gatepost, he paused to wipe the sweat from his brow and enjoy the cooling breeze that stirred in the meadow. He closed his eyes and tilted his head toward the heavens, inhaling the earthy, flower-laden fragrance that filled the air. There was nowhere on earth more glorious, no place he would rather be.

Savouring the moment, the king let the air rush from his lungs and opened his eyes to behold the view before him. He smiled at the rainbow of colour that greeted his gaze. Fuchsia-coloured roses and emerald ivy twined about the arbour, while clusters of purple irises and orange tiger lilies bobbed among the rhododendrons on the banks of the River of Delights. A pair of blue butterflies darting amid a field of yellow chrysanthemums and crimson poppies caught his eye and his smile grew fond. It was breathtaking. Exquisite. The perfect place for his children to flourish and grow.

A peal of laughter intruded upon his thoughts and he reached for the gate, his heart leaping in response to the carefree abandon of his children. *They are such a joy. Such an incredible joy.* The corners of his eyes crinkled as he listened to their playful shouts and he shook his head. *So loving, so trusting, so sweet.* Hastening across the threshold, he scanned the garden, eager to locate the source of their mirth. Drawn by a flash of gold, his eyes locked upon a towheaded girl tumbling about with her friend in the meadow. He chuckled as he watched them frolic in the long grass, chasing feather-winged butterflies from flower to flower. *Whatever would I do without them?*

Like an errant cloud obscuring the light of the sun, a sudden tightness gripped his heart as the shadow of coming sorrows threatened to steal from him the joy of the moment. Shaking it off, he glanced once more around the garden. His heart warmed at the sight of his children at work and at play, their glowing smiles and twinkling eyes but a reflection of the joy that radiated from deep within his own heart.

Thrilled by their exuberance, the king watched as a handful of boys splashed about beneath the waterfall while others dabbled their feet in the shallows, admiring the glittering rocks strewn across the beach. He laughed aloud as dozens of boys and girls ran screeching through the greenwood, clambering up the gnarled trees to stuff their pockets with handfuls of luscious fruit. He grinned as their gangly arms swung wildly from one twisted branch to the next and their cries of exhilaration rang through the air. His children were everywhere—laughing, singing, delighting in the life of privilege he had always meant for them to enjoy.

Reaching the arbour, the king sat in the shade of its arching walls and reclined against its sun-warmed vines. He savoured the mingled scents of honeysuckle and rose that engulfed him as he enjoyed the antics of his dear ones and he fought to keep his heavy lids from closing. Life was good.

Roused by the insistent drone of a bumblebee buzzing past his nose, the king jumped and waved it away with a bemused smile. Life was very good. Very good, indeed. With a yawn, he let his eyes slip shut. *The kind of life one could live forever.*

Barely had his eyelids closed, when a quiet rustle whispered past his ear. Feigning surprise, the king opened his left eye to survey the surrounding green and was rewarded by a childlike giggle. His children were coming. At last. One by one, then in groups of two or three, they came leaping from every corner of the garden, their faces shining as they rushed to take their places at his feet. Their eager response pleased the king. He knew this was their favourite time of day. It was likewise, his own.

* * *

A cacophony of breathless voices clamoured for the king's attention as the chatter of happy children filled the air. Enthralled by their endless tales, the king's heart danced as he patiently listened to each one. With the wink of an eye here and a nod of his head there, a friendly jibe, a teasing wave, he eagerly shared in the excitement of his children and rejoiced that they belonged to him.

As the shadow on the sundial crept forward, he surveyed the spirited group of youngsters bouncing about his feet and wagged his head appreciatively. He adored every one of them and relished the pleasure they so obviously took in his attentions. No longer able to contain his joy, the king threw back his head and opened his mouth in song. Sweeter than the singing of angels, more thrilling than the meadowlark's springtime serenade, the notes bubbled from his lips and echoed from the heavens. Within moments, the rippling melody filled the garden, its glorious timbre infusing his children with a jubilance that could not be silenced. The soul-stirring harmonies of childlike voices trilled in his ears as one by one his children raised their voices to join his happy song. Hands clapped in time to the music, toes began to tap, and then the dancing began.

Leaping to his feet, the king reeled across the green. His robe flapped in the breeze as he wove between the dancers, swinging them in his arms and spinning them about to the accompaniment of gleeful laughter and whoops of joy. On and on they danced until, little by little, the children fell exhausted to the ground. Their faces were flushed with exertion and contented smiles parted their lips as they lay panting upon the grass, their hearts galloping in their chests.

Finally, all was still. Tired bodies sprawled across the green, gasping for breath as they revelled in the coolness of the lush, fragrant grass. The king stood smiling in their midst, a chuckle falling from his lips as he took in the scene before him. How great was his love for his children! Suddenly exhausted, he lowered himself to his seat in the arbour as a comfortable quietness stole over the garden. What a blessing it was to love and be loved.

* * *

Enjoying the rare opportunity to observe his children at rest, the king rubbed a sweaty palm across his face, wondering if they would ever truly grasp the depth of love he bore for them. A shudder shivered down his spine as a sudden chill filled the air, and he shifted in his seat. Looking up, he scanned the heavens. A lone cloud drifted past the sun, veiling its life-giving rays. The king lowered his head as a flicker of sadness lashed his heart. It seemed somehow prophetic.

His smile faded as tears pooled in his eyes, and his shoulders sagged. The sorrow he knew must soon be endured would be great, both for him and for his children. This he knew, though he could hardly bear to acknowledge it. Leaning forward, he rested his arms on his knees and bowed his head. He knew the time was near. He had seen the signs, witnessed the subtle hints of unrest needling his children as they explored their glorious domain. Though he had clearly instructed them never to venture into the desert lands beyond the Oaken Hills, he could see their ripening curiosity as they skirted its borders. How it pained him to watch them gaze upon its sun-bedazzled sands, a dreamlike expression clouding their eyes. They didn't know about the war that raged beyond the borders of their homeland. How could they? He hadn't even tried to explain it to them, knowing that any explanation would only serve to confuse. It was too far beyond the realm of their knowledge and experience. They couldn't possibly be expected to understand; they would simply have to trust. Yet every day his heart sank further as he watched them increasingly abandon the safety and wonder of their home to gather at the edge of the shimmering savannah. His heart splintered with each wistful glance they visited upon the forbidden lands and shattered at the look of puzzlement that furrowed their brows as they tried to make sense of his restrictions. While none dared question his authority openly, the king could sense their growing resolve to disregard his command in the shadowed looks they cast his way, in the whispered communications meant not for his ears. It was only a matter of time. A lone tear escaped his eye as he contemplated the choices he knew his children would make. *If only they would just obey. Why could they not simply trust?*

A heavy sigh shuddered through him and he settled his chin in his hands. He could, he supposed, *make* them obey, but the idea of forcing his will upon his children repulsed him. While dictatorships brooked no room for disobedience, they lent themselves little to love and that was what the king desired from his children above all else. Ultimately, unless they were freed to make their own choices, his children would forever hold him suspect and aloof, a threatening dictator bent on forcing his will upon theirs, heedless of the needs and desires of their hearts. Whether or not it was true.

"No," he groaned, raising his eyes to the heavens, "they never truly will be mine unless I let them decide for themselves." Removing his crown, the king raked a hand through his hair and shook his head in dismay. He could not bear to force his will upon them, yet he knew what they would choose, and he knew what that choice would cost them—and himself.

A taunting snarl intruded upon his thoughts, sending a shiver of dread up his spine. Instantly alert, the king jerked his head upward and trained his eyes on the forbidden lands as he absently stroked the gooseflesh pimpling his arms. The hair on the back of his neck bristled and he leapt to his feet. *It won't be long now.*

Replacing his crown firmly atop his head, the king stared into the distance and bowed his head in grief. The adversary was on the prowl.

* * *

One of the last children to dance in the arms of the king, Cosette finally fell to the ground, panting. She giggled as she wiped a grass-stained sleeve across her brow and wriggled into the soft, cool grass of the meadow. A satisfied sigh escaped her lips as she relished the earthy aroma that engulfed her. Could any place be more glorious? Any day more sublime? Stretching both arms above her head, she rolled onto her belly to study the king. He was magnificent. His face radiated purest joy, his eyes, love beyond imagining. Strong and sure and true he stood, a stunning portrait of goodness and glory. She loved the way the sun danced upon the surface of his robe, suffusing it with every colour of the rainbow and making it sparkle with the light of a thousand stars. And to think that she was his and he was hers. Her daddy.

Smiling up at him, she basked in the glow of his presence, her heart swelling with joy when his eye caught hers and he winked. A volley of uncontrollable giggles erupted from deep within her and she propped her head upon her hands, contorting her face in an attempt to return the gesture. An answering laugh broke from the lips of the king when, at last, she resorted to using the first two fingers of each hand to hold open her left eye while batting the other shut in a lopsided wink. Giggling anew, she crossed her arms in front of her to cushion her head and bent her knees to waggle her legs in the air. No one could possibly compare to her daddy.

Cosette watched as he took his accustomed seat in the arbour. He seemed different somehow. Her head tilted as she studied his features, wondering what to make of the changing expressions that clouded his face. There was something foreign in the way his shoulders slumped, in the way he rested his face in his hands, in the wrinkles that creased his forehead. The heavy sighs that left his shoulders shuddering in their wake perplexed her. She had never seen her daddy look like that before; she had never seen *any*one look like that before. She knew no words to describe it. Curious, Cosette rose and tiptoed to his side. Eager to see what had captured her daddy's attention, she followed his gaze to the Oaken Hills, squinting to see what he saw. A spotted fawn frolicked at the edge of the meadow while its mother grazed beneath the trees, but other than that, she saw nothing unusual. Surely the deer weren't the cause of her daddy's peculiar behaviour.

Startled by a sudden movement, Cosette jumped aside as the king rose. Something was definitely wrong. An odd feeling niggled at the edge of her heart and she raised her eyes to gaze upon his face before slipping her hand into his. Why did her daddy look so... so... strange?

* * *

As quickly as it had come, the moment passed. Tearing his eyes from the desert lands, the king turned to face Cosette. Touched by her obvious affection, he gave her hand a reassuring squeeze and bent to lift her into his arms. He stilled when she traced a river of shimmering wetness down the contours of his face, wondering what she would make of his tears.

Soon you will know, little one. He tucked a wisp of golden hair behind her ear as she peered at her dampened finger. *If only I could spare you...*

"Daddy?" Her childlike voice was even higher than usual. Eyes narrowing, her gaze flitted between her finger and his face. "Why is your face wet?"

"Oh, little lamb..." His head bobbed gently as the words sighed from his lips. "You are such a treasure. Don't ever forget that, Cosette. Not ever." His eyes bore into hers, willing her to remember each word. "No matter what," he insisted, lifting a finger to punctuate his plea. His voice softened and he cradled her face in his hand. "I love you, Cosette. Nothing will ever change that. Do you understand?"

Cosette nodded uncertainly, never taking her eyes from his face.

"I love you and I always will. If you remember nothing else, remember that, dear one. I love you because you are mine."

Cosette cocked her head and wrinkled her nose as she tried to process her daddy's words. How could she ever forget such a thing? Of course he loved her; he was her daddy. He loved her and she loved him. Smiling shyly, she placed a hand on either side of his face and leaned in to place a kiss on the tip of his nose. What was her daddy thinking?

* * *

The ragtag gathering of children that converged at the edge of the Oaken Hills had steadily grown as the king's beloved ones cautiously began to leave the pleasures of the paradise he had prepared for them to gaze longingly upon the forbidden lands beyond. The fact that their daddy had commanded them never to cross the border into those lands was such a puzzle. After all, he had given them all things to enjoy. Why not this? And so the assembly grew, and with it, a subtle discontent, previously unknown, began to take hold of the hearts of the king's children. Gazing longingly into a land meant not for them to share, they could almost hear the sand calling them to bury their feet in the tingling warmth of its dunes, the spreading baobabs beckoning them to rest in their lingering shade, the tall desert grasses—so unlike those of their homeland—drawing their imaginations and summoning them to unearth the secrets hidden within their shadows. The mind-numbing allure was almost more than the children could bear.

Struggling to deny the nagging urge to join the others in checking out the forbidden lands, Cosette lagged behind, kicking a stone mindlessly along the path with her big toe. Her daddy had instructed them not to venture into the desert lands, but surely just a peek across the border wouldn't hurt. She bent to pick up the stone and tossed it into the undergrowth. He hadn't said they couldn't look. Assuring herself that, despite what the others might do, she would never disobey her daddy, Cosette timidly stole after her friends.

Standing beneath the boughs of the great oak trees edging the savannah, Cosette froze. She gazed upon the desert lands, so foreign, yet so inexplicably desirable, and caught her breath as a confusing melee of unfamiliar emotions arose within her. Her heart raced as she surveyed the beauty of the land stretching out before her. It was different from the land of her home. Perhaps that was why it piqued her curiosity so. Its rippling sands intrigued her; its austere beauty entranced. Cosette clenched her fists at her sides and forced herself to breathe. Squeezing her eyes shut, she shook her head hard, determined to erase the tantalizing scene from her mind as she spun from the sight that consumed her imagination.

"I-will-not-dis-obey-my-daddy. I-will-not-dis-obey-my-daddy," she chanted, gritting her teeth with each stilted syllable. Determined to keep her word, she ducked further into the trees, fighting the urge to turn back with every step. *What kind of place is this?*

Her hands trembled as she recalled her decision to obey no matter what, and she turned to glance one last time upon the lands she so longed to explore. *What have I done?* She raised her hand to scratch at an unusual tickle winding its way down her cheek and came to an abrupt stop. Her eyes widened as she stared at her fingertips. They were wet. Lips parting, she rubbed her fingers uncertainly with her thumb. Where was her daddy? She had to see him. Now!

Hastening through the woods, Cosette ran across the meadow, a gentle breeze fanning her hair as she hurried to meet him. But something had changed. Suddenly timid, she stopped short of the green and gasped, raising her thumbnail to her lips.

"Cosette?" The voice of the king startled her. Slowly, she raised her eyes in response to his call, swallowing the lump that had formed in her throat. His eyes glistened in the light of the setting sun. They were wet. Like hers. Only more so.

* * *

It took but a moment for her daddy to come, quickly closing the distance between them. He swung her into his arms and embraced her fondly before returning to the arbour and settling her comfortably upon his knee. Cosette sighed as the unaccustomed emotions that had so confused her heart began to subside and she relaxed into her daddy's arms. This was where she belonged. Here. With her daddy. In the home he had prepared for her. She snuggled further into his embrace as he stroked her hair with his calloused hand and pressed her close to his chest. This was what she longed for, the joy for which she yearned. Gradually, her ragged breathing slowed and, with the soothing words of her daddy thrumming in her ear, her eyes slipped shut.

"Remember, dear one—take heart, my Cosette. I love you and I always will—no matter what."

* * *

Creeping through the brittle scrub of the sun-baked savannah, the adversary inched closer to its prey, its piercing eyes trained on the curious group of children huddled at the edge of the Oaken Hills. The time had come; it wouldn't be long now. There were very few things upon which he and the king could agree, but this was one of them. He licked his lips in anticipation and edged closer to the witless urchins. They'd never know what hit them.

A PEOPLE AT WAR

chapter one

We are a people at war. Granted, it is not a war of our own making, but it is war nonetheless. A war far greater than we know, waged between the God of all glory and His most glorious creation; a war in which we enlisted our hearts when first we chose to disobey the One who made us for Himself; a war that, by the grace of God alone, has already been won.

This we know; yet how blinded we are to the day-to-day assaults of the enemy, not to mention the insidious list of weapons that comprise his mind-numbing arsenal. Merciless in his attacks, the adversary targets the hearts and minds of God's children and lures us to join forces with him in a life of separation from the Father who loves us. He knows that it will destroy us, but that does not concern him. The adversary does not care about the welfare of his troops. He cares only about vengeance against the One who, in his mind, stole from him his glory and banished him from the realms of Heaven.

Nothing is too sacred to him, no depth of depravity too great, if it will work his will and wound the heart of the One he abhors. That's why he sets his sights upon God's children. There is no greater way for him to wound the heart of God than by turning God's own children against Him. And that's just what he aims to do.

The master of deception, he wheedles his way into our hearts and minds, spouting lie after treacherous lie and a spate of beguiling partial truths. He robes himself as an angel of light and appeals to the ignorance and fallen nature of humanity, all in a bid to tear our loyalty away from our Lord. And the worst of it is, we fall for it. We wonder how we could be so naïve, yet we cannot deny the truth. If we are honest, a day does not go by in which we do not find ourselves struggling to loose ourselves from his evil clutches.

But with subtlety his watchword and deceit his weapon of choice, the devil is a powerful enemy. Clouding the minds of God's children, he chooses his weapons with care and mounts his offensive, stalking his prey with such stealth that it often succumbs before it even realizes it is under attack. And so it is, our spiritual battles far too often become commonplace before our eyes are opened to recognize them as assaults of the enemy. How easily we become inured to the endless barrage of temptation the evil one heaps upon us.

That's the way it was for me this morning. Standing before the mirror, I absently stroked a brush through my hair as I prepared for another day of camping. I grimaced at the familiar wail of an angry child whose will had once more been crossed. Sleep had evaded us all as the youngster pitched tantrum after tantrum the evening before, and now he was at it again. A tight-lipped scowl contorted my face and I rolled my eyes in annoyance. *Would somebody silence that bratty kid!* I seethed inwardly. *Someone needs to teach those parents a thing or two about paren...*

A sharp intake of breath accompanied my sudden realization that I was under attack. The passionate and authoritative "NO!" that exploded from my lips was more a gut reaction than a planned response, but it was effective. Those were not *my* thoughts, of that I was very sure. Yet though they were certainly not a reflection of my heart, the quiet prayer of affirmation that leapt from my heart to my lips in the wake of my refusal to entertain them, surprised even me. *Good for you, Mom and Dad, for not giving in to the dictates of your child's will.* With a sigh, I set down my brush and bowed my head. *O Lord, grant them wisdom and rest, and help them to persevere.*

I could almost hear the enemy's chortle of triumph die on his lips when he realized his plan had been thwarted. His prey had recognized the assault for what it was and was prepared to resist. Yet how often it is not so. To my shame, I far too frequently fall prey to the schemes of the evil one, totally unaware that a battle is being waged. Grudgingly accepting the sinful motivations and attitudes of my heart as a product of my fallen human nature, the thoughtless and destructive words of my mouth as undeniably wrong but understandably normal, the loveless and inglorious acts of my hands as unfortunate yet natural outgrowths of the circumstances of life, I miss the fact that I am under attack and concede defeat before even engaging in battle. But that's the way the adversary likes it. If he can keep us unmindful of the battle, he knows he will win, thrusting yet another spike through the heart of the One he abhors. And so he strikes his blows subtlety, depending upon the ignorance of his prey to ensure the success of his schemes. He knows that when we recognize our danger, his odds of winning the fray decrease markedly, but should we recognize his ploys and choose to resist, his defeat is assured.

It is crucial, then, for us to recognize the everyday attacks of the enemy and learn to resist those attacks, for resistance alone leads to victory. By acknowledging the many ways the evil one assaults the hearts and minds of God's children, we are less likely to be caught off guard and can better understand what it means to resist his advances in our daily lives. May God open our eyes to see and our hearts to understand, that we might stand firm in the battle for our hearts and claim the victory that is ours in Christ Jesus, our Lord.

Evie led the furtive band of children as it threaded its way across the forested slopes of the Oaken Hills. The narrow path all but disappeared in places and she grew weary of pushing her way through the undergrowth, but their need for secrecy outweighed her desire for comfort, and she pressed on. She slowed when at last they came to the grassy sward bordering the forbidden lands and raised an arm to wipe the sweat from her brow. The noon day sun beat upon her shoulders and she thrust out her lip to direct a stream of cooling air across her face.

"A–ddie... are you coming?" She turned to glare at the dark-haired boy who trailed her and balled her fists on her hips. "I'm going with or without you. Are you coming or not?" Feigning nonchalance, Evie spun to face the foreign plain and stepped boldly onto its beckoning sands. She wriggled her toes appreciatively in the grainy warmth of its rippled surface and squealed in delight. "Come on!" She grasped Addie's outstretched hand and tugged. Curiosity flamed in his eyes, yet still he hesitated. She beat her toe imperiously against the sand and rolled her eyes as Addie stared across the great expanse. *Surely he isn't going to leave me to explore alone.* She raised an eyebrow questioningly at him. "A–ddie, what's the big deal?"

With a final glance over his shoulder, Addie turned to fix his eyes upon the forbidden lands stretching before him. He had to make a decision. Fast. Evie was waiting; he couldn't let her go alone. What *was* the big deal, anyway? Heart racing, he leapt across the border and landed with a thud by her side.

"See?" Evie crowed. She spun in ever-widening circles, her arms upraised to the heavens. "It's good!"

Saddened, the king pursed his lips as he watched the drama unfolding at the edge of the Oaken Hills. He had known it was only a matter of time before the curiosity and desire of his children betrayed them into the hands of the adversary, yet it pained him nonetheless.

A collective gasp rising from the hills startled him from his thoughts and he turned to see his beloved ones peeking around the trees, their eyes fixed on Evie as she spun gleefully across the sand with Addie close behind. Blinking back a tear, the king shook his head slowly. He could sense the questions lurking in his children's minds as they studied the grin that puckered Evie's face. He imagined the quiver of their lips as they watched her eyes darken with the excitement of forbidden pleasures, and smiled ruefully when their hands leapt to cover their gaping mouths. They knew what Evie and Addie did was wrong. The guilty looks they cast over their shoulders left no doubt about that. If only that knowledge would keep them from making the same mistake.

Shoulders hunched, the children froze, their eyes locked on Evie as she spun across the sand. A minute passed, then two. When nothing seemed to happen, the tension broke like a wave on the shore. Catapulted from their silence, the children resumed their excited chatter as Addie joined Evie on the sandy plain. Suddenly aware of options they'd never known before, they found themselves considering whether or not to follow their friends into the unknown wilderness. Surely their daddy wouldn't have forbidden them entrance to the desert lands if he had known what they were like. Evie and Addie were right; the forbidden lands were good! Why should they avoid them just because their daddy forbade them to enter? If he really wanted the best for them as he claimed...

* * *

The king laid a steadying hand upon the latticed arch as he watched his children huddle at the edge of the trees, fervently debating their options. One young man stepped away from the rest and pointed toward Evie, his animated gestures clearly suggesting they should follow. The others bobbed their heads excitedly in response. The king knew it wouldn't take much for them to convince themselves of their right—even need—to explore the desert lands, regardless of the unmistakable command he had given them to remain within the borders of their garden home. If only they could comprehend the consequences their disobedience would bring. But they could not. Some things could only be understood through the lens of experience.

Consensus obviously reached, it wasn't long before a torrent of eager children poured from the borders of their magnificent home to join their friends on the burning sands of the desert. The king sighed as he watched them hasten to their fate. Even Cosette, blinded by the thrill of adventure, had joined the throng of children carelessly fleeing the land he had so lovingly prepared for them. He cringed as, eyes fixed firmly upon the land of unknown wonders, her feet scurried through the trees until at last, with a final leap, they buried themselves in the desert's shifting sands. "Even Cosette," he mumbled into his beard.

Abandoned and alone, the king welcomed the salty tears that coursed down his face as his children capered about in the sand. *And so it begins.* Fists clenched, he threw his head back and loosed the heart-rending wail that clawed its way up from deep within his soul. He had known it would be this way, but now that it had happened, the pain of betrayal was almost more than he could bear. Spent, he lowered his head and forced himself to watch once more as his beloved Cosette danced eagerly across the sandy plain with the others. "Even Cosette," he repeated sadly. "If only they..."

Wearily the king rubbed the tears from his eyes and exhaled a long, painful breath. He alone could see the shadow of the adversary creeping toward his children; he alone could hear its snarl of triumph as its eyes sought to pin his opponent with its deadly glare; he alone could protect his dear ones and rescue them from a fate for which they were totally unprepared. And, he alone would—when the time was right.

IS SATAN REALLY AT WORK IN THE WORLD TODAY?

Do you have a hard time believing that the evil one is actively stalking the hearts of God's children today? Do you wonder if this is all some kind of conspiracy theory aimed at the gullible and promoted by fanatics? Let God's Word convince you. Check out the references below to see what the Bible has to say about the activities of the evil one in the world today.

Genesis 3:13: Right from the beginning, the evil one has been at work in God's people. "Then the Lord God asked the woman, 'What have you done?' 'The serpent deceived me,' she replied. 'That's why I ate it.'"

Job 1:7: Job's story begins in the courts of heaven. It reminds us of how actively and vehemently Satan pursues God's children. "'Where have you come from?' the Lord asked Satan. Satan answered the Lord, 'I have been patrolling the earth, watching everything that's going on.'"

Matthew 6:13: When Jesus teaches His disciples to pray, He tells them to pray that they would be delivered from the evil one. Why would He do that if the evil one was not at work in the world? "And don't let us yield to temptation, but rescue us from the evil one."

Matthew 13:19: In the parable of the sower, Jesus tells His disciples plainly that the evil one is working hard to keep God's Word from taking root in our hearts. "The seed that fell on the footpath represents those who hear the message about the Kingdom and don't understand it. Then the evil one comes and snatches away the seed that was planted in their hearts."

Matthew 13:25-26: In the parable of the weeds, Jesus speaks figuratively of His children as wheat seeds that He has sown in His field, His Kingdom. "But that night as the workers slept, his enemy came and planted weeds among the wheat, then slipped away. When the crop began to grow and produce grain, the weeds also grew." In verse 39, He explains, "The enemy who planted the weeds among the wheat is the devil."

Matthew 16:23: Jesus recognizes the work of Satan in His daily life. When Peter rebukes Him for saying He will die, Jesus responds vehemently, knowing it is not Peter who speaks, but the evil one speaking through him. "'Get away from me, Satan! You are a dangerous trap to me. You are seeing things merely from a human point of view, not from God's.'"

John 13:2: Later, we read: "It was time for supper, and the devil had already prompted Judas, son of Simon Iscariot, to betray Jesus."

I Corinthians 7:5: Paul gives many warnings about the reality of the evil one's attacks in our everyday lives. In speaking of the marital relationship, he exhorts husbands and wives: "Afterward, you should come together again so that Satan won't be able to tempt you because of your lack of control."

II Corinthians 2:10-11: When speaking about forgiveness, he writes: "Anyone you forgive, I also forgive. And what I have forgiven—if there was anything to forgive—I have forgiven in the sight of Christ for your sake, in order that Satan might not outwit us. For we are not unaware of his schemes." (NIV)

II Corinthians 4:4: When speaking about unbelievers, he laments: "Satan, who is the god of this world, has blinded the minds of those who don't believe. They are unable to see the glorious light of the Good News. They don't understand this message about the glory of Christ, who is the exact likeness of God."

II Corinthians 11:14-15a: In warning about false prophets, he notes: "But I am not surprised! Even Satan disguises himself as an angel of light. So it is no wonder that his servants also disguise themselves as servants of righteousness."

II Corinthians 12:7: Here, Paul speaks personally about a *thorn in the flesh*, the exact nature of which he does not reveal. Yet the source of that thorn, he plainly states. "...So to keep me from becoming proud, I was given a thorn in my flesh, a messenger from Satan to torment me and keep me from becoming proud."

Ephesians 2:1-2: In speaking about our lives before coming to Jesus, Paul reminds us that Satan is clearly at work in this world. "Once you were dead because of your disobedience and your many sins. You used to live in sin, just like the rest of the world, obeying the devil—the commander of the powers in the unseen world. He is the spirit at work in the hearts of those who refuse to obey God."

Ephesians 4:26-27: He also reminds us to be careful lest the evil one get a foothold in our lives. "And 'don't sin by letting anger control you.' Don't let the sun go down while you are still angry, for anger gives a foothold to the devil."

Ephesians 6:10-12: And he pleads with us: "A final word: Be strong in the Lord and in his mighty power. Put on all of God's armour so that you will be able to stand firm against all strategies of the devil. For we are not fighting against flesh-and-blood enemies, but against evil rulers and authorities of the unseen world, against mighty powers in this dark world, and against evil spirits in the heavenly places."

I Thessalonians 2:18: In addressing the people of Thessalonica, he explains: "We wanted very much to come to you, and I, Paul, tried again and again, but Satan prevented us."

I Thessalonians 3:5: And again: "...I was afraid that the tempter had gotten the best of you and that our work had been useless."

I Timothy 4:1: In addressing church leaders, he writes: "Now the Holy Spirit tells us clearly that in the last times some will turn away from the true faith; they will follow deceptive spirits and teachings that come from demons."

II Timothy 2:25-26: In speaking about how to address those who oppose the truth, he says: "Gently instruct those who oppose the truth. Perhaps God will change those people's hearts, and they will learn the truth. Then they will come to their senses and escape from the devil's trap. For they have been held captive by him to do whatever he wants."

I Peter 5:8: Peter's warnings are also clear. "Stay alert! Watch out for your great enemy, the devil. He prowls around like a roaring lion, looking for someone to devour."

Revelation 12:12: And finally, while I do not pretend to understand the full context of this verse, it seems to me that it clearly tells us that the evil one is at work in this world. "Therefore, rejoice, O heavens! And you who live in the heavens, rejoice! But terror will come on the earth and the sea, for the devil has come down to you in great anger, knowing that he has little time."

part ii

THE BATTLE PLAN OF THE EVIL ONE

Lurking in the undergrowth, the adversary slowly blinked his hooded eyes as he lowered himself to rest upon the cooling sands. The deed was done. It had been even easier than he had anticipated. Far easier. A sinister laugh rattled through his frame, a malevolent snicker of deep-seated malice. The king was a fool! The very thought of the old dotard ruling anything elicited a snort of disdain from the throat of the evil one. *As if anyone would submit to the decrees of such a demanding taskmaster.* Crouching in the shadows, he surveyed the scene before him and rubbed his chin. A growl hissed through his teeth as his eyes came to rest upon the objects of the king's affections and his lip curled. What was so special about that riotous group of hoodlums that they should lay such claim to the heart of the king? His eyes narrowed as his attention shifted beyond the witless children intruding upon his domain to settle upon the distant figure of the king. He looked so amusingly crestfallen. *As if he hadn't known what to expect!*

Barely able to contain his rage, the adversary spewed a bevy of snarled epithets into the wind. How dare the king so ruthlessly inflict upon him the indignity of life within the confines of this failing mortal domain! His stomach churned as the cauldron of bitterness simmering in his belly threatened to overflow, and his lip twitched in a haughty sneer. The war was on and he would win—no matter what the cost.

* * *

The king's children had long since ceased their frenzied dance across the desert sands and collapsed, sweaty and exhausted, beneath the skimpy shade of a gnarled baobab tree. How they yearned for a long, satisfying dip in the River of Delights. Heat and thirst unlike any they had ever known compelled them to return to the garden, yet still they hesitated, reticent to abandon their adventures so soon. Whyever would their daddy forbid them such pleasure?

Restless, they rolled about aimlessly in the sand, a fine layer of grit clinging to their clothing and coating their sweat-stained faces. The unbearable heat of the afternoon sun bit at their reddened skin and left them listless and uncomfortable as they crowded within the final shreds of shadow afforded by the scrawny tree. Only then did it begin to dawn on them that perhaps the desert lands weren't quite as wonderful as at first they had supposed. Maybe their daddy had been right; they did not belong in this wild place.

* * *

Cosette sneezed twice, her nostrils clogged with choking grit, her parched throat screaming for a life-giving sip of water. *What was I thinking? This isn't where I belong! I should never have followed the others. I want to go home.* Despite the blistering heat, she shivered as another sinister growl split the afternoon air, her heart fearing to dwell upon its source. She wrapped her arms tightly around her knees and bit her lower lip as she studied the goosebumps that rose to ripple across her skin. *Doesn't anyone else want to go home? Am I the only one who doesn't like this place?* Her eyes shifted nervously from side to side, hoping to find a friend in her distress, but dismayed to find her brothers and sisters still enjoying their adventure. *I've got to get out of here! This isn't right. I need to go home.*

Unable to abide another moment of the foreign land's desolation, Cosette jumped to her feet and sprinted toward the safety of her homeland. *I have to get back. Now.* She clasped a hand to her side as she ran, her breath rasping from her lungs in short, ragged puffs. *I have to find my daddy!*

* * *

Halfway to the borderlands, Cosette lurched to a halt as an ear-splitting roar shrieked across the savannah. The earth beneath her feet began to dance, leaping and cavorting like a young lamb at play, and she froze in alarm. Clapping open palms to her ears, her eyes widened in horror. The blistering sands, so stable moments before, pitched beneath her feet and she froze, mesmerised by the shower of sand crumbling beneath her toes as the earth began to give way.

Suddenly aware of the danger, Cosette stumbled backward, desperate to regain her balance as a final shudder rocked the foreign plain, sweeping yet more of the treacherous sand from beneath her feet. And then there was silence.

As suddenly as it had begun, the deafening thunder subsided and an eerie calm took its place. Cosette stiffened at the sight before her. Where once there had been sand, she now gazed into a terrifying abyss. Her head whirled as she teetered on the edge of the great chasm, struggling to keep from tumbling into its cavernous depths. "Da-ddy!" she wailed. "Help me!"

The chaotic screeching of panic-stricken children reached her ears and she turned to see a handful of her brothers and sisters stumbling toward her. Hands clasped, they stepped timidly toward the great abyss and peered into its depths.

"We're trapped." Addie's wobbly voice boomed in the silence. "We can't get back."

"What are we going to do?" Evie whispered.

A chorus of whimpered cries filled the air as the children looked from the great abyss to their homeland and back. Cosette drew a fist to her mouth and gasped, a fiery stream of tears gushing from her eyes as she remembered her daddy. *There has to be a way.* She pinched herself, hoping she would awaken to find it all a dream, but she knew she would not.

"Da-ddy…" she whimpered, "Don't leave us." Great, wrenching sobs lurched from the depths of her heart and she crumpled to the ground in a heap. "I want to go home."

* * *

A cruel laugh issued from the lips of the evil one as he waited for the violent quaking to subside. He couldn't help but enjoy the horrifying plight of the king's children. It served them right. Now they belonged to him.

Stepping from beneath the shelter of the underbrush, he padded gracefully across the shifting plain toward the dishevelled group of children gathered at the edge of the abyss. They were frightened, agitated, alone in a strange new land. They needed a friend...

LIKE A LION HE PROWLS

chapter two

Sleek, regal, powerful. The lion is a magnificent beast. Lordly and majestic, mighty and merciless, ferocious and terrifying—the uncontested king of the jungle. A study in contrasts, the lion is a creature we can't help but admire. Enthralled by its regal bearing and muscular prowess, we are drawn by its graceful agility and captivated by its beauty. Yet we are also repulsed. Disturbed by its ferocity and cunning, we despise its predatory instincts and abhor its deadly cruelty. It is no mistake that the writers of the Scriptures so often make reference to the lion as they seek to convey the truths of God to His people.

Like a lion, he prowls—The words of Peter still resonate. "Stay alert! Watch out for your great enemy, the devil. He prowls around like a roaring lion, looking for someone to devour" (I Peter 5:8).

What a scary image. To be stalked, threatened, attacked by an unseen predator eager for the kill is almost more than our hearts can bear, yet the threat is a disconcerting reality for the child of God. Job knew it. Paul knew it. Peter knew it. Even Jesus knew it. Intent on the destruction of God's people, the enemy hounded each of them. Relentless in his determination to snatch them from the hand of the Almighty, he mounted attack after cruel attack against them, huddling in the shadows of their lives and awaiting their moments of greatest vulnerability to launch his offensive and take down his prey. Such is the way of lions.

The majestic pride rested on the shady banks of the waterhole, basking lazily in the heat of the midday sun. They were hungry; it had been almost three days since their last feed. Hunger for the kill lay heavily upon them as they stretched upon the sand, their apparent docility and feigned disinterest daring their prey to approach.

Intimidated by the presence of the majestic beasts, the gentler creatures of the savannah hung back, reticent to approach the waterhole. Something had to give. Growing thirst raged within as they edged closer to the muddy waters, alert to the slightest twitch of the enemy's tail. Ever vigilant, they blinked in surprise as they watched the patriarch of the pride rise and stretch its agile physique then pad across the sand. Their hearts hammered in their chests when the regal animal neared a weak and foolish wildebeest slinking toward the banks of the waterhole. Yet their wariness gradually turned to hope as, hardly seeming to notice, the wild one paced on, leaving the lone wildebeest to scuttle its retreat.

A whicker of relief rustled through the gathering animals and their rigid muscles began to relax. Perhaps the lions weren't hungry today; perhaps they had already eaten.

Emboldened by the disinterest of the ferocious felines, the animals drew near, braving the presence of the lions to assuage their thirst at the life-giving pool. Moment by moment, their confidence grew as the wild ones made no move to attack, and the vigilance of the hunted grew slack, their boldness escalating with every step.

Noting their prey's growing confidence, the lions watched through half-lidded eyes, readying themselves for the attack. Their ruse had worked. Again. Unnoticed, they rose from their repose and crept through the undergrowth to hide themselves in the scraggly scrub. Bodies tensed in readiness, their eyes never left the docile herd as they crouched in the shadows, waiting for the moment of attack.

Meanwhile, the lone male, certain his pride would not fail him, resumed his position on the banks of the waterhole, licking his lips in anticipation. The scent of victory was in the air.

A chilling silence descended upon the skittish gathering of animals as a low, guttural snarl rumbled from the throat of the great one, and they froze. The lions had disappeared. A second passed. Then two. Suddenly, chaos erupted in a whirlwind of hooves and tails as the animals took flight. Hearts thumping, they galloped across the grassy plain in a frantic race to elude the deadly beasts, the hair bristling on the back of every neck.

Leaping from their hiding places, the lions took to the chase, converging on the terrified animals as they attempted to flee. Today there would be food enough for all, and then some. Bloodlust drove the raging lions forward as one by one, they pounced on the slow and the weak, snatching at the vulnerable with dagger-like claws.

Overwhelmed by fear, an exhausted young zebra slowed and turned back to gauge the approach of the wild ones. When he saw the advancing beasts, he pivoted mid-step to resume his frenzied flight, but it was too late. Within seconds, the lions had surrounded him, their claws ripping his skin as they threw themselves upon him.

His struggle was short-lived. Fear froze in his throat as blood poured from his veins and the life drained from his body. His fate unnoticed by the retreating herds, he succumbed to the feeding frenzy of the lions, never to rise again. His foolishness had cost him his life.

Sated at last, the lions rested in the golden glow of the late afternoon sun, leisurely licking the blood from their tawny fur. Nearby, yearling cubs cavorted on the sand, honing their skills in preparation as the adults conserved their energy for future attacks. Licking the final traces of blood from their chops, the lions settled lazily upon the banks of the waterhole, their minds churning in anticipation of their next kill, even now devising a plan of attack. The life of a lion was good.

It's quite the picture, isn't it? When we really stop to consider it, the image of the prowling lion is more alarming than we would like to admit. A malevolent presence freely roaming the earth, lying in wait to capture the weak and defenceless? A ferocious beast, ever seeking to devour as it cunningly lures its prey into the jaws of death? It is not without reason that chilling metaphors like *into the mouth of the lion* fill our hearts with dread. The lion is a mighty and powerful beast. So, too, is the adversary.

Peter is right. Like a roaring lion, the adversary roams the earth, seeking to destroy. Driven by hatred, he wages war against the Almighty by mercilessly attacking the beloved children of the Most High, the children the Almighty One cannot bear to lose. Deceptively he charms us, exploiting our vulnerabilities and disguising himself as a friend, courting our favour until we find ourselves hopelessly enmeshed in his schemes.

Yes, the prowling lion is an apt description for a vicious foe. A description the wise would do well to remember. For, like a roaring lion, the evil one prowls, preying upon the unsuspecting soul. With bone-chilling accuracy, he strikes the vulnerable heart with fear and lures his prey into a state of complacency, fooling the unwary into thinking him harmless. He is deceptive, cunning, cruel, and bent on the destruction of God's children.

Yet, instead of recognizing the evil one for what he is, we mindlessly succumb to his attacks, for we are, nonetheless, enthralled by the beauty of the image he portrays. And so we wallow in ignorance, enamoured by his tantalizing offers and repeatedly falling for his wiles.

Yes, the lion analogy provides a very apt description of the adversary—the ancient enemy of our souls—the foe who would fool us into calling him a friend. Understanding this is a very important part of learning to resist his ploys and experiencing victory in the war zone.

In any war, a wealth of time, expertise and resources are wisely devoted to intercepting and outmanoeuvring the battle plan of the enemy. The side that can best anticipate the tactics of its foe has the advantage, for in recognizing the plan, it can more readily counteract its deceits and win the battle. With that in mind, the next chapter will examine a selection of the most common, yet insidious, tactics used by the evil one to attack God's children. By engaging us in skirmish after skirmish, he effectively erodes our defences in order that we might fall prey to his cunning and wander from the path of victory.

It is important to recognize, however, that the Great War—the War of Eternity, if you like—has already been won. When our Lord, our Saviour, Jesus Christ, defeated Satan on the cross, He won a resounding, once-for-all victory in that war. A victory that no amount of cunning or resolve on the part of the evil one can reverse. He does not have the power. But neither does he give up easily. The question is, are we allowing him to bully us into submission as a result of ignorance, or are we skilled in recognizing and resisting his attacks?

Sadly, I fear we are too often guilty of the former, and allow the adversary to hold far too much sway in our lives. At least, I am. Not because I consciously fall prey to his attacks, but because I so rarely recognize them for what they truly are until it is too late. Perhaps it is the same with you. So join me as we examine some of the specific weapons that comprise the enemy's arsenal, that our awareness might be heightened and we might be better equipped to recognize the attacks of the adversary and resist his attempts to defeat us. May God open our eyes to see, our ears to hear and our minds to understand all that He would reveal to our hearts.

THE ARSENAL OF THE ADVERSARY
chapter three

As far as I can tell, there are two basic types of warfare: the kind that confronts the enemy, challenging him face to face in the horrors of armed conflict, and the less bloody kind that chips away at the enemy's defences until utter defeat is assured. As a teacher of young children, I might describe the two somewhat more practically as *boyfare* versus *girlfare*.[1] Although there are definite exceptions, when little boys fight, they push and they shove and they hit and they kick until a victor emerges triumphant. Then they put their quarrels behind them and go back to being friends. Most little girls, on the other hand, fight more deviously. Verbal slights, subtle snubs, and reprehensible rumours meant to devastate the heart of the enemy are the weapons of girlfare. These are not so easily forgiven or forgotten.

When we think of it that way, it is no surprise that our adversary favours the latter. While we tend to live our lives expecting a barrage of head-on, confrontational spiritual boyfare, we instead find ourselves ambushed from behind in wave after wave of subtle, yet insidious,

---

[1] Study after study verifies that boys and girls *do* fight differently. If you wish to explore the topic of gender differences more fully, I suggest you refer to the book *Why Gender Matters* by Leonard Sax. Be aware that you may find some of the content of his chapters to be a little more enlightening than you might appreciate.

spiritual girlfare meant to wear us down and destroy us from within. The evil one is a master at it. It is just the kind of warfare in which he specializes—that deviously deceptive, arrow-in-your-back kind of warfare that we so despise for, sullied though our hearts may be, we yet bear enough of the image of the Almighty that we cannot help but abhor its injustice.

I once heard it said that the evil one often seems, from our human standpoint, to have the upper hand in this world. Not because he does, but because there is no depth of depravity to which he will not sink in his desperation to get his own way. God, in contrast, will never betray His own holiness by combating evil with evil, for He is always faithful—not only to His children, but more significantly, to Himself. Besides, He knows what the adversary refuses to admit: the war has already been won and the glory days of the evil one are numbered.

Let us, then, look at some of our enemy's most universally effective weapons that we might not become victims of his unrelenting hatred. Some of his tactics you will recognize immediately as those he aims regularly and mercilessly at your heart, while others you may find less familiar. Each will be illustrated by an image drawn from our animal friends and accompanied by a prayer. While you will have to decide how best to approach the reading of this chapter, you might consider reading one segment a day as part of your daily devotional time. The segments do not need to be read in order and you do not need to complete them before reading on. Be sure to ask God to speak His truth to your heart, though, and open your eyes to see areas in which you may be under attack. This is not a chapter for the faint of heart, but it contains timeless truths which I have found to be worthy of attention. Remember: Only when we can reliably recognize the attacks of the evil one for what they are, will we be ready and able to resist his ploys. As long as we remain ignorant of the attack, we allow ourselves to become unwitting and unwilling accomplices in the enemy's plan to wound the heart of God.

DECEPTION: THE PLIGHT OF THE FLEDGLING BUTTERFLY

Glorying in her newfound freedom, the fledgling butterfly fanned her wings as she pirouetted from one colourful blossom to the next. She could hardly believe it was true, yet neither could she deny the marvellous changes that had graced her form. Freed from the bondage of her past, she could fly! Where once she had but stubby buds to creep from place to place, she now had glorious wings just aching to take flight. The amazing transformation of her body thrilled her. She was a new creature. A new creation. A masterpiece beyond compare.

Heart pounding, she spread her wings once more to soar through the cerulean skies. Forgetting for a time the wormy estate from which she had been lifted, she exalted in the sweet sensations bombarding her senses and an unaccustomed giddiness swept over her. The old had passed away and all had been made new. It was a dream come true. Her earthbound fetters were broken and she was free.

Rising unrestrained, she took to the air, enthralled by the breathtaking new world that opened up beneath her. For hours she fluttered over meadows and flitted among the trees, lost in a haze of wonderment and joy, enveloped by a quiet contentment no words could describe.

But it was not to last.

Dancing through the air along the banks of a stream, she chanced to glance at the waters below and her wings skipped a beat. Mirrored in the surface of the stream, was the skeletal reflection of a would-be butterfly. Appalled, she swooped to take a closer look. The image bore little resemblance to the radiant being she had become. Or did it? Insecurities engulfed her as she contemplated the watery likeness. Was that her *reflection? Really? Was the grandeur she had imagined only a dream? Was* that *the reality of her newfound beauty? It couldn't be.*

Disappointment clouded her vision as doubts assailed her. If this was what it meant to be a butterfly, she would have been better off to have remained a worm. How could her heart so deceive her senses? Or was it her senses that deceived her heart? After all, she could fly. If only she knew what was real.

Deception is one of the most destructive and frequently-wielded weapons in the arsenal of the evil one. It is doubtful that a day goes by in which our hearts and minds are not accosted by it. Repeatedly. The problem is, most of the time we don't recognize the lies of the evil one as attacks from without, and believe them to be truths welling up from within. That is, if we actually think about them at all. More often than not, we simply act upon the lies he fires our way without stopping to consider their veracity.

This weapon goes by many names: deception, falsehood, deceit, delusion, misdirection, subterfuge. Yet, regardless of the word we choose to describe it, there is one that embodies them all: lies. Not just the lies we tell, but even more concerning, the lies we are told. Nothing delights the evil one more than to lie to the children of God, especially when we so naïvely fail to recognize his schemes and so eagerly disregard the truths God would whisper to our hearts. How convincing, indeed, are the lies of the evil one. It is not without reason that the first piece of armour in the Armour of God described by Paul is the Belt of Truth. Nor is it in error that Jesus referred to the adversary as the father of lies (John 8:44). Undoubtedly, deception is the deadliest and most pervasive weapon wielded by the evil one. It makes me wonder how much of our lives are based upon the lies the enemy so subtly tries to convince us are truths.

Father, grant us Your eyes to see the glory You have hidden within us, that we might not be led astray by the lies of the enemy. Deliver us, we pray, from the deceptions of the evil one and enlighten us with Your truth, that we might live the victorious lives you created us to enjoy. Show us where we are mistaking lies for truth this day and teach us to recognize and separate the two, rejecting the one and embracing the other. Bind us about with the Belt of Truth and, by Your grace, let us not be deceived.

SEDUCTION: THE FOLLY OF THE SLEEPING SWAN

With a distraught cry, the frantic cob flew to his feet and rushed toward his beloved, desperate to save her from the evil presence that threatened to engulf her. He could not, would not, surrender her to the beastly apparition. Not now. Not ever. The thought of the skeletal bird luring her vulnerable heart away from his enraged him. He would not give her over to the lust of the enemy. She was his.

A string of piercing shrieks broke from his throat as he drew near, determined to rouse her before it was too late. Yet still she slept on, her elegant neck curved sensuously across her graceful body, her restless heart adrift on the seas of slumber.

With a final cry, the cob rose to the height of his glory and beat the air with his powerful wings, his pulsating shrieks intensifying with each wild stroke. The seducer was now between them, standing seductively before the sleeping form of his beloved and impregnating her dreams with a host of vile thoughts and tormenting desires, infiltrating her mind with a bevy of tantalizing questions and enticing suggestions.

Enraged, the swan surged toward his mate who, unaware of the intrusion, slept on. He had to awaken her before it was too late, before she succumbed to the lure of the enemy, before the foul beast could imprison her heart. Why did she not wake up? Surely she wasn't that anaesthetized to the lurid schemes of the evil one.

She was only a wingspan away now. Exhaustion threatened to overwhelm him, yet still he pressed on, thrusting himself forward with every vestige of determination his wounded heart could grasp.

"Awaken my love. Awaken and flee. The enemy is upon you!"

Beguilement. Seduction. They imperil us all. Enticing dreams, tantalizing images, sensual pleasures, lurid fantasies, lustful thoughts, dark passions, unholy desires, harlotry. The adversary is master of them all. Constantly aiming to seduce our hearts away from our Bridegroom, he chips away at our desires, purposely perverting them that they might lead us to stray from the One who alone can satisfy our longing hearts.

The evil one knows exactly what he is doing. If he can use the deepest desires of our hearts to woo us from the Father who loves us and yearns for us to be His alone, the adversary has won, and he knows it. Hence, seduction is one of his favourite weapons, for like deception, it is deadly and none are immune to its devastating blows. He doesn't even need to tempt us to engage in immoral behaviour to wreak havoc in the lives of the saints; he only needs to seduce our hearts and minds away from our Father for his plan to succeed. A stray thought here, an obsession or two there—it doesn't take much. Materialism, gluttony, athleticism, sensuality, ambition, lust—they all spring from the same root. With promises of glory and pleasures untold, the evil one lures the hearts of God's children away from the only One who can meet their needs, knowing it will destroy them. But that's okay with him. In fact, it's more than okay; it is his plan. After all, what could devastate the heart of God more than to see the children He loves so easily seduced by the enemy? Oh, that we were less vulnerable to attack.

Father, awaken our hearts to recognize the seductions of the adversary and grant us Your grace to flee. Guard our hearts that we might not succumb to the devices and desires of his unholy heart, no matter how alluring they might appear, and protect our wandering hearts with Your Breastplate of Righteousness. Seduce us, O Lord, with Your glory and lure our hungry hearts with Your limitless love that our gaze might be fixed upon You alone, both now and forevermore.

FEAR: THE FALCON'S DOWNFALL

The majestic falcon eyed the hideous apparition with disdain as a familiar sense of foreboding gripped his heart. Tendrils of fear shivered up his spine and rippled the feathers at the base of his neck whenever the shadowy bird appeared. His heart raced at the sight. Would that he could escape its ominous presence. Would that he could banish the growing sense of terror that threatened to overwhelm his regal frame. Would that he had the courage to confront the dastardly fiend and flee its presence forever. Wherever he went, it was there, its menacing gaze eroding his courage and heightening his dread. No matter how hard he tried to avoid its icy glare, it loomed before him, its disquieting presence terrorizing him at every turn. The mere thought of it fairly froze his blood. He simply could not shake the paralyzing fear that crept over him whenever it was near, no matter how tenaciously he tried to ignore the spectral stalker. Though he was loath to admit it, panic was his constant companion and terror stalked his days.

With a sigh, the mighty falcon squeezed his eyes shut, hoping for a reprieve. If he didn't look at it, perhaps it would go away. And then again, maybe it would only make things worse. Would the nightmare never end?

Fear. It threatens to accompany us wherever we go. We forever seem to be at its mercy in some shape or form. At least, I do. Whether it comes in the form of nagging concern or restless worry, mind-numbing anxiety or abject terror, the results are the same. Fear chills the heart with dread and immobilizes the soul with its poison. It's fight or flight or pull a scared rabbit and wait for the enemy to descend upon us.

The arrows of fear affect us all: fear of what is, fear of what may be, fear of what could have been, fear of what is to come. There seems to be no end of things to fear in this fallen world. Yet, that is not how God wills it. He does not want His children to live in fear, for the life lived in fear is a life lived in the shadows of the adversary's regime. How it must hurt His heart when we fail to live our lives trusting in the assurance of His love for us. And the adversary knows it.

Father, loose the chains of terror that bind our battered hearts and release us from the clutches of fear. Let us not be bound in the shadows of a world commandeered by the evil one, but let us live freely in the light of Your love in accordance with Your will. Grant us trusting hearts, we pray, that we might be freed from the worries that accost our hearts and teach us to cling to You alone.

BUSYNESS: THE BEAVER'S OBSESSION

Endless obligations consumed the beaver's every moment. The dam needed building, the lodge required repairs, there were mouths to feed and kits to protect, a pond to defend and a mate to support. His every waking minute was accounted for, and still there was more to do. Exhausted, the noble beast surveyed his riverside kingdom and shook his head in dismay. Then, bound by the duties before him, he bent his back to the monotony of unending labour, painfully aware of the escalating cycle of ceaseless activity his weary life had become. There was no time to rest or play, to listen, to think, or even, it seemed, to pray. Not that he could actually remember what it was like to do such things. It was all he could do to fulfil the most urgent demands of each day, and far too often, he couldn't even do that.

But maybe it was better that way. Maybe he even liked it that way. After all, he was never bored and besides, he was needed. Of what use to him was mindless frivolity or the pursuit of pleasure when there was work to be done? Did not the holy words themselves commend a man to work? Was it not then a most godly pursuit? Did not the Maker Himself condemn sloth?

A baleful sigh escaped him as he shifted his burden and resumed the work before him, his eyes fixed upon the days and years yet to come. Yes, he supposed a rest would do him good, but it was hardly necessary. He could relax when his work was complete. And besides, who would do the work if he did not? Some things just had to be done.

Yet, he couldn't quite shake the twinge of holy desire that hounded his heart as the evening sun began its descent. Could it be that it was the call of the Eternal to be still, the summons of his Maker to commune with Him? Would his work not always be there? Perhaps it was *time to rest.*

Busyness is, unarguably, a wearisome reality of the world in which we live, yet it is also a subtle, and disconcertingly successful, weapon in the hands of the evil one. Much to the adversary's delight, the pace of life in this world seems to accelerate with each passing year, sweeping God's children along in a whirlwind of frenetic activity. With countless responsibilities and obligations clamouring for our attention, we are daily bombarded by a barrage of duties as we seek to fulfil all that is required of us. The adversary can't help but laugh as he witnesses the chaotic world of commotion in which we immerse ourselves.

How ironic that the proper, and God-honouring, pursuit of good works should leave mankind so dreadfully short of time and energy to invest in developing a meaningful relationship with the One who longs for our devotion and love. But if the adversary can keep God's people occupied with endless lists of good, though ultimately meaningless tasks, then success is his. And we fall for it every day.

Drivenness characterizes the people of God every bit as much as it does the world in which we live, often keeping us from doing the very things God has called us to do. We try to prioritize, but it is always the most urgent tasks that get the attention, regardless of their importance. It is no wonder the evil one rejoices in the busyness of God's children. Accomplishment and success have become vital, regardless of what must be sacrificed to achieve them. And sacrifice we do. Constantly jumping from job to job, we willfully resist the need to rest and thoughtlessly ignore the call of our Father to come away and spend time with Him. It is a sacrifice far too great.

Father, forgive us we pray, for the times when we have succumbed to the busyness of life and missed the opportunity to serve and worship You. Give us discerning hearts, to distinguish between the tasks that You have called us to do and those that are mere diversions, for we are so easily led astray. We want to make a difference; we long to have an eternal impact upon this world and the people in it; we yearn to serve You with all our hearts and fulfil every task to which You have called us. Yet we allow ourselves to become so infernally busy with meaningless tasks that seem so important to the eyes of our humanity. Give us the courage we need to set aside time to be with You, and the resources we need to accomplish the work it pleases You to give us. Grant us, O Lord, the wisdom and strength to live lives paced according to Your timetable and help us to prioritize our time by Your standards alone.

REASON: THE RAVEN'S DEBATE
"But listen," its soothing voice countered. "You say that He is good; you say that He is God. But open your eyes! Would a good God really have given humanity charge over all creation? Would not say, the raven have been a better choice? Why, He ought to have given dominion to a creature with at least some intelligence!"

The debate had gone on for hours, days—or had it actually been years? The harried raven sank onto his perch and picked at his glossy, black feathers. The problem was, the spectral bird spoke so intelligently, so reasonably, so logically. It made sense, though its every word ran counter to the throbbing impulse of the raven's heart. How could something so blatantly wrong seem so incredibly right? Yet, how could the intelligence of thoughtful logic be in error? His mind told him it was true; his heart shouted, "Falsehood!"

Confusion tugged at the corners of the raven's mind as, bereft of answers, his heart succumbed to doubt. Could it truly be that the peculiar bird was right? Could the whispering voice of his own heart be mistaken? Shaking his head, he stretched his wings and hurled himself from his perch. What, indeed, was he to trust—his head, it being the seat of knowledge, or his heart, wherein was understanding? In which did the real *truth lie?*

Logic, knowledge, intelligence. What wonderful gifts these are to humanity. If only they weren't so dangerous. It was for good reason God allowed his new creation to partake of every tree in the Garden of Eden other than the Tree of Knowledge. The fruit of the forbidden tree was withheld for a purpose far wiser than the human mind could grasp.

That the Tree of Life and the Tree of Knowledge were two different trees is a fact worth noting for, in our humanity, too often we equate the two, concluding that to have knowledge is to know life. Yet it is not true. That is one of the adversary's greatest lies. That it is our right to know, our due to understand, is a deception beyond all comprehension. I cringe whenever I hear the words.

Yet knowledge itself is not evil. It is important; it is good. It is a gift from God to be used in His time and for His purposes. Our willful dependence upon it is what gets us into trouble. When we begin to depend more upon what we see than upon the truths of God, which can only be revealed, we are trapped. Just because we cannot understand or explain something, it does not mean it isn't true, yet that is exactly what the ruler of this world would have us believe. And he does such a good job of convincing us. He is a master at inciting doubt in the minds of God's people by planting seeds of uncertainty and watering them with just enough reason and knowledge to make them grow. He doesn't even have to resort to lies. He only needs to hide a few elements of the truth or leave out a few key principles for his plan to succeed. He knows how easily we are led astray, our fallen eyes occluded as they are by the cataracts of sin. And so he wields his arsenal of logic, knowing few can resist its appeal. Blinding our eyes to the realities of the spiritual world, he simply leaves out anything that might damage his cause and hopes we'll never notice. And the sad thing is, we rarely disappoint him. We love our knowledge. We can reason our way into and out of anything we please as we elevate logic to the highest levels of human attainment. And we think we're so smart.

Father, give us courage to live in faith though the wisdom of humanity may call it folly. Impress upon us the truths of Your Word and guard our minds lest we fall prey to the deceptive clutches of human understanding. O Lord, may Your wisdom rule our minds and hearts this day, that we might truly know the secrets of eternity as You see fit to reveal them. Increase in us true faith that, believing, we might see, and cause us to grow daily in the grace and the knowledge of our Lord, Jesus Christ.

PRIDE: THE ARROGANCE OF THE ELK

Reclining its head ever so slightly, the skeletal creature settled into the brittle prairie grass, a ghost of a smile playing upon its wizened face. With an amused snort, it surveyed the grassy plain and absently chewed its cud. Who could have imagined the hunt would have proven to be so easy? It had but to make the merest suggestion and the conceited elk fell for it. Just look at him standing there, it mused, his powerful form poised majestically on the rise, his chest puffed out, his nose in the air. It is true he is an elegant beast, but one would think from his stance that the world itself should bow before his lordliness.

Shaking its head, the shadowy beast licked its lips and grinned at the unmitigated arrogance that exuded from the elk as he towered above the plain. It never failed to be amazed by the ease with which it could convince its prey of its own godhood, despite the blatant falsehood of the claim.

"It's a shame they are all so easily deluded." It sighed contentedly. "It ruins the challenge of the hunt. Yet, I suppose it doesn't really matter, so long as their pride reigns victorious. It's a wonder such a regal beast could remain so oblivious to the truth."

But, oblivious the elk was. As pride swelled the heart of the foolish beast, he stood erect, shamelessly flaunting his self-proclaimed glory to the world, completely unaware of his folly.

Pride has to be the greatest bane of the human heart. Pride, vanity, arrogance, pomposity, conceit, piety. They all walk hand in hand, each one as distasteful and ugly as the one before. Not only in the eyes of humanity, but even more so, in the eyes of God. Yet how incredibly vulnerable we are to its crippling attack. Tricking us into believing ourselves to be greater than we truly are, the evil one blinds our eyes to the plight of our sinful, selfish hearts and fools us into thinking we need no God. By building within us an exalted—though faulty—sense of our own glory, he steals from us the very thing we need most: the desire to bow before, and submit ourselves to, the God who created us.

It is the most hideous sin of the adversary's own heart that he seeks so vehemently to visit upon the children of his nemesis. Maybe that is why it is so pervasive. As the evil one lures our hearts and works to fashion our minds after his own, is it any wonder he would try to foist his own greatest depravity upon the people of God? Yet obvious, he is not. Pride is one of those things that sneaks up on a person, devouring the heart before its presence is recognized. Oh, that we could see ourselves for what we truly are.

Father, give us Your eyes to see ourselves in the light of Your truth. Let us not succumb to the pride that so easily ensnares our hearts, but grant us the grace to submit ourselves ever and only unto You, in full acknowledgement of who we are both in You and to You. Let us not think more highly of ourselves than we ought, for You alone are holy, You alone are the Lord, and You have made us for Yourself.

IGNORANCE: THE FISH'S FOLLY

The aging fish swam contentedly through the sun-dappled shallows of the stagnant pond, heedless of the monstrosity that lurked among them. They had dwelt in these waters all their days—swimming in their murky shadows, frolicking near their grassy banks, hunting in their chilling depths. It was home. Yet they knew nothing of its most menacing inhabitant. Life for them was what they knew, what they saw, what they felt. Never did it cross their minds that they might not be alone. The thought that there might be a whole world around them of which they were unaware was beyond comprehension. That a malevolent entity lurked among them enslaving their hearts without their knowledge was a thought no sane fish would entertain. They had no idea of the threat which, even then, held them in its deadly grasp and blinded them to the truth. But that's the way the skeletal ichthyoid liked it. The more ignorant the prey, and the more oblivious it was to its presence, the easier it was to trap. And so the fish swam on, daily losing more of their territory to the unseen enemy, never knowing something was desperately amiss.

What you don't know can't hurt you is one of those time-honoured axioms passed down from generation to generation, though why that should be is a question worth pondering. For it isn't true; it's a lie, and the evil one knows it. Even we can see the falsehood in it, yet that doesn't seem to stop us from living our lives as if it were true. *Hide our heads in the sand long enough and the unpleasantries we so desperately wish to deny just might go away* tends to be the approach we prefer, despite its obvious dangers.

While most of us would think it foolish to apply such a principle in the physical realm of this world, how sad it is that we seem to apply it so thoughtlessly in the realm of the spiritual. So blinded have we become to the unseen world around us, that we rarely acknowledge the possibility of something beyond the scope of our limited understanding, let alone consider it to be a threat. Yet all the while, the adversary lurks, waiting for the best opportunity to attack.

Selective ignorance is one of his greatest allies in the battle for our hearts for it gives him the freedom and space to do his work without the hindrance of human resistance. While we have no shortage of curiosity about the spiritual world, the lack of knowledge inherent in our understanding of it puts us all at risk of ambush. The adversary is very real—though he would rather we believe he is not—and, as Peter reminds us, he still roams the earth seeking those he can devour (I Peter 5:8). Let us not close our eyes to his presence.

Father, fill us with Your wisdom that we might be alert to the presence of the enemy. Grant us Your courage to stand against his ploys and Your strength to resist his advances; may he never be granted admittance.

Open the eyes of our hearts, O Lord, to recognize the realities of the spiritual realm, confident in Your matchless sovereignty, and let us not be bound by the fear of that which You see fit to reveal. Free us from the folly of ignorance, we pray, and let us never take for granted that which our eyes cannot see.

COMPROMISE: THE SEAGULL'S DECISION

"Leave? We can't leave! This is our home." *The agitated seagull flapped her wings, hoping to scare the avian intruder from her roost.* "Surely you could make an exception."

"Maybe," *came the silken reply of the unwelcome guest.* "I suppose we could consider it. It is true it isn't quite what I had in mind, but I suppose an exception might be in order—after all, compromise is to be applauded." *The hint of a smile toyed at the corners of its skeletal eyes as it paused to ponder the options.* "Come, let us negotiate."

Relieved, the seagull nodded her head. Her eyes flickered back to the handful of birds huddled on the ledge behind her and she wondered for a moment what she had gotten herself into. Eager as she was to please them, she could not risk offending her outspoken visitor. Yet how could she possibly please both?

"Suppose we…" *As if in a dream, she listened to herself push for compromise, ignoring the persistent voice within urging her to stand firm. Some things simply were not meant to be compromised. A long pause filled the air as she strove to clear her thoughts.*

"What would it matter," *the skeletal bird asked,* "if we do it this way or that, then or now, with or without their consent? Does it really matter if we have to fib a little in the process? Why, is it not the result that truly counts?" *Pacing back and forth along the ledge, it stopped to give the seagull a conspiratorial wink.* "Who would begrudge us a little profit on the side? You can't possibly think it would really matter." *Sensing the seagull's discomfort, the strange bird chuckled.* "Why, you don't actually have to give up on your convictions—just fudge them a little. No one will know. Not that they would care if they did. Besides, surely you can't be so narrow-minded as to think the convictions you hold so dear are absolutely *sacred. Just* give *a little. You don't have to abandon them altogether. It's called compromise."*

What could the stalwart seagull say? The intruder's words were outrageously untrue; yet the more passionately she protested, the more patronizing its reply and the more convincing seemed its argument. Maybe compromise was the only option. Maybe, as the skeletal bird had said, it really didn't matter. Perhaps it was *the only solution to her predicament.*

The seagull gulped, willing herself to remain calm. The choice was hers alone, and a more daunting decision she had never known. To compromise or not to compromise—that was the question.

From our earliest interactions, we have been encouraged—and at times even forced—to perfect the art of compromise. And there's not a thing wrong with that. In fact, it is a good and right thing to do. Most of the time. For people to live together harmoniously, compromise is a given; our uniqueness demands it.

Yet there are things that should never be compromised, although the world, in its wisdom, would argue differently. How insidiously the evil one works his will on humanity. If he can get us to compromise on the little things—the things we *ought* not to compromise—then when the big things come along—the things we *dare* not compromise—we'll be so well practised in the art that we won't even think to resist.

How carelessly we risk compromising the Word of God and the life of the Spirit within us. Like the proverbial frog stewing in the cooking pot, the compromise occurs so gradually, we hardly know it is happening at all. Compromise is a wonderful thing, but compromising the truth is deadly. That is why the enemy spends so much time honing this most valuable weapon. Inoculate us little by little with venom from its barbed arrows and maybe, just maybe, we will succumb to its poison when we are called to stand for the truth.

Father, grant us Your wisdom to recognize when compromise is the necessary and right thing to do and when it is destined to destroy. Fill us, we pray, with Your courage that we might stand firm in the truths of Your Word, even when compromise would seem to be the easier route. Alert our hearts to areas of compromise in our lives that need to be addressed and illumine them by Your truth that we might boldly cast them aside and stand firm in our faith. O Lord, by Your grace, keep our consciences clear and let us not fail You in the time of temptation.

ACCUSATION: THE CURSE OF THE RAVENOUS MOUNTAIN LION

The shadowy creature was everywhere the wretched wildcat went. Looming beyond each corner, it stalked her every move, forever lying in wait, poised to ambush her trembling heart. There was no escaping its insidious presence. Wherever she went, it was there, hissing accusations in her tender ears and scourging her heart with shame.

"You'll never be good enough to gain His favour. Do you know how many defenceless little animals you've killed in your life? They all belong to Him, you know. And what about the ones you've merely maimed?" An oily smile crept across the sinister creature's face. "You're despicable, evil, ugly to the core. Oh, beauty may show itself in your feline grace, but what of your heart? Ye-esss..." It paused, nodding, gauging her response. "What of your heart? Your very nature betrays you."

The weary mountain lion sank to the ground and lowered her eyes. Self-contempt was her constant companion these days. With a sigh, she rested her whiskers on her paws and gazed into the shallow stream. The accuser was right. She could never hope to win the favour of her Maker; she didn't deserve it. Her every impulse confirmed it. She was ugly. Reprehensible. Evil to the core. If only it were not so.

The eyes of the tawny beast drooped as she crouched at the edge of her dreams, hating the monster she had become. Who could abide such a foul beast? Who would embrace such a loathsome fiend? Raising her head, she peered once more at the stream. Her reflection taunted her as it rippled across the surface of the water and she cringed. The shadowy creature was right. There was no denying what she knew to be true. With a snarl, she flicked out a paw and swatted at the offending image, scattering it in a volley of choppy waves. If only her past could be eradicated so easily.

Guilt. Shame. Self-hatred. Caught in its steely grip, we cannot help but despair. We know we are unrighteous; we recognize the seeds of sin growing in our hearts. We don't need to be told that we are far from the holy people God calls us to be. Night and day, our hearts condemn us, for not only do we not measure up to the righteousness of our God, we are helpless to make ourselves righteous before Him. Over and over, our hearts are laid bare in His presence as we plead for His forgiveness, scourging ourselves with the agony of regret and writhing in the throes of self-hatred. And to this, the evil one adds his own accusations, gleefully heaping condemnation upon our broken hearts. Is there no hope for us?

Desperately grasping after the favour of our God, we cry out for His mercy while tenaciously clinging to our own guilt, unwilling to accept the absolution He so graciously provides. It is one of the great paradoxes of life: We desperately want to be rid of our sin so we might stand guiltless before our Father. Willing to take our unrighteousness upon Himself, our Father invites us to lay our sins at His feet that He might rid our hearts of them forever, just as we desire. But the accuser stands ever near, badgering the hearts of God's children with accusations and convincing us that we are unfit to lay our sins at the feet of a holy and righteous God. How it must hurt the heart of God to see the children he has suffered so much to free wallowing in shame as we cling to the guilt He yearns to absolve.

In John 3:17 (KJV), the apostle John notes, "God sent not his Son into the world to condemn the world; but that the world through Him might be saved." If Jesus does not condemn us, what right have we to condemn ourselves? Our righteousness is not dependent upon the things we have or have not done, but upon the righteousness of Jesus. When Paul says, "...there is now no condemnation for those who are in Christ Jesus," he means what he says (Romans 8:1, NIV). It isn't up to us.

The adversary is right; we are guilty. But where he would have us wallow in our guilt and bury our hearts in shame, God invites us to come boldly into His presence, confident that in Jesus, we will not be condemned. It sounds too good to be true, but it's not. In Christ Jesus, *nothing* is too good to be true.

Free us, Father, we pray, from the merciless hold of the accuser, that we might stand with confidence in the light of Your grace. Let us not be destroyed by the condemnation he would heap upon our hearts, for You have borne our guilt and freed us from its burden forever. Precious Jesus, Tireless Burden-Bearer, Faithful Advocate, shield our hearts from the arrows of the Evil One and fill us with Your peace.

CONFORMITY: THE ERROR OF THE GEESE

It seemed like the right thing to do at the time; all the other geese were doing it. Why, even now three more approached, their powerful wings carrying them upward and onward to places unknown, to opportunities no goose could afford to miss. Curious, the young geese looked on, enthralled by the mass migration, wondering where the majestic birds were going and what their exodus might mean. They needed to act quickly if they didn't want to be left behind.

With an excited nod, the young ones rose, beating their wings in determined synchronization with the strange, yet powerful, birds before them. Thrilled to be in the company of such magnificent geese, the courageous duo soared across the sunlit meadows in a haze of delighted oblivion.

"I wonder where we are going," the first one puffed.

"I wonder when we're going to get there," came the breathless reply of the other.

Numbed by the unaccustomed exertion, the birds fell silent and the rhythmic beating of their wings began to slow. With each determined stroke, they struggled to close the widening gap that opened before them, but their aching wings would carry them no farther.

"Where do they get all their energy?" the first bird asked.

The two young geese peered at the fast fading flock and shrugged. The birds they trailed were definitely odd. There was a certain illusiveness about them that the two youngsters couldn't quite define. Exhausted, they ceased their frenzied attempt to keep up and glided to the ground on the banks of a rocky bay. They peered again at the retreating flock, but the more they looked, the less they liked what they saw. The strange birds were unlike any the two had ever seen. They seemed somehow ghostly, skeletal, almost lifeless. In fact, one might hardly call them geese at all.

With a sigh, the young ones turned their attention to the unfamiliar landscape. "Do you know where we are?" the largest of the two whispered frantically.

Alarmed, they scanned the little bay. In their pursuit of the ghostly birds, they had somehow lost their way and had no idea how to find their way back. Maybe joining the mass migration hadn't been such a good idea after all, though little they would gain from their remorse. They were caught. Caught between continuing down a path destined to lead to destruction and navigating a perilous course through the loneliness of the wilderness in the hope of finding the abundant life they had so thoughtlessly forsaken.

"What should we do?"

The young goose could barely hear the raspy voice of his terrified companion above the beating of his own heart. "I want—I want to go home..."

Conformity is comforting. To stand out in a crowd, to walk the paths of resistance, to stand alone in the face of opposition—these are not feats to which we aspire. In fact, most of us would rather avoid them at all cost; the consequences of non-conformity can be scary. When the apostle Paul urges us to "be not conformed to this world," he does not do so lightly (Romans 12:2, KJV). He knows firsthand the sorrows to which a life of non-conformity can lead, having suffered much for his own refusal to comply with the norms of the society in which he lived. Conformity is the easy way in a difficult world, for non-conformity demands a price few are willing to pay. That's what makes it such a perfect weapon.

The adversary knows that the greater the opposition—the more unrelenting the ridicule, the sharper the discomfort, the greater the sorrow—the harder it is to resist the desire to comply with the dictates of the world around us. And, he can be very convincing. But Paul gives us a better way. We are not to pledge conformity to the people and things of this world, he says, but rather, we are to allow Jesus to transform our hearts and minds that we might conform to the wonders of the Kingdom to come (Romans 12:2). Bowing to the wisdom and ways of this world is not the way our Father would have us go, no matter how convincingly the adversary may present the option. The way of destruction is paved by conformity. Wide is the road and many are they who travel it (Matthew 7:13).

Father, grant us the courage to choose life, the determination to stand alone in the face of opposition, the will to walk the lonely path of obedience. Grant us wise and discerning hearts to recognize the pathway of life You have set before us, and the courage to walk upon it, even when it means we must walk alone. Provide for us, we pray, good friends along the way that we might help each other to stay on track and strengthen our hearts to finish the race that we might receive the Crown of Life promised to all who follow You.

COMPLACENCY: THE OTTER'S INDIFFERENCE
The whispering wind haunted the lonely otter as he stretched upon the pebbled beach, its gentle caress beckoning him with the promise of impending joy. Shifting his muscular body, he stretched, turning sleepy eyes from the rhythmic waves to peer along the shore. He could almost hear his name warbled on the wind's gentle breath and he lifted his graceful neck in answer to its call. He longed to hear more, yet lulled by the comforts of his seaside home, he couldn't seem to rouse himself to pursue the summons.

With a quiet sigh, he closed his eyes and rolled onto his side, basking in the music of the spheres, yet never quite heeding its call. Listening to the voice of promise, but never rousing to follow its command. Settling for a glimpse of the eternal while rooting himself in the shallow oblivion of life as he knew it. Neither hot nor cold, he lay on the stony pier and succumbed to the passionless existence that enfolded him, oblivious to the pangs of desire that promised him fullness of joy.

Complacency, indifference, apathy. They are a dangerous trio. A powerful triad that afflicts each one of us at one time or another. Lulled into a false sense of satisfaction, how easy it is for us to content ourselves with passionless lives, dead to the desires that would drive us to the Source of Life. But that's how the enemy likes it. Satisfaction is integral to the adversary's success. Satisfaction in the strength and resources of humanity, satisfaction in the paltry pleasures and pastimes of this world, satisfaction in anything but the presence and love of our Father. Even those who have tasted the wondrous glory of our Lord are not immune. It's just so much easier some days to accept the mundane and ignore the magnificence for which we were created. Less exciting perhaps, but easier. Oh, let us not be fooled.

Father, kindle our hearts with the fervency of holy desire and awaken in us a well-spring of everlasting love that cannot be quenched. Grant us the courage, the passion, the will to abandon the comforts of this world, ever mindful of the glories of eternity that await us. Let us not be lulled into complacency, O Lord, but fill us with the urgency of undying love that, forsaking all else, our desire would be for You alone.

INDULGENCE: THE INSATIABLE THIRST OF THE WOLF
Touching parched lips to the cool water, the silver-maned wolf lapped eagerly in a futile attempt to sate his mounting thirst. How strange that, no matter how much he drank, his thirst could not be assuaged. Plunging his snout further into the blue-green depths, he drank deeply—wanting, needing, demanding more. Not that it would do him any good. Lately it seemed that the more he drank, the thirstier he felt. Shaking the shimmering droplets from his face, he backed away from the quiet pool. The need for water consumed his every thought. Many moons had waxed and waned since he had surrendered himself to its demand, yet fulfilment always seemed to be just beyond reach. Tail drooping, he turned toward the trees. There was a stream not far beyond them that flowed into the sea. Maybe he would stop to get a drink there.

It never crossed the wolf's mind that there might be something wrong with the water. In fact, in his haste to slake his fiery thirst, he hardly noticed the bitter tang that left him longing for more. Nor had his eyes beheld the spectral shadow lapping the coveted water from his mouth as he sought to satiate his longing. He didn't know he was lapping from the wrong stream, or to be more exact, the wrong streams, for had he not, in desperation, tried them all? All but the great waterfall that cascaded from the clouds. Who, but a fool would try to drink from that?

Head bowed, the wolf sank his snout back into the water, ignoring the cataract that gushed but a heartbeat away. Water was water.

Indulgence is the hallmark of the society in which we live. A people of myriad appetites and desires, we yearn for gratification and will do almost anything in our power to see our longings fulfilled. We were made for something better—something perfect, something glorious—and we cannot help but pine for it. We know there is something we are missing, something we cannot live without, and yet we cannot seem to isolate exactly what that something is.

The idea that our desire is an invitation from our Heavenly Father to return to the paradise for which we were created, escapes us. But it does not escape the adversary. He knows the best way to snare the hearts of God's children is to pervert something good into something unspeakably profane. And so he uses our thirst for all that is good to trick us into seeking fulfilment in a world of alluring alternatives, carefully blinding our eyes to the fact that God alone can fulfil the desires of our hearts.

The evil one knows how easy it is for us to succumb to the lure of things that cannot satisfy. That is why indulgence is such a successful tool in his hands. It works every bit as effectively today as it did so long ago in Eden. Drawn to the passing pleasures of this world, we immerse our hearts in our drug of choice: food, alcohol, labour, consumerism, fantasy, eroticism, sports, hobbies, fame, good works. The list is as varied as it is endless, but the items on that list are similar in that they all lure our hearts away from the only true source of fulfilment by promising to satisfy our every longing. Yet, while they might relieve our thirst for a time, the relief never lasts. It can't. For only when we bring our desires to God will our thirsty souls be quenched; in Him alone flows the River of Life.

Father, draw our hearts that we might find the satisfaction of our desires in You alone. Reveal to us, we pray, the substitute pleasures in which we indulge in our quest to satisfy the desires that drive us, and grant us Your grace to cast them aside. May they not rule over us. O Lord, increase in us a desire for righteousness and truth, and fill us with a passion for You surpassed only by Your passion for us.

ENTITLEMENT: THE PETULANCE OF THE SELFISH OTTER

Curiosity piqued the otter's interest as her eyes fell upon the unusual sea creature. Lounging on the crest of the waves, the skeletal apparition rocked contentedly on its back, the final rays of the dying sun gilding its belly. It looked rather alarming with its cavernous eyes and skeletal frame, yet there was something intensely intriguing about it nonetheless. An irresistible impulse drew the otter's attention toward the shadowy animal so like herself and yet, so inexplicably different.

Absently nibbling a pawful of rosy urchins, she studied the beast before her, troubled by the host of disturbing questions that gnawed at the corners of her mind. What was it doing here in her private waters? How dared it enter unbidden? Just look at the way it loafed around, floating so idly and effortlessly upon the waves and stealing her sun, no less. The nerve of some creatures! She could think of a few choice words she'd like to share with the brassy thing—if only she dared.

A thousand angry thoughts assaulted her as, one by one, she rehearsed her grievances. An otter had rights. There were rules to govern such things. One simply did not infringe upon the rights of others like that. It wasn't right. It wasn't fair. It wasn't done. Her irritation increased with each pronouncement, feeding the resentment within and stoking her ire. She wouldn't even think of infringing upon the territory of another like that. It was just plain wrong.

With an angry huff, the otter scanned the horizon. It was getting late; the sun would soon set. Once again, her resentment overflowed in the heat of internal dialogue, her eyes darkening with the chill of animosity as she stared at the unwelcome apparition. And, like a splinter festering in the depths of her heart, her sense of entitlement grew. She didn't know yet what she would do, but she would do something. Perhaps the intruder would be gone by morning.

Entitlement surrounds us. We only need to look within to see its insidious tentacles gripping our hearts and spewing their bitter lies to all who would listen. Increasingly, our world is driven by it. The more we have, the more we want, and sadly, the more we imagine it to be our right to possess. Selfishness and greed pervade the world in which we live, and when the expectations of that self-centredness are not fulfilled, bitterness and resentment take root. We accept it as a fact of life, but it is not; it is the buckshot of the adversary seeding God's children with the spirit of discontentment.

More pervasive than we would like to admit, it is everywhere we look. *You deserve it. They have no right. Stand up for yourself. Who are they to stand in your way?* Every day the call of entitlement tugs at our hearts, and blinded to the real story, we believe its lies. If our eyes were only open to the truth; how blessed we are that we do *not* get what we deserve.

We have no rights—at least, not before our Lord. We gave up any rights we might have had long ago when we first walked away from the Father who loves us. Our rights are nothing but an illusion. What we imagine to be rights are really *privileges*—privileges given to us by a patient and compassionate Father who loves us dearly and bears with our infirmities, unwilling to surrender His children as casualties of war.

We know this, yet entitlement continues to hound us, crippling our hearts with the perils of self-absorption. A powerful weapon, it leads to a host of evils so subtle they can take root and bear fruit before we even realize they have been planted. But the real secret to the success of this weapon is the way it takes our eyes off our Father and focuses them inward upon ourselves. That is the true threat of entitlement. *It's all about us,* our culture claims, but it is wrong. It's really all about *Him.*

Father, release us from the sins of entitlement which so subtly, yet persistently, attack the hearts of Your beloved; free us, we pray, from the bitterness and resentment they beget. Remove from us the selfishness and greed that so easily displace the love You have rooted in our hearts and fill us from the wellspring of Your love, that compassion and understanding might overflow from our hearts to touch the lives of all we meet. Focus our eyes on You, we pray, and let us not be drawn into the web of destruction the evil one has set for us, for we belong to You.

SELF-SUFFICIENCY: THE BANE OF THE ELEGANT SWAN

An aura of confidence surrounded the glorious swan as she paddled down the tranquil stream, her head held high, her eyes fixed firmly upon the future. Elegance embodied her every move. Elegance, beauty, power, majesty. An angel itself could not compare to her glory, and she knew it. Lowering her eyes, she smiled at the statuesque reflection mirrored in the quiet waters and congratulated herself on her poise.

She was not, she supposed, like other swans, though one might be fooled at first glance. She stifled a snort as she watched them paddling about in the shallows, shepherding their cygnets in the hollows, glued to the sides of their mates. No, she was not like them at all, she assured herself. She travelled alone—just the way she liked it. "What need do I have of them?" She rose, stretching her wings. "I don't need their strength. I have no use for their companionship. They're nothing but fools."

The sun's final rays wreathed the swan in splendour, as she slid through the twilit waters. Glancing once more at her reflection, she smiled. The image was strong, stately, steady. Like her. Yet, there was something about it that troubled her. Her feet stilled as she dipped her slender neck to get a better view. While reminiscent of her beauty, there was a lifeless quality to it that could not be ignored. Stark and skeletal, the watery image hinted at a heart filled with chaos and writhing with conflicting emotions. That couldn't be right. Something was wrong. Perhaps she was seeing the reflection of one of the other birds. She scanned the stream, disturbed to find herself alone. It couldn't really be her reflection, could it?

With a menacing hiss, the swan rose, beating the water with her wings. Relieved, she watched as the offending image dissipated in a flurry of ripples. Yet as soon as the water calmed, the likeness returned and her studied poise faltered. Determined to ignore the shadowy spectre, she straightened her neck and paddled on, her head held high as she willed the reflection to go away. Yet, much to her chagrin, it followed her wherever she went and there was nothing she could do to stop it. Perhaps independence was not quite as alluring as she had supposed.

Independence and self-sufficiency are two of the most deadly weapons the evil one levels against us. We were created to be dependent—dependent upon the God who made us for Himself, dependent upon the One who loves us and wants us for His own—and there is nothing that chafes the heart of the adversary more. And so he mounts his attack. If he can drive a wedge between the Father and His beloved by fostering a spirit of independence within the hearts and minds of God's people, he can deal a savage blow to the heart of God. And that's just what he aims to do.

Independence is one of those sure-fire weapons that embeds itself deeply and effortlessly in the hearts of all mankind. The arrow strikes early—we need only spend time with a two or three year old to see that—and slowly releases its poison into our hearts and minds with each passing day. *If you want something done right, do it yourself. Look out for yourself; no one else will. Depend on another and you will be disappointed.*

The evil one delights in each calculated attack for he understands what we do not, that when independence blossoms, our relationships begin to wither. Independence and relationship, by definition, cannot coexist. Introduce independence to our relationships and they will be destroyed; introduce it to our relationship with God, and the adversary's goal is achieved. The heart ruled by independence cannot help but scorn the intimacy God so longs to share with His children. If we are convinced we must look to ourselves alone for the fulfilment of our deepest needs, we will never turn to our Father for His most glorious provision.

This weapon, however, can be confusing, for there is a certain independence that is healthy and necessary and right as we grow from childhood into adulthood. Respect for the time and desires of others dictates that we learn to tie our own shoes, zip our own coats, do our own laundry; we do not exist to be served. Yet for most of us, our self-sufficiency does not end there. I often wonder if the attribute that Jesus lauded in children was their dependence. Children know they need others to look after them; it is not hard for them to turn to others for support. The same cannot be said for most adults, though. Somehow, as we mature, we start to fool ourselves into thinking that we can make it on our own, that we don't really need anyone but ourselves, that dependence is only for the weak. But we are wrong. We *do* need each other, and even more so, we need our Father. It is He who made us for Himself and we are incomplete until we find our completion in Him.

Father, we are an independent people, afraid to trust and bent upon going our own way. Forgive us for our lack of trust and grant that we may live lives dependent upon You alone. Where we have deliberately wandered away from Your care and held ourselves aloof, draw us near. Where we have shrunk back in reluctance from fear of Your hand, give us the courage to turn to You. Where we have willfully chosen to depend upon none but ourselves, grant us mercy. You made us for Yourself and we belong to You. Protect us from the poison of the evil one, we pray, and let us not by entrapped by the subtlety of his attacks. Keep us ever dependent upon You, O Lord, for we need You far more than we know.

DISCORD: THE PUFFIN'S FURY

Anger simmered in the gizzard of the furious puffin as he recalled the fiery interchange. The constant discord was wearing, the intolerance exhausting. If it wasn't one source of contention, it was another. Would he and his fine-feathered beauty never see eye-to-eye? The pain of disharmony deepened with each passing day, numbing him to the love they once shared, and he found himself wondering if there was any hope of reconciliation. Were they forever destined to bicker?

Irritation quickened his breath as he rehearsed his argument yet again. He was right and he knew it; he held not a whisker of doubt about that. He was right and she was wrong and no one could convince him otherwise. The lines of division had been drawn, the walls of enmity laid, and with them, the joy of unity destroyed.

The puffin cringed beneath the disapproving glare of his mate as she winged past his perch, her burning stare fuelling the fires of wrath simmering within his heart. Compromise was not an option. He had taken his stand and, right or wrong, he would not budge from it. The fact that he couldn't quite remember what the argument was about served only to strengthen his resolve. The breach in their relationship had rapidly widened to a yawning gulf and he simply was not prepared to bridge the gap. Nor, he suspected, was she.

And so they fought on, the intensity of their discord mounting with no resolution in sight, the source of their contention long forgotten. And with each razor-tipped word, the evil one smirked in triumph. The only thing better than an enemy at war with its adversary was an enemy at war with its friend.

Discord, disharmony, contention. It all boils down to a lack of unity. Disputes arise, tempers flare, arguments erupt and wars are waged in which no party wins. Meanwhile, our hearts and minds are so diverted from the real war raging around us that we allow our rearguard to slip, opening ourselves up to further attack. A host of different perspectives combine with heightened passions and simmering indignation to bury the beleaguered soul in dispute after weary dispute, robbing it of the joy of selfless love for which it was created. This is not the way we were meant to live. "Divide and conquer," is the victory cry of the evil one. "United you stand, divided you fall," is our Father's plea. And He's right. It is no wonder the enemy takes such delight in creating and nurturing tension among God's people. It is so much easier for him to destroy God's children when they are vulnerable and alone than it is when they are united as one.

Disunity is a powerful weapon and it serves the enemy remarkably well, for oblivious to the part we have to play in the great War of Eternity, we far too often give the enemy our full cooperation. If only we were better at turning the contention back to its source.

Father, how easily we give ourselves over to the schemes of the evil one. Free us from the spirit of disharmony that divides Your people and forgive us for falling prey to the divisive arrows of the enemy. Unite our hearts with Yours, O Lord, that Your thoughts might be our thoughts, Your ways, our ways, and Your desires, our desires. Unify us, we pray, and make us one with You—and each other.

FORGETFULNESS: THE BEAR'S DOWNFALL

A blissful sigh escaped the weary bear as she settled herself on the sun-baked rock. Mesmerized by the rhythmic stroking of unseen hands, she lay entranced, oblivious to the world around her. She was comfortable... relaxed... content... at ease. Ever so slowly, her mind and will succumbed to the soothing whispers of the shadow as it urged her to surrender to the haze of forgetfulness pressing upon her, and a numbing calm closed in around her. Still, a niggling memory fluttered at the edge of her consciousness, only half awakening her from the dream-like stupor that blanketed her mind.

The great bear shifted as the pressure of a tiny paw nudged insistently at her hulking frame. It crossed her mind that she might be forgetting something, though what it might be she did not know. Struggling to open her bleary eyes, she lifted her nose to sniff the air. The fleeting memory was just beyond reach. With a noisy yawn, she rubbed her belly on the rock and gave in to the overpowering weariness that pervaded her soul as forgetfulness cast its spell upon her heart. If it was important, it would come to her later. Probably. Heedless of her cub's insistence, the hulking bear rolled onto her side and lost herself to slumber. Maybe come summer...

Forgetfulness is one of the most subtle, yet deadly poisons that tip the arrows of the evil one. If he can just get God's children to forget—to forget who we are, to forget the glory that once was ours, to forget the Father who loves us and desires us for His own—then he has won. If we forget who we are, and to whom we belong, he can make us believe any lie he would concoct to drive a wedge between our hearts and the heart of the One who loves us more than life.

It is a terrible thing to be forgotten, and the evil one knows it. He knows there is little that can so keenly rend the heart of God than to be forgotten by His beloved and to see her wandering, frightened and alone, believing herself abandoned and bereft of all hope. He knows God is, by nature, Love, and in the Father's yearning to comfort His beloved, His heart can't help but ache with the torment of lost love when His every advance is denied. That is what makes forgetfulness such a valuable weapon. That, and the fact that it is so difficult to detect. Forgetfulness is a trap that captures us unaware, and anaesthetizes us to its sting until its work is complete. Consider how easy it is for us to get caught up in the challenges of day-to-day living and forget the life for which we were created, the life to which our Father has called us. As the adversary draws the veil of forgetfulness ever tighter around our hearts and minds, the memories of our truest selves grow dim, enshrouding us in a haze of loneliness and uncertainty. It is as if we have been torn from the side of our Beloved and our hearts rent asunder, for our memories have been taken captive and replaced by lies.

O Lord, rouse our hearts from their slumber and awaken us to Your truth, that we might live each day in the awareness of Your beloved presence. Let us not be lulled into the realm of forgetfulness by the hypnotic charms of the evil one, but instead be aroused to do battle, ever mindful of who we are both in You and to You. O Lord, may we daily be partakers of the abundant life You promise to all who would follow You for we long to be fully alive, our hearts awakened to Your love, our souls attuned to every movement of Your Spirit within us. Father, awaken our hearts to our peril and grant us Your power to resist the mesmerizing appeal of the enemy.

CONFRONTATION: THE DILEMMA OF THE CORNERED RACCOON

The trembling raccoon froze, staring at the grisly apparition before him. His whiskers quivered as his eyes darted from side to side and his nose began to twitch. There had to be some way of escape. The hideous creature blocking his path loomed before him, poised for the kill. The raccoon cringed at the steely determination etched upon the skeletal features of the unwelcome beast and edged back a step. The once powerful dictator of the masked marauder's heart, though long evicted from its foul throne, had returned.

Shrinking back in alarm, the raccoon considered his options, silently willing the oppressor to depart while stubbornly resisting the urge to flee. Fur bristled on the back of his neck as the intruder closed the space between them. One step. Two. Three. He was cornered. Trapped. To hide would be useless; to flee, in vain. Yet did he have within him the courage—or the will—to resist? The choice was his. His heart quaked at the menacing sneer that spread across the face of his enemy as it took another step forward. What was a raccoon to do?

While it would appear that the evil one prefers the subtle approach, it is clear he does not limit himself to that approach alone. If the direct approach works, he will use it. If he can corner God's children and intimidate us into adopting his will as our own, he will do so.

Challenging our loyalty and resolve, the evil one shrewdly opts for direct assault whenever it suits his purposes—whenever he thinks he can cow us into doing his will. Which leaves us with a difficult decision. Not because we do not know what to do, but because he can be so incredibly persuasive. It is not a trick that we fall for, or a trap we fall into, but a clear choice we are called to make.

Should we, or shouldn't we? That part is usually clear.

Will we, or won't we? That's the part with which we struggle.

It is our way or God's way, and it is a choice we are all called to make. Repeatedly. Just where *does* our allegiance lie? Will we give way to the prodding of the evil one or obey the voice of our Father? The choice is ours. Ours and ours alone. If only it wasn't so easy to give way to the enemy.

Father, grant us Your strength to resist the advances of the evil one that we might not fall prey to his imperious demands. Infuse us with Your courage to endure, Your wisdom to discern, and Your will to choose with certainty the way we should go. Grant us Your grace, O Lord, to stand firm in the knowledge that You alone are the rightful King and ruler of our hearts, and help us to walk in righteousness before You, no matter how convincingly the evil one might tempt us to stray. Provide for us a way of escape when the adversary strikes, and grant us Your grace to take it, as You teach us to cling to You.

DISTRACTION: THE CONFUSION OF THE LOON

The bewildered loon stared in confusion at the cacophony of shifting images bombarding her senses. Crooning in distress, she squinted her eyes and strained to discern the vacillating reflections that danced in the shadows before her, but she could not make them out. Slowly she blinked her eyes. If only she could discern what was real from what was mere fancy, what required her attention from what held no import, what she saw from the threat of what she could not see. She cocked her head to one side and exhaled in frustration. Never had she seen anything like it.

Growing agitation assailed the regal bird as she eyed the fluctuating spectre. The ghostly curtain aroused in her an odd mingling of curiosity and fear. Whatever could it mean? She paddled through the darkening night, struggling to banish the puzzling scene from her mind, but she couldn't. As if drawn by a magnet, the loon peered at the eerie pattern of illusive shadows, her eyes darting wildly from one fluid scene to the next as she steered herself closer to the shore.

And so it was that, riveted by the ever-changing montage, the loon lost herself in the peculiar world of formless phantasms and failed to see the trees of the shoreline grove upon which the array of broken reflections flickered. And, in missing the trees, she also missed the loon-like apparition that peered from between them, snickering at the wary bird's befuddlement as her attention snapped from one startling image to the next. It worked every time!

Distraction is a powerful tool—anyone who works with young children knows that—yet, in the hands of the adversary, it is also a formidable weapon. I shake my head when I realize it has taken me weeks, perhaps even months, to begin work on this meditation. Talk about distraction! So many good, and seemingly essential, things have laid claim to my attention each day and kept me from the task, not to mention the trivialities that have ceaselessly clamoured for my time. A computer game here, an e-mail check there, endless marking and planning and preparation for school, a concert to organize, a newsletter to write, a book to read, a party to attend, a letter to write... There always seems to be something to take my focus away from the work set before me. Something necessary. Something worthwhile. Something *good*.

I didn't realize how distracted I had become until, casting sheer busyness aside, I finally took the opportunity to sit before my computer and write. Filled with excitement at the prospect of finally giving myself permission to do something I so enjoyed, I sat before the screen and set my fingers to the keys, bursting to get started. But instead of writing, I checked my e-mail, played a few games, did a little unnecessary research on the internet and finished off with a phone call, after which I decided it was time for a nap. It wasn't until then that I realized I was under attack. I am, as I expect we all are, notoriously slow to pick up on these things at times. That is the nature of distraction.

Focus is such an easy thing to divert. I'm a teacher; I fight the battle for my students' attention every day. I know what focus issues look like and I know the devastating impact they can have upon a person's life. Yet I have never thought of myself as a person who struggles with focus or attention issues. Until now.

However one describes it—diversion, distraction, inattentiveness, procrastination—lack of focus is perhaps the easiest and most dangerous weapon in the arsenal of the evil one. It finds its mark easily, for it is practically impossible to detect and it does not present itself as being evil. It entices our hearts and minds to wander without leave, and if its aim is true, the battle is lost before we even know we have strayed from the path. Distraction is a valuable weapon in the hands of the evil one, for the world is filled with things that distract us from the mission to which we have been called. But as we all know, things that appear harmless often prove to be the source of great harm. Oh, let our hearts beware.

Father, focus our hearts and minds fully upon You that we might not be distracted from the commission You have entrusted to us. Let us not be drawn astray by the trivialities that bid for our attention, but keep our eyes on You, that we might be sensitive to Your call and quick to respond to Your command. Forgive us, we pray, for allowing ourselves to fall prey to the endless distractions that seek to consume us, and let us never wander from the paths of glory You have prepared for us to follow.

ANALYSING THE ATTACK

chapter four

The arsenal of the enemy is formidable and strong, yet we do not need to succumb to its deadly power. The adversary, while he may refuse to admit it, knows that the war is already forfeit and that his glory days are numbered. We know this too, yet so often we live as though the outcome is uncertain. And so the attacks of the evil one intensify, for he will not accept defeat without a fight.

Remember the image of the roaring lion Peter introduces? It is not a question of *if* a roaring lion will strike, but of *when* and *how* it will do so. Lions are predatory beasts that prey on the life-blood of others. Yet for a lion to grow to maturity in the wild, it must not only be adept at the kill, it must also know its quarry. The ability to target the specific weaknesses of its prey is one of the key factors in its success. Though it may be vicious and calculating and cold, the lion hunts not for sport, but to sate the voracious appetite that drives it to the kill. Failure is not an option for the mighty beast; if it is to survive, it must defeat its prey. And so it studies its quarry until it can anticipate its every move, patiently waiting for it to let down its guard. Only then will the lion rush in to exploit every last vulnerability its victim has to offer.

It doesn't take much to see the parallels, does it? The evil one, driven by an insatiable hunger for revenge, roams the earth, honing in on his prey. He cows us into obedience to his will by amassing all the weapons of his arsenal against us, and lies in wait, eager to ambush the weak, the unsuspecting, the alone.

It can't help but chill our hearts to realize that he is an expert at recognizing and exploiting our vulnerabilities and that he knows us far better than we know ourselves. After all, he's had millennia to perfect his skills. Well acquainted with the evil propensities of our fallen nature, he recognizes the signs of our weakness with ease and mounts his offensive, expertly anticipating our responses and ruthlessly going in for the kill. It follows, then, that if we are to render useless the weapons he would use against us, we must clearly recognize and acknowledge our weaknesses so that we might be prepared to resist. We need to know ourselves every bit as well as the enemy knows us—and more so—if we are to withstand the weapons levelled against us.

Before moving on, I suggest that you take time to meditate upon the following questions, prayerfully identifying specific areas of weakness in your own life. Review the meditations in this chapter and note areas in which you think you might be most vulnerable to attack. Undoubtedly, there will be areas not covered in the devotionals in which you realize you are being targeted. That's okay. Each time I try to wrap up the devotional segment of this section, it seems God opens my eyes to yet another weapon to add to the list. The enemy is nothing if not adaptable. After reading Part III, we will revisit your answers to these questions and look at creating a plan of resistance, for as we will see in the chapters to come, we do not need to despair; our Father has not left us defenceless.

1. The adversary is the biggest button-pusher of all time. He skillfully hones in on our vulnerabilities and shamelessly exploits them to decimate our hearts and separate us from our Father. What are the buttons the evil one insists upon pushing in your life? Try to identify the five or six areas of vulnerability that plague you most.

_____
_____
_____
_____

2. Consider the weapons of the evil one discussed in Chapter Three. List those with which you identify most keenly.

3. Reflect upon your answers to questions one and two. Do you see a connection between the two? Record your reflections here.

4. How does the wartime analogy impact your understanding of the trials and temptations that touch your life?

Leaning against the mouldering sill of the tower window, Cosette peered through the bars of her cell at the highlands surrounding the ancient fortress. Grey and lifeless. Just like her heart. With each passing year, it seemed the hills grew more bleak, more unfriendly, more hopeless. A shudder lifted her shoulders as a parade of endless days wandered across her mind. No beginning. No end. Just one dreary day following another. Empty. Purposeless. Depressing. Had there never been anything else?

Clenching her fists, she rattled the bars before her and scowled. No matter how viciously she scoured the recesses of her memory for something—anything—that would lend a hint to a life before the hell she now endured, her efforts met with nothing but frustration. With a grunt, she dashed an angry tear from the corner of her eye and pushed herself away from the sill, but not before a sudden movement near the hangman's tree drew her eyes away from the accursed wilderness. Apparently some poor soul had managed to infuriate the master yet again. She cringed at the sound of laughter floating across the courtyard. The hangman grinned as the tyrant chuckled and clapped him on the back, then turned to stride purposefully from the still-struggling form dangling from the Tree of Death. *I wonder who it was this time.* Cosette shook her head and sighed. *Probably some wandering troubadour. Those travelling minstrels seem to be forever raising his ire.* The fact that they kept coming back troubled her. Everyone knew what happened to those who crossed the will of the self-appointed monarch of the Fortress of Fear. Did they not value their lives?

Turning from the grisly scene, Cosette snugged her threadbare blanket more tightly around her shoulders and hobbled across the fetid chamber toward the cot in the corner. Dragging her manacled legs onto the flea-ridden mat, she hugged her knees to her belly and rocked, swiping at the river of tears that found a familiar pathway down her cheek.

Perhaps there wasn't much in life worth valuing. Not for her, anyway. Her chest tightened as a maelstrom of sobs erupted from deep within and she raised her arms, circling them around her head. Was this all there was to life? Endless drudgery and merciless abuse? Nauseating pain and mind-numbing discomfort? Outright injustice and undisguised evil? How much longer could she live like this—one hopeless day following another, each new tomorrow promising to be bleaker than the one before?

* * *

Startled into wakefulness by the sinister rap of her captor's hobnailed boots, Cosette stifled a cry of alarm. Her chains tore at her chafed ankles as she struggled to gain her feet before he could invade the sorry sanctuary of her prison cell, and she prayed that he would, for once, pass her by. But she knew that he would not. When had he ever overlooked an opportunity to torment her?

Tugging her blanket around her shoulders like a shield, she steeled herself for the inevitable, abhorring the helpless wretch she had become. Her heart pounded as she stood, fists balled around the tattered hem of her wrap. He was taking an awfully long time—longer than usual. Beads of sweat gathered on her brow as she waited, painfully aware that his footfalls had ceased. What evils did he have in store for her this time? Swallowing hard, she leaned her head against the wall and forced her rapid breaths to slow. How had she ever gotten mixed up with the bloodthirsty tyrant in the first place?

As the seconds turned to minutes and all remained still, the panic that had gripped her began to subside and her mind started to wander. The dream had come again last night. Not that it was really a dream, exactly. It was more like a series of images, related in some way she was certain, though how, she did not know. It scared her just to think of it. Scared *and* comforted her at the same time.

First there was an amazing garden filled with exotic flowers and plants of every kind. The blending of colours and fragrances was beyond any her feeble mind could imagine. Then there was the whirling—around and around and around in the arms of some undefined someone her eyes could not quite see—and the delirious excitement that enveloped her as she fell to the ground, giggling with joy. *Oh, to be so blissfully happy and gloriously at peace.* She sighed, shaking her head in dismay. *What I wouldn't giv...*

Her mind recoiled as a new image replaced the breathtaking scene that awakened in her such desire. Searing heat. Brittle grass. Moving earth. An incessant roaring that grew and grew until she clapped her hands to her ears and fell to her knees. Then silence. Ominous, intense silence.

Cosette's heart raced as the silence gave way, replaced by the horror that inevitably followed. Without warning, a vast pit opened before her—a massive chasm—slippery, deep, uncrossable. Breathless, she watched herself teeter on its edge, scrambling to make it to stable ground. It annoyed her that she could never tell if she made it to safety or not, for the final image always rushed in before she could see what happened. Hands—strong, work-worn hands—extended toward her. Small, childlike hands reaching out in response. Neither quite able to touch. Glistening tears scalded the curious fingers of the child and somehow she knew they were her own. Then came the voice. Gentle. Sad. Imploring. "Don't ever forget that, dear one. Not ever. No matter what."

"Don't ever forget?" Cosette sniffed, willing herself not to cry. "Don't ever forget what?"

Her captor forgotten, Cosette staggered back to her bed, striving to ignore the kernel of recognition that fluttered in her heart whenever she heard those words. The troubling plea was vague. Dreamlike. Hazy. Like something she might once have imagined. Like something someone once might have said.

A staccato rap at the door interrupted her thoughts, sending a rush of adrenalin surging through her system. She knew that knock—all too well. Tensing, she edged herself backward, her eyes never leaving the door as the knob began to turn. Eyes wide, she shrank into the corner as the dreaded footsteps drew near.

"Cosette," a sugary voice sneered. She loathed the air of disdain with which her captor so pointedly laced her name. "Nursing our dreams again, are we?"

Devastated by her own transparency, Cosette drew her legs to her chest and lowered her face into her waiting arms. Her shoulders quivered as she strove to control her sobs and corral her anxious thoughts.

"Listening to the stories of the wandering troubadours, I see," he continued menacingly. Lunging toward her, he grabbed her arms and yanked her upward, forcing her to stand before him, daring her to defy his unspoken command. She lowered her eyes to focus on his feet, his hands, his chest—anywhere but his face. He was not one to tolerate insubordination. A vision of the hanging tree flitted through her mind and darkness consumed her. What did it feel like to die? To take life's final breath and know it was the end? The incessant grinding of his teeth was deafening in the quiet room and her heartbeat hammered in her ears.

"I told you they are but lies." He shook her. Hard. Until dizziness overwhelmed her and her head slumped to her chest. "Surely you're not stupid enough to believe them. Grow up, girl! You want me to leave you alone? Start doing what I say—and leave the lying minstrels to me. I'll see that they are silenced."

With another violent shake, the evil tyrant hurled her to the ground and strode toward the open door. Biting back the tears, Cosette forced herself to watch as he paused in the hallway, his keys dangling from his finely-sculpted hand, his smouldering eyes fixed on hers. "Never forget who's in charge here, Cosette," the evil one hissed. His serpentine eyes narrowed threateningly. "You are mine now, *my dear*. You'd be wise to remember that."

* * *

Jaired heard it all—the terrified whimpers, the convulsive cries, the bone-chilling threats, and that final, sickening thud. It wasn't the first time he had heard such things, and he was sure it would not be the last. Not as long as the adversary was on the loose.

Slinging his mandolin over his shoulder, he crept stealthily down the corridor toward the source of the latest commotion. Careful to keep within the shadow of the towering stone wall, he peered cautiously around the corner, the rattling of keys alerting him to impending danger, the voice of the enemy filling him with dread.

"You are mine now, *my dear*. You'd be wise to remember that."

Jaired cringed at the audacity of the enemy. That the evil one would dare to threaten the king's children with such obvious lies infuriated him. If only his brothers and sisters could see the truth. A quiet sigh escaped his lips as he contemplated the sorrows they endured at the hands of the adversary. Great was the grief they had unwittingly brought upon themselves *and* the king.

Jaired tensed as a door slammed shut and the snick of a key turning in a lock echoed through the lonely corridor. It was difficult to tell exactly which cell the beleaguered prisoner inhabited, but Jaired was sure it was nearby. Sounds could be deceiving in the cavernous compound, though. Braving a peek around the corner, he breathed a prayer of thanksgiving when he noted the adversary's dark eyes still focused on the door of the cell, his hand resting upon the knob. He knew the room well. Many times he had sought to enter it, but never had he succeeded.

Gripped by a sudden urge to flee, Jaired stifled the cry that rose from his throat and pressed himself back into the shadows. He could not give himself away; there was too much at stake. The slow, cruel smile that parted the lips of the adversary sickened him. He didn't even want to imagine the sordid plot that had given birth to such a wicked grin. Slowly exhaling the breath he had been holding, Jaired clung to the wall as the adversary turned and strode down the hall, the tuneless whistle issuing from his lips sending shivers of dread coursing down the minstrel's spine.

The moments crept by as Jaired waited for the retreating footsteps of the adversary to recede into silence, concern for his sister mounting with each torturous second. Even when complete silence echoed in his ears, he still waited, carefully measuring the minutes before he edged around the corner and tiptoed to the great oaken door from which the adversary had come.

* * *

Tap, tap, tap. Jaired's knuckles rapped lightly on the wooden planks. *Tap, tap, tap.* No answer. Shifting his mandolin to his other shoulder, he searched the pockets of his travelling robe for the rusty awl hidden within its folds. It was a crude tool in many ways, but an effective one, nonetheless. He'd had many opportunities to use it over the years and he never went anywhere without it. Sliding its tip gently into the lock, he patiently twisted it until a tell-tale click ricocheted through the corridor, releasing the lock and announcing his presence to any who cared to notice.

Glancing furtively down the hall, Jaired twisted the tarnished handle and darted into the cell, closing the heavy door carefully behind him. He leaned against its wooden planks for a moment, his hand pressed to his heaving chest, his eyes squeezed shut, his ears alert to any indication that the enemy might be near. He could only pray that his presence had gone undetected.

The room was cold and damp and it took a moment for Jaired's eyes to become accustomed to the darkened cell. The smell of stale urine and unwashed flesh assailed his nostrils as he surveyed his ghastly surroundings. A dishevelled cot filled most of the room, leaving little space to move about. A putrid bucket, the contents of which he could but guess, stood beside the bed next to an untouched trencher of blackened bread and a jug full of brackish water. Stomach churning, his eyes turned to the uneven flagstone of the floor. The dim light filtering in from the narrow window was barely enough to illuminate the prostrate form awkwardly sprawled on the stone, not two steps from where he stood.

Dropping his mandolin, Jaired narrowly missed dumping the bucket as he rushed to her side. Like an abandoned rag doll, she lay, her long, stringy hair matted with blood, her body still as the grave. Straining his ears for the slightest sign of life, he willed her to breathe, desperate to see colour return to her pallid features. Surely he wasn't too late!

Gently shaking her shoulder, Jaired called her name as his expert fingers probed for wounds. He had recognized her as soon as his eyes had seen her. Though aged by the hardships and suffering she had endured, and ravaged by the ill choices she had made, her identity could not be hidden. He had found Cosette. Finally. Sweet, beautiful Cosette. Who could have imagined the depths to which she had fallen?

Pulling a wrinkled handkerchief from the pocket of his robe, Jaired dabbed gently at her fevered brow, tenderly wiping the blood from a jagged cut behind her left ear. The wound was deep and she had lost a lot of blood, but her heart yet beat. *She must have hit her head when she fell.* Tearing a narrow strip of cloth from the hem of his tunic, Jaired bound it about her head, knotting it securely over the deepest part of the wound. Her body was broken beyond his power to repair, her spirit beyond his power to revive, but in her yet lay the soul of a princess, no matter how deeply it was buried.

Cradling her limp body in his arms, he lifted her from the floor, careful to avoid the bloody pool congealing beneath her head. He'd have to do something about that later. In the meantime, he placed her on the bed and covered her with the worn and bloodied blanket he found abandoned on the floor. He reached for his mandolin. Music was a great healer, but even more so, was truth; she was badly in need of both.

Clearing a space on the edge of the bed, he sat by her side and fingered the strings of his mandolin. Soon a haunting ballad rose to his lips, the grief-laden tale of a heart-broken monarch abandoned by his beloved.

> The king approached his garden fair
> Where once he'd danced with joy,
> Reliving mem'ries sad and sweet
> No thief could e'er destroy.
>
> With grief, his noble head was bowed,
> Bright tears adorned his face.
> His children had abandoned him—
> He longed for their embrace.

He watched them from his garden home;
He saw their pain and wept.
He yearned to meet their every need,
Disarm each evil threat.

He could not leave them desolate;
He would not let them go.
Though steep, indeed, would be the cost,
He would defeat their foe.

He saw his children as they'd be,
Bright shining as the stars.
T'were laughing, dancing, filled with joy,
By glory, set apart.

Not a smudge their beauty marred,
No wrinkle scarred their clothes.
The glory of the king's own heart
Within their bosoms glowed.

He was their father; they were his,
Despite their wayward hearts.
He'd woo them, love them, draw them close,
His grace to them impart.

With joy he raised his voice in song;
The time at last had come
To bring his children home again
Where they'd, with him, be one.

Oh, laughing, dancing, see them shine!
Filled with love divine.
Cherished jewels, bright and fine,
Cries their loving father, "They are mine!"

* * *

A lone tear trickling down her nose. The fleeting remnants of a tattered dream flickering at the edge of her memory. The achingly familiar strain of a soothing baritone voice. Cosette's eyes fluttered open as her mind drifted into wakefulness. Dim shapes danced in the shadows, fighting for a piece of the light as she strove to make sense of her surroundings. Her head pounded against her skull and her stomach churned in response. What was wrong with her?

Exhausted, Cosette let her eyes slip shut once more, enveloping her in the welcome oblivion of darkness as the gentle voice chased away the shadows. The sound seemed so close, and yet so far away. If only the infernal throbbing behind her ear would cease. Raising timid fingers to investigate the source of the pain, Cosette carefully probed the area, her hand coming to rest upon the knotted cloth carefully wound about her head.

Without warning, a torrent of memories bombarded her, stealing from her the glorious peace that had settled in her heart. The unfounded accusations and scathing threats of her captor clanged in her ears, a dissonant counterpoint to the soothing song stroking her heart from without. Oh, how she hated this place!

A weary groan escaped her as the memories continued. She winced as she recalled the confrontation with her jailer. He had shaken her like a rag doll and tossed her across the room. She remembered hitting her head on the floor and the sickening sensation of spurting blood. Her head spun as she relived the moments and she whimpered aloud. She had wanted to die. Desperately. The darkness that had crept over her had been a welcome relief, but then had come the dream. Again. If only she knew what it meant.

Tears gushed from beneath her lidded eyes, wetting the mattress beneath her head. There was more. A click in the lock. A tender voice calling her name. Gentle hands tending her wound and lifting her to her bed. A song more beautiful than any she had ever known.

Pierced by a sudden pang of anxiety, Cosette struggled to sit, terrifyingly aware that she was not alone. Someone was in the room with her. Someone she did not know.

***

The music had stopped. A gentle hand swept the limp strands of Cosette's once-golden hair from her face and drew her into the waiting embrace of the mysterious stranger. Her whimpered protests went unheeded as he dabbed the tears from her eyes and crooned her name.

"Oh, Cosette—dear, dear Cosette—you are, indeed, a lamb. Our daddy named you well, little one..." His voice trailed off into silence.

Adrenalin coursed through her veins as her clouded mind registered his words. The strange man thought he knew her. The poor man was confused. He thought she was his sister. Funny that his sister and she should share the same name; she had never known another Cosette before.

Hardly daring to breathe, Cosette contemplated her options. He seemed like a kind man, gentle and compassionate of heart. She could reveal to him his error and presume upon his mercy, or she could humour his delusions and submit to his ministrations. Unless, of course, she were to turn him over to her captor, perchance to earn the tyrant's favour and buy her way out of this hole. That, too, was a possibility, she supposed, although not one her heart was willing to acknowledge. No one deserved a fate so cruel, especially one who was so obviously guileless and had shown her nothing but kindness. No, only one thing would do. She would have to tell him the truth.

Cosette's eyes widened in disbelief at the claims of the wandering troubadour. They were ridiculous, absurd, yet somehow they bore the ring of truth. It was the fact that he denied with such certainty her assertions that she was not the person he presumed her to be that troubled her most, though. Of course she wasn't his Cosette. She had never laid eyes on him before in her life.

"Cosette, don't you remember?" He leaned his mandolin against the side of the bed and reached to take her hands in his. "You must remember. How can you possibly have forgotten?" Deep creases lined his brow as he spoke. "The garden—don't you remember the garden? I was there; you were there. We both were there together. Swinging from the trees of the great Oaken Hills, swimming in the waters of the River of Delights, reeling through the meadow in the arms of the king. It was wonderful! More wonderful than words can tell."

She sighed as his words reverberated in her head.

"Try, Cosette. Try! You have to remember."

She hadn't been able to bring herself to admit to him, or to herself, how closely his stories resembled the images that dogged her dreams and caused her such distress. If the pictures his stories had evoked were more than mere dreams, it followed that the rest of her dream was the product of long repressed memories as well. A shiver of dread shuddered down her spine at the thought. Some things were just too horrifying to dwell upon. Relaxing back against her pillow, she listened to the lilting cadence of his voice, losing herself in the stories the troubadour told of a long-forgotten king, convincing herself they were but the imaginings of a heart out of touch with reality.

And then he was gone. And she was alone. Loneliness scourged her heart as an unexpected emptiness enshrouded her soul. Which was worse—the loneliness or the lies?

* * *

Cosette paced the confines of her squalid cell, fingering the snake-like scar behind her ear. Her mind whirled with questions as lingering uncertainties assailed her heart. What if Jaired was right? What if she wasn't the person she thought she was? Could his stories possibly be true? She paused, gazing out the window at the hills beyond the castle compound. What if she really did have a daddy out there looking for her, a king determined to bring her home and make her his own, no matter what the cost?

A click at the door shook her from her contemplations. He was late, but at least he had come. Relieved, Cosette turned to greet her clandestine guest, eager to bombard him with the questions that consumed her.

"Waiting for someone, *my dear?*" a familiar voice sneered.

Stiffening at the sight of the intruder, Cosette paled, her smile fading as she pressed her back against the wall.

"Expecting a visitor?" her captor taunted, his silken voice infused with innocence. "What kind of lies has that blasted minstrel been feeding you?" he snapped.

She cowered as he stepped toward her, his hand raised.

"I thought I warned you about those travelling minstrels," he spat. "Now where is he?"

Cosette froze in terror. That he expected an answer, she knew, yet what answer could she give that would not incriminate her? She wasn't that good of a liar. "Wh–where's who?" she stuttered.

"Where's who?" The evil one snorted and clapped a hand on her shoulder. "That's a good one." Without warning, his face darkened and he pinched her. Hard. "Don't play with me, Cosette. You *will* pay for this. Now tell me where he is."

She cringed at the growled epithets he hurled her way, her mind racing for a means of escape. But she could think of none. She heard the nauseating crack of flesh against flesh a heartbeat before she felt the stinging blow. Staggering to her knees, her hand leapt to the fiery welt numbing her cheek and a pitiful wail rose in her throat.

"Don't hurt me, my lord! Please don't hurt me!" Scalding tears poured from her eyes as Cosette bowed her head in shame, loathing the lily-livered woman she had become. Would the nightmare never end?

Dragging her to her feet, the evil one dug his nails into her arm. She shuddered at the malevolent snarl that curled his lip as his handsome face contorted with rage. She had never seen him so incensed. "You will not defy me again, Cosette." His threatening hiss chilled her heart. "You are mine and no one—do you hear me?—no one has the power to take you out of my hands. Now..."

Like the shifting of the wind in a storm, his demeanor suddenly softened. Gone was the blood-thirsty glint in his eyes, the simmering hatred in his voice, the vice-like grip of his hands. Breathing rapidly, Cosette drew back, perplexed by the unexpected transformation. Though it wasn't the first time she had witnessed such a change in her captor, it never failed to surprise her. Suddenly fatherly and kind, the tyrant approached, drawing her gently into his arms, smoothing her straw-like hair with his hand, kissing away her tears. Lifting her as easily as he would a child, he carried her to the bed and stretched out beside her, his head upon her breast.

"Oh, Cosette, my poor, dear Cosette. It isn't your fault," he purred. "You couldn't have known." Lifting his head, he traced soothing spirals on her shoulder with his finger as he waited for her sobs to subside. "You must understand, my dear, it is for your good that I seek him."

Helpless to resist the voice of compassion, she laid her head dejectedly upon her captor's shoulder and wept. Thirsty for the comfort he offered, though her heart knew it to be false, Cosette clung to him, forgetting her fears and basking in the kindness of his touch. Anything, no matter how repugnant, was better than the emptiness that hounded her days and the nightmares that terrorized her nights. Maybe. She whimpered as he lifted her head from his shoulder and cradled her swollen cheek in his hand. She was afraid to trust, yet powerless to resist.

"What did he tell you, that has so enamoured your heart, Cosette? Was it the daddy story again? The glorious garden paradise where the perfect daddy awaits his perfect little children that they might live with him forever and ever in his great garden home?"

It sounded ludicrous from the lips of her jailer. Cosette's heart sagged at the hint of mockery lifting the corners of his mouth.

"You can't possibly have believed him." He snickered, shaking his head. His eyes glinted in the light of the oil lamp. "Honestly, Cosette. Look at yourself! You're hardly the perfect little child now, are you?" His steely eyes glanced pointedly down the length of her body and back, finally coming to rest on her puffy, bloodshot eyes. "Of course you didn't believe him. Why, you were only pretending, weren't you?" He grinned. "After all, we aren't exactly a prize now, are we?"

His condescension crushed her. Sickened, she stiffened in his arms and pulled away from the kisses he pressed to her neck. There was too much truth in what he said. Exhaling sharply, she pushed him away and stumbled from the bed, ignoring the satisfied smirk that slid across his face. Who was she to think she might be special? To deign to imagine some foreign monarch would, sullied as she was, stoop to call her precious? Who was she trying to fool?

Reaching for the bucket, she retched again and again until, exhausted, she sank to the floor. The acrid odour of vomit overwhelmed her, but no more than the putrid stench of self-loathing that filled her with disdain. Hatred—rabid and malignant—erupted within her and she hurled the bucket across the room.

Rising unsteadily to her feet, she struggled for a moment to keep from sliding on the flagstones, now slick with the vile contents of the bucket. There was only so much a person could take. Teeth clenched as tightly as the fists at her sides, Cosette fixed furious eyes upon the only one she hated more than herself and took a menacing step forward. Then, with an unearthly screech, she flew toward her astonished jailer and fell upon him, pummelling his chest with her fists and scratching at his face with her ragged nails.

Over and over she struck until his vice-like hands tightened around her wrists and pinned her flailing arms to her chest. In a final bid to free herself, Cosette thrust her head forward and bit his shoulder. The coppery taste of blood filled her mouth and she spat in horror, disgusted by the thought of what she had done. Wrestling her arms from his grasp, she swiped a sleeve across her mouth and spat again, striving to rid herself of the foul gore. *Breathe in. Breathe out. Breathe in. Breathe out.* Slowly her stomach began to settle and she licked her parched lips, afraid to look at her foe.

And then she heard it. Laughter—deep, throaty, appreciative—issuing from the mouth of her jailer. She looked up to see his hand clapped over his injured shoulder, his eyes alight with amusement.

"Very good, Cosette," he managed between snorts. "Some little lamb you turned out to be. Maybe there's hope for you yet."

Cosette squeezed her eyes shut and let the tears fall as his laughter echoed in the tiny room. Whatever was she trying to prove?

* * *

Jaired stumbled in his haste, sending his precious mandolin skidding across the flagstones of the courtyard and careening into a dank, mossy wall. He tensed as the piercing wail came again, resisting the urge to clap his hands tightly over his ears.

Cosette had been on his mind since the first cock crowed. He knew the time had finally come to free her from the bonds of the adversary, but all day long he had been forced to deal with one obstacle after another. One would have thought they had been purposefully designed to impede his task, as indeed, they probably were. There was no level to which the adversary would not stoop.

First it was the oxen. Loose in the cornfield, they carelessly trampled the corn, threatening to wipe out the entire food supply for the coming winter. Somebody had to stop them. Then there was the elderly merchant whose wagon had been overturned when a passing soldier had spooked his horse with a cruel flick of his whip. None but a rogue would leave the old man to collect the precious cargo strewn across the dusty road himself. Next there was the little girl enmired in the malodorous filth of the village cesspool, the scantily clad serving wench cornered behind the village inn and the simpering cries of the ragged urchin being dragged across the grainy cobbles of the village square. The accompanying shouts and wild applause of a crowd bent on revenge still made him shudder. The boy had pitied a hungry stranger and shared with him a half-penny roll he had stolen from a local vendor.

It had been one thing after another. Yet, how could he leave those dear people to suffer and die when he had the power to free them from their bonds? And so he did what he had to do and prayed that Cosette could hold her own until he arrived.

Retrieving his mandolin from the alcove in which it had come to rest, Jaired sprinted past the well and leapt over a pile of sodden refuse. He had recognized Cosette's tortured pleas before he even got to the gate and knew there was no time to waste. Mounting the flagstone steps two at a time, he flew toward the source of the wails, heedless of the curious on-lookers watching his every move. His chest heaved with every step and he squeezed his elbow to his ribs, hoping to stem the mounting spasm in his side. He was almost there.

The wailing had stopped, replaced by sounds Jaired could not identify, and familiar laughter he wished he could silence forever. Scurrying the final few steps, he mopped the sweat from his brow and swept an unruly lock of hair from his eyes. He smiled in relief when he saw the open door of Cosette's room come into view, rejoicing in the impeccable timing of their daddy. He took a long, deep breath and peered into the squalid cell. He wasn't too late. Cosette was ready—at last. There wasn't a moment to lose.

* * *

"ENOUGH!"

The single word, commanding and powerful, reverberated through the tiny cell, echoing in the sudden silence that greeted it. Speechless, Cosette stared at the forbidding warrior blocking the entrance to her prison. He looked familiar, somehow, although she couldn't quite place him. Rubbing a hand across her face, she blinked, confused. It was his eyes—so passionate, so kind, so... "Jaired?" she breathed. Horrified that he should see her in such a state, she bowed her head, wishing he would go away, yet at the same time, praying he would stay.

As if waking from a dream, the jailer grabbed Cosette's arm and jerked her to her feet. "Jaired?" he parroted, his voice dripping with disdain.

Cosette bit her lip and struggled to keep from crying out as his nails sank into her skin.

"I distinctly recall you telling me that you didn't know this man." Yanking her forward, her captor eyed the silent minstrel warily. "Out of my way, troubadour," he growled, his teeth clenched. "She's mine and you know it."

"You deceive yourself, oh pretender to the realm." Jaired took a single step forward and planted his fists on his hips. "The king's children belong to none but him."

Jaired's calm, yet authoritative, words puzzled Cosette, though they also brought her comfort. Who was this man? She flinched as her captor's cruel fingers tightened on her arm, biting further into her bruised flesh as she struggled to free herself from his grasp.

"Release her, in the name of the king." The words rang powerfully through the room.

Cosette stilled as a tremor moved through her jailer, relieved to feel his grip lose some of its strength.

"Take your hands off her and be gone, oh ancient enemy of the king. Now." Jaired bellowed. "You may not have her."

Cosette's heart pounded in her chest as the mighty tyrant faltered.

His hesitation lasted only a moment before he released his death grip on her arm and shoved her into the waiting arms of the minstrel. Spewing a torrent of threats, the evil one pushed his way past them and stormed into the corridor. "This isn't over, troubadour," he snarled. "The girl is *mine*."

* * *

Silence.

A quiet calm enfolded Cosette's spirit and a flicker of hope flamed within her. Strong, gentle arms held her, supporting her when her wobbly legs gave way. Tender hands caressed her face, soothing her tattered nerves and wiping her tears. Slowly she opened her eyes. *Jaired. How had he known she needed him?* He scooped her up, effortlessly carrying her out of the dark, dank chamber and into the stale air of the corridor. For the first time she could remember, Cosette felt safe. Safe and warm and cherished. His rhythmic footfalls calmed her as he strode down the hall and out into the night. *Jaired's here. He'll take care of me. I'm not going to die.* A gentle breeze brushed against her cheek and she breathed deeply of the cool, fresh air. It smelled good. Clean. Untouched by the stench of the cell to which she had been confined for so many years.

With a satisfied sigh, Cosette expelled the welcome air from her lungs and savoured the replenishing breath that took its place. How could she have lived with the rancid air of that cell all these years? Had she really become so inured to it that she hardly even noted its presence? What was wrong with her that she had not fought back sooner? A gentle breeze whispered past her ear and she lowered her head, resting it upon the troubadour's muscular shoulder. Maybe there was something to the fanciful tales he told after all. Perhaps he was going to take her to his king.

Jaired's footsteps slowed, drawing her thoughts from their tangled wanderings. Cosette forced her heavy lids to flutter open once more and eyed her surroundings. It seemed they were in the courtyard—a place she had seen often enough from her window, but never entered herself. Jaired stopped as they neared the well to set her upon a low stone bench almost hidden from sight by a pile of discarded rocks and beams.

"Cosette," he whispered urgently. "Cosette? Are you alright?" He patted her cheek. "You've got to wake up now. We have a lot to talk about. Can you sit?"

Cosette groaned her assent and forced her eyes to focus on his face as she teetered on the edge of the bench. Jaired knelt in front of her, his hands holding hers as he looked beseechingly into her eyes.

"Cosette, it is time that you left this place." His voice was hoarse, yet intense. Freeing his hands from hers, he fumbled in the pocket of his robe and brought out a small, rusty awl. Her brow furrowed as she watched him slide its well-worn tip expertly into the keyhole of the manacles that bound her ankles. She tensed as he twisted the awl back and forth in the lock and jumped when a quiet click echoed through the silence of the deserted courtyard. The deafening clatter of her shackles as they fell from her ankles sent her diving to the ground, pressing herself into the space beneath the bench. Frantically, she jerked her head from side to side, her eyes alert to any movement, her heart bumping wildly against her chest.

"It's okay, Cosette." Jaired's hushed voice gradually wended its way into her panicked thoughts and her pulse began to slow. "No one is following us. You don't need to be afraid."

Cosette yielded to his gentle touch as he lifted her back onto the bench and tenderly massaged her chafed and swollen ankles. Exhaling deeply, she willed her body to relax and tossed a stubborn strand of matted hair from her face. The warmth of his hands comforted her and she let her eyes slide shut as the minstrel's soothing voice danced at the edge of her consciousness.

"Laughing, dancing, see them shine!
Filled with love divine.

Cherished jewels, bright and fine,
Cries their loving father, 'They are mine!'"

Cosette recognized the song immediately. It was the same song he had sung to her on the night they first met. Tears rolled down her cheeks unchecked as its golden notes wound its way around her heart and she began to hum quietly, until, in a moment of uninhibited passion, her raspy voice joined his on the final strain, surprising them both.

* * *

It was just after dawn when Cosette finally arrived in the infamous town of Malefborough. She shivered as she approached the city limits, well aware of its reputation for wickedness. The place had been well named. Cautiously, she rounded the corner of the old tavern and nearly collided with a tipsy greybeard leaving the foul place. He stumbled as he stepped into the street, still nursing his precious ale, and cast her a leering smirk. Staring after him, Cosette groaned, her hand clapped against her chest. What was she doing here? The events of the night before hung hazily in her mind as she struggled to make sense of everything that had happened since Jaired had set her free. It all seemed so very long ago.

After freeing her legs from the manacles, Jaired had tenderly washed her face with a corner of his tunic before producing from a worn satchel a meal worthy of a queen. She smiled at the pleasant memory. The choicest wine had met her lips as she sipped from the leather flask he handed her. The sweetness of the ruby liquor delighted her tongue and warmed her belly, but to her chagrin, he hadn't allowed her much before he replaced it with a cup of cool, clear water drawn from the nearby well. Suddenly alert to her thirst, she drained the cup, her vigour returning as she watched him refill it from the massive cistern. There had been chunks of bread, soft and fresh, and thick slabs of salty hardened cream he called cheese. The savoury flavours had begged her to eat more, even after her belly was full, but time had been short.

Pressing a flask of well water into her hands, Jaired had helped her to her feet and led her toward the postern gate, encouraging her feeble efforts even as he urged her to make haste. Her steps, though slow and unsteady at first, had grown in strength as she followed close behind the minstrel and her heart had soared the further she got from her cell.

"The adversary has held you captive long enough, Cosette," Jaired whispered. "It's time you left this place and headed for home."

Cosette looked at him askance, confused by his cryptic words.

"Just go one step at a time, little lamb. One step at a time," he crooned. "After you pass through the gate, travel straight until you reach the deserted mine shaft at the edge of the great abyss. Don't worry, you'll recognize it," he assured her when her gaping mouth betrayed her alarm. "You've been there before. That's where the adversary first befriended you and lured you into his lair."

The phantom-like memory that had played about the corners of Cosette's mind as she processed his words began to surface yet again and a nameless fear clawed at her heart.

"You must be wary," Jaired had continued, "lest you lose your footing and fall into one of the mine's many traps. The enemy will not let you go easily, Cosette, and those shafts lead straight to the Dungeons of Doom."

The Dungeons of Doom. The name sent shivers up her spine. Those she knew about. All too well. "But aren't you coming with me?" she pleaded, alarm tingeing her voice.

"I'm sorry, Cosette. My place is here with my brothers and sisters." He paused, his eyes intense. "They need me, Cosette—like you needed me. They, too, are in bondage and must be freed. You'll be okay without me. I promise."

Cosette had fought against the rising panic that threatened to undo her as Jaired hurried on.

"Listen carefully. Turn due west at the entrance to the old mine and head toward Malefborough. First you'll come to The Inn of the Thirsty Traveller, a busy tavern near the edge of the village square. Whatever you do, Cosette, do not go through those doors. The servants of the evil one frequent it, preying upon unsuspecting travellers. They snare them with false promises and lure them with forbidden pleasures, only to deliver them into the waiting hands of the adversary."

Cosette shuddered as she remembered his warning and glanced at the forbidden tavern before her, certain his words held more truth than he realized. With a shake of her head, she let her mind drift back to their parting. Jaired had gone on to instruct her to find the house of their sister, Ilana, on the edge of the city square across from the cobbler's shop, just beyond the lone baobab tree. There had been such passion in his eyes as he spoke.

"She will be watching for you, Cosette. She'll know what to do." He had opened the gate for her to pass through. "She'll introduce you to Manuél."

"Manuél?" Something in her jumped in recognition at the mention of the unusual name.

"Yes, Manuél. You remember him, don't you? The great prince? He's going to be so happy to see you. He's been looking for you for so long."

"Looking for me?" Her confusion finally found a voice. "Why would a prince be looking for me?"

"Not just any prince, Cosette. Manuél!" Jaired's blue eyes glittered with excitement when he spoke of the prince—as if he knew him well and loved him even more. "Don't you understand? He's here to take you home. That's the reason he came. Our father sent him to bring you home."

"But I don't have a home," she murmured.

"Oh yes, you do, Little Lamb. A home and a family and a daddy who loves you and misses you terribly." A ragged sigh had escaped him then and he let his hand fall from the handle of the gate. "Oh Cosette, how I wish you could remember." A moment of quietness had passed between them as he willed her to recall.

Cosette's eyes pooled as the memory engulfed her.

A single tear had slid down her nose and she lifted her shoulder in a helpless shrug. "I wish I could, too."

He studied her in silence for a moment, as if hoping she would say more. "It's time for you to go." His voice softened as he reached out and brushed a lock of hair from her face. "Don't worry. You'll remember. Now be sure to give Ilana my love when you see her, and tell Manuél I miss him."

With that, the gate had swung shut, locking Cosette out of the compound and her only friend within. Renewed fears had watered her soul as she turned her back on the only life she had ever known and headed into the darkness of the wilderness. All she could do now was hope that Jaired was right. About everything.

* * *

The town drunk long gone, Cosette cast a final glance at the open door of The Inn of the Thirsty Traveller. With her last drops of water now but a memory, she wet her parched lips with her tongue, yearning for something, anything, to quench her thirst. Tantalising aromas wafted from the doorway of the tavern, awakening her empty belly and calling her to partake. *What could it really hurt?* The unwelcome thought plagued her. Jaired had warned her about this place; she knew it was corrupt. But she was so hungry.

Toying with the options before her, Cosette stepped closer to the door and let the golden light of the great room wash over her. How she longed to sate her growing appetite, but she could not bring herself to disregard Jaired's warning. Even so, it took every ounce of will she could muster to turn from the door of the inn and resume her trek toward the village square. She was miserable. Her feet, raw and blistered from her long walk through the unforgiving sand of the desert, throbbed as her empty stomach growled its displeasure. She had to find Ilana before it was too late—before her wanton flesh betrayed her.

Step by step, Cosette edged her way past the tavern and into the dusty square. Despite the early hour, eager merchants filled the grimy marketplace with their wares in anticipation of the day's business. She watched in wonder as they arranged an endless array of merchandise beneath striped tents and canvas awnings, jostling for space along the crowded rows. It wasn't long before the shouts of greedy vendors competed with each other as they sought to draw early shoppers to their stalls.

A bell tolling nearby startled Cosette. *Five... Six... Seven. Seven of the clock.* Cosette pushed past the hawkers' stalls, her blistered feet all but forgotten in her haste. Jaired had said Ilana's house was at the far end of the square opposite the cobbler's shop, just beyond the lone baobab on the other side of the village well. Cosette skidded to a halt and scanned the village square, wondering which way to head. She strained to see the faded boards hailing the shops along the edge of the square, but nowhere could she see any sign of a cobbler.

By now, the bustling marketplace was teeming with people haggling with the merchants and counting out their coins. Wide-eyed, Cosette watched as a scantily clad woman paraded her wares before an assembly of leering men, gyrating her hips seductively as she lifted her brow in invitation. The raucous laughter and lewd remarks of the men brought colour to Cosette's face and she averted her eyes. They sounded so much like the wretched tyrant who had abused her for so long. They looked like him, too. Anger simmered in her gut at the startling realization. Were all men the same?

Hugging the remnants of her tattered wrap more tightly around her shoulders, Cosette turned aside, desperate to distance herself from the lurid fantasies of the evil men. Was there no escape from the madness? She stumbled down a narrow alley just south of the fishmonger's stall, not caring where it might take her. The pungent odour of day old smelt and salted sardines enveloped her, sending a wave of nausea crashing over her empty belly and she retched violently. Perhaps it was a blessing she had eaten so little.

Ignoring the silent glare of the fishmonger, Cosette collected herself and headed on, skirting the open kegs of fish lining the alley as she pressed a corner of her wrap tightly against her nose. She exhaled sharply when she finally made it to the other end of the alley and let her wrap fall to her side. Throngs of people bustled along the thoroughfare, bumping her on all sides as she pushed her way into their midst. The crowds were exhilarating, albeit a little frightening.

Her raging thirst forgotten, Cosette wandered leisurely from stall to stall, fascinated by the exotic opulence surrounding her. Never had she seen such things before, not even in her wildest dreams. A colourful scarf at the weaver's kiosk caught her eye, its jewel-like colours shimmering in the morning sun, and she reached for it without thinking. Longingly, she fingered its silky weave, reverently lifting it to her cheek as she closed her eyes and sighed. It was so soft. Softer than anything she had ever felt before.

An angry voice infiltrated her thoughts and she jumped as the storekeeper wrenched the coveted scarf from her hands. "Two Minas!"

Shaking her head sadly, Cosette retreated. She had no money, no hope, and no place to go. Except Ilana's. Brightening, she scanned the village square for the landmark baobab, but it was nowhere in sight. Perhaps it would be easier to look for the well. Her steps faltered as she pushed her way down aisle after aisle of crowded stalls, desperate to find her way to the shelter of Ilana's home.

"How could I have been so stupid?" she chided herself as she succumbed to the never-ending sea of humanity jostling her forward. "How could I possibly have let such worthless distractions keep me from following Jaired's instructions?"

Minutes turned to hours as Cosette searched the marketplace for the landmarks Jaired had given, but they seemed nowhere to be found. Twice she stopped to ask for directions, though no one seemed inclined to help. Perhaps they didn't know the way either. Finally, snagging the hood of a passing urchin, she demanded he be her guide. Surely he would know the whereabouts of this illusive cobbler's shop. He looked like the kind of kid that would know everything there was to know about this despicable town.

* * *

Cosette's stomach lurched when she surveyed the empty crossroads to which the child had led her. Obviously, he had not been the one to go to for assistance. There was no cobbler's shop here. She grimaced as his retreating form disappeared behind the only building in sight and she muttered a curse. *How am I supposed to find Ilana now? I don't even know where the square is.*

Hopeless and alone, she sank to her knees. Her stomach growled and she wondered for a moment when she had last eaten. Could it really have been just last night? With a sigh, she buried her face in her hands and wept. *What am I going to do?*

How long she had knelt there, Cosette could not tell. The occasional wagon clambered by as the midday sun paraded across the sky, but not one stopped to see if she needed aid. A freshening breeze stirred her hair and she lifted her swollen eyes to gaze at her surroundings. She was at a crossroads, the meeting of two unknown streets, far from the center of town and the promised safety of Ilana's home on the square. Swallowing hard, she pressed a fist to her mouth, willing herself not to cry. She was lost. She had no money. No food. No place to stay. And no one to blame but herself.

An uneasy feeling crept over Cosette as she surveyed the crossroads, desperately striving to focus her thoughts. Someone was watching her. She could tell. The hair on the back of her neck prickled and she pressed herself further into the shadows cast by the bushes lining the road. Readying herself to flee, she looked cautiously down each road, clawing back the scream that threatened to rip from her throat as rising hysteria claimed her.

Her stomach tightened when she saw the strange man leaning casually against the central pole of the open livery shed opposite her. He was perhaps ten years her senior, although his weathered features made it hard to tell. A paradoxical calm stole over her when their eyes met, and her fear melted into confusion. He reminded her of Jaired. Perhaps it was his eyes. She sighed, perplexed. Even from a distance, she could see tears tracking his face and disappearing into his beard. Who was this man?

Suddenly conscious of her dishevelled appearance, Cosette lifted her hands to comb through her tangled hair. Acutely aware of the stranger's eyes on her, she scrubbed at the stains on her tattered rags and tried to smooth out the stubborn wrinkles, but it only took a glance to see that her efforts were fruitless. Her cheeks burned as she splayed her hands across her chest and lifted her gaze to meet his.

The light of compassion radiating from the eyes of the stranger pierced her soul and she let out a long, slow breath. A fleeting memory nudged her to speak. "Manuél?" She rose to her feet and took a tentative step his way as a slow blink of his eyes and the barest nod of his head acknowledged her cry. It was him. It had to be.

The moment Cosette's foot touched the street, the stranger stiffened and she knew she had made a mistake in coming out of the shadows.

"Cosette."

Cosette froze. Only one person could speak her name with such venom. Her eyes widened as the lord of the fortress she had so recently fled rounded the corner flanked by two burly henchmen. His cloak fluttered behind him as he strode toward her, his hands firmly planted on his hips. A pain knifed through her chest and her eyes rose to meet those of Manuél. Was he just going to stand there and do nothing? With a shudder, Cosette turned to face the one who had held her captive for so long.

"Did you really think I would let you go so easily?"

His honeyed voice petrified her. How had he found her? Shrinking from his gaze, she cast a fleeting look over her shoulder in a silent plea for help, but the stranger was gone and she was alone. Manuél was nowhere in sight.

"Take her, men," her adversary bellowed, his voice dripping with undisguised animosity.

Cosette flinched when the iron fists of her captor's henchmen grabbed her arms and dragged her toward her tormentor. "No-o-o-o-o!" she wailed. She dug her heels into the gravel and fought to hold her ground. "Manuél, come save me! Don't let them take me away!"

part iii

HE HAS NOT LEFT US DEFENCELESS

"Manuél, come save me!"

The heart-rending urgency of her cry quickened his pulse and tore at his soul.

"Don't let them take me away!"

Even from across the street, Manuél could see the fear in Cosette's eyes as they darted frantically from post to post, scanning the livery where moments before they had first met his. Sweat beaded on her forehead as she fought to free herself from the grasp of her attackers and he tensed at the desperation in her panicked cries. But it wasn't time. Not yet. Not quite.

His shoulders sagged as he lowered his head into his hands, knowing she was looking for him, certain she would think he had abandoned her like everyone else she had ever trusted. Oh, that she could see his heart.

With a heavy sigh, Manuél pushed himself further into the shadows of the open stable until the last of her wails echoed only in his heart. It would not do for the adversary to see him before the time was right, yet he couldn't help but sense the time for action was upon him. She needed him. His beloved Cosette, so recently freed from the clutches of the adversary, would be back in the enemy's stronghold within the hour if he didn't do something fast. He scowled at the audacity of the enemy, repulsed by the thought of abandoning her to the evil one's abominable schemes. To do so was unthinkable. He had to act. Now.

Leaning heavily against the support beam, Manuél peered into the street, preparing himself for the horrors his next move would incite. He knew what he had to do, though every ounce of his humanity forbade it. Squeezing his eyes shut, he breathed deeply, willing courage to his heart, even as he prayed that another way would be opened to save his beloved.

But there was no other way. With a prayer for strength, he turned to watch the scene unfolding in the street.

Having ceased the frenzied struggle to free herself, Cosette shuffled between the guards, her head bowed low as if a great weight hung about her neck. He imagined the disillusionment clouding her soul and suppressed the desire to cry out to her. He could wait no longer; the time *had* come. It was for this he had left the sanctuary of his father's realm.

Exhaling sharply, Manuél pushed himself from the post and stepped out of the shelter of the livery. Avoiding the route of the retreating guards, he slipped like a shadow across the road and loped down the nearest side street. He had to get to the Inn of the Thirsty Traveller.

* * *

He was gone. Hope bled from Cosette's soul as the truth of her plight pierced the tender flesh of her heart. He was gone, and she was alone—alone, weary, defenceless. Angry tears pooled in her eyes as she cursed her insufferable vulnerability. *How could I have been so stupid?*

Gradually, her frenzied cries gave way to whimpers as hopelessness engulfed her. *I should have known the tyrant would never let me go.* The guards slowed, their rough hands loosening their grip as she doubled over, retching violently at their feet. *What was I thinking?* Cosette bit her lip, determined to stifle the scream that rang between her ears as the guards jerked her to her feet and prodded her forward. Her head bumped limply against her chest and the world spun around her. *Jaired is wrong. Manuél doesn't care about me. I never should have left the compound.*

Cosette yelped at the sudden tightening of the guards' hands on her arms and stumbled to a halt between them. Waves of nausea rocked her belly when she considered the horrors that awaited her, but it was the unexpected silence echoing in her ears that gnawed at her sanity the most. With a deep, steadying breath, she squared her shoulders and lifted her face to peer around her, intent upon finding a way of escape. Just ahead lay the village tavern. A golden glow spilled from its doorway, tracing a pale pathway to her feet in the dusky light of the early evening. An involuntary shudder shivered through her as she sensed the evil emanating from its interior and she hung her head, recalling the impassioned allure the inn had held for her but hours before. Gorge burned her throat at the memory. Had that only been this morning?

A slight movement at the edge of the path caught her attention and her eyes fell upon the form of her captor. Despite her determination to be strong, her face slackened at the sight of him. There was something odd about the way he stood. He looked stiff. Defensive. Aloof. The breath caught in her throat and she swallowed hard. This was a side of her captor she had never seen.

Following his gaze, Cosette's eyes came to rest upon the figure of a man silhouetted against the wan light of the tavern. She glanced back to her captor. His eyes had narrowed and a menacing sneer contorted his face. It relieved her to have the evil one's ire focused upon someone other than herself, for once. Turning once more to study the object of her captor's fury, she gasped in recognition. "Manuél?" Her swollen tongue could barely form his name. He was larger than he had appeared when first she had seen him at the stable—taller, broader, more muscular. Again, he reminded her of Jaired, or perhaps it was Jaired who reminded her of Manuél. She shook her head in confusion. Could her eyes be deceiving her? What was he doing here?

* * *

An unnatural silence descended upon the street outside the tavern as every head turned to watch the unfolding drama. Few had publicly confronted the evil tyrant, and of those who had, none had lived to tell the story. This Manuél knew, but it changed nothing. Die he would, if he must, but the enemy's claim to the king's children would be denied once and for all.

Tension choked the silence as the crowd leaned in to witness the confrontation. Manuél stared into the ashen face of his nemesis and stepped forward, his feet crunching on the pebbled pathway. Cringing in anticipation, the crowd gaped as Manuél neared the place where his foe stood glowering. The tyrant bared his teeth in response, his fists clenched at his sides.

"Nyoke."

The evil one's face dropped at the sound of his name.

"Nyoke?" The single word shot through the crowd, releasing the pall of silence that had enshrouded them since the moment the mysterious stranger had appeared.

"Nyoke?"

"Is that the maniac's name? Snake?"

A wave of nervous laughter rippled through the group of eager onlookers.

"Fits him, don't ya think?"

"Like a glove! No wonder he's never mentioned it."

Manuél ignored the quiet whicker of the crowd, his eyes focused intently upon his opponent. Nyoke's eyes shifted rapidly from side to side and Manuél wondered how long it had been since he had heard his own name. "Release her, Nyoke. Now. She is not the one you want."

The words, quiet, yet commanding, rippled through the crowd, leaving a breathless silence in their wake. Manuél noted the spark of rebellion that flared in his foe's obsidian eyes before it flickered and died.

With a begrudging nod, Nyoke signalled his henchmen. Immediately, the burly guards loosened their hold on Cosette and flung her to the cobbles before striding to their master's side.

His eyes never leaving his opponent, Manuél stood motionless, certain a counter-attack would follow. Nyoke was a man accustomed to having his own way, to issuing commands, to being obeyed. Defeat would only stoke the fires of hatred that simmered in his soul.

Nyoke's jaw slackened and a mirthless grin replaced the sneer that disfigured his face as he raised an eyebrow at Manuél. The next moment, the evil one threw back his head and chortled gleefully. Slowly and deliberately, he clapped his hands until the quickening of his applause thundered with the pace of his mounting laughter. "What a magnificent performance!" he exulted. "Bravo! Bravo!"

A smattering of applause rippled through the crowd as the slack-jawed faces of the onlookers bounced from tyrant to hero and back.

Manuél sighed and crossed his arms, waiting for his opponent's charade to end. Did Nyoke really think such theatrics would change anything? A few quiet snickers riffled through the crowd as the last of the adversary's laughter subsided.

"Now, what was it you were saying?" Nyoke brushed an imaginary tear from his eye with a bejewelled finger.

In a trice, Manuél closed the gap between them, his shoulders squared, his eyes blazing. Unlike his opponent, he exuded an air of calmness, of confidence, of uncontested authority. "You cannot have her, Nyoke." His powerful voice echoed through the silent crowd. "She is not yours to command. She does not belong to you."

A rush of subdued voices rose from the crowd. Incredulous. Hopeful. Afraid.

"I hereby grant freedom to my sister, Cosette," he continued, his thunderous voice stilling the crowd. "Freedom that you are powerless to revoke."

Tension mounted as the two stood face to face, their eyes locked in silent combat. Seconds turned to minutes and still neither moved. Breathless, the crowd edged closer. Could it be the great tyrant had met his match?

The barest flicker of Nyoke's eyes ended the contest and Manuél nodded his head in assent. "Now, let's get this over with once and for all. *I* am the one you want."

VICTORY IS ASSURED—GOD IS IN CONTROL

chapter five

So, you are willing to concede that we are in the midst of a war and grant that we are daily under attack by the legions of the adversary. You are even willing to admit that the choices we make have a far greater impact upon the heart of God than we could ever have imagined. But what are we supposed to do about it? We cannot undo the past; the choices made by us, and by others, cannot be unmade. Caught in the middle, we are trapped. Powerless to escape, we are the prisoners of a war so vast our human hearts can only glimpse hints of its shadow. It is a weight too great for us to bear. If only we hadn't so willfully entered the fray to begin with. If only we had listened to the voice of our Father rather than the voice of the enemy. If only we had chosen to trust His word and the love that He lavished upon us. If only, if only, if only.

But we did not listen to our Father's voice, nor did we trust His heart, and we did—of our own free will—enter the war. Whether we like it or not, that war is very real and we, betrayed by our own willfulness, have been conscripted. The question is: will we ignore what we know to be true and live as if that war is a distant reality unrelated to our daily lives, or will we acknowledge it for what it is, strap on our armour and stand firm in the face of attack?

It is easy for us to lose heart when we think of such things. The mere thought of war fills our hearts with fear. It is so much bigger than we are, and we know it. God is God, the creator of all things, and we are but His creatures, fashioned from dust and corrupted by sin. And the adversary—we don't even know what to think about him. How easy it is for us to forget that he, too, is but a creature, fashioned by our Lord. The angel of light forever fallen into darkness. He may intimidate us, but he does not hold our fate in his hands. The fact is, we may be at war, but that war has already been won. Unwilling to abandon us to the foe, our Father sacrificed Himself to ransom our souls. He defeated the power of the evil one once and for all by sending Jesus, His only begotten Son, to pay the penalty for our sin. By sending His Beloved One to bring us home where we belong, He has brought an end to the War of Eternity.

The contest is over; the cards are spread across the table for all to see. The war is won and our Father reigns victorious. Yet still the adversary, incensed by his failure and unwilling to concede defeat, goes about in a show of power, ambushing God's children and doing as much damage as he can before his fate is sealed in the hell-fires of eternity.

God is almighty; the evil one, much to his own chagrin, is not. He can only go so far, for he merely has as much power as our Father sees fit to allow him. I smile when I recall the day God so vividly reminded me that He, and not the evil one, is in control.

> Tail twitching wildly, the cheeky chipmunk beat his paw in fury, his dark eyes riveted to the rival chipmunk invading his domain. A volley of deafening chirps shot from his pulsating throat, a veritable war cry warning the bravest intruder of imminent attack. Not that it did much good. So focused was he upon defending his territory, that he did not see the deadly peril that awaited him. Yet peril, indeed, was near.
>
> Fierce golden eyes followed the unwary chipmunk's every move—alert, unblinking, intense—as a curious wildcat crept near. Its muscles taut with restrained energy, it patiently awaited the moment of greatest advantage, its cunning mind alive with visions of fresh meat. The cat's teeth clacked sharply together

in anticipation of the prize, though the chipmunk's indignant cries overpowered the quiet warning that might have saved it from its miserable fate. And so the cat, unnoticed, drew near.

That would have been the end—of the chipmunk, at least—but it wasn't. For the cat, though far from harmless, was not quite as free as at first he might have seemed. Tethered by a length of rope, he was securely leashed, his harness held by someone greater than them both. The someone who provided the peanuts. The someone who so patiently delighted in taming the fearful hearts of the tiny woodland beasts that they might enjoy to its fullest the wealth bestowed upon them. The someone who called them her friends and thrilled to the warmth of their companionship. The someone who, unbeknownst to them, held their fate in her hands and protected them from dangers their earth-bound eyes could not see. It was she who held the leash of the cat. A word from her mouth could halt its advance, a tug on its leash, rein it in. She was in command and would not abandon her friends to the wiles of their feline pursuer. She wouldn't dream of it.

And so the little chipmunk continued its incensed tirade, heedless of the greater drama unfolding around him and never fully aware of the danger that threatened, nor the power that prevailed.

How easy it is for us to forget, in the reality of our daily lives, that God is in control. We see but a part of the picture. We see a world driven by evil, its inhabitants overcome by wickedness, and wonder how a holy God could allow such abomination. What God sees, we cannot know, except that He sees many things to which we are as oblivious as that chipmunk. Things that soar beyond the scope of our finite understanding. Things too big for our human hearts to comprehend, let alone appreciate. It is He who is in control of all things—big and small, seen and unseen—for He is the uncontested Ruler of them all. None can topple Him from the throne of victory. Not one. The evil one tried, and failed. And so the war is won for now, and forever. The Victor has emerged victorious and all has changed. The tide has turned. We are no longer at the mercy of the evil one. We need no longer be his pawn, for we are defenceless no longer. The enemy has been stripped of his power and we have been set free.

This is the truth of the Gospel—the glorious message of God's triumph over the adversary—the truth in which God's children find life and victory over the ravages of sin. At least, that is the way it is supposed to be. It doesn't take much to realize that God's people, while freed from the tyranny of the evil one, too often still live beneath the shadow of his will. For, enraged by his own impotence and feverishly licking the oozing sores of his wounded pride, the evil one has not abandoned the fight. Instead, relieved of any vestige of true power, he has resorted to the only tools available to him, the tools of cowards—intimidation, fear, deception—to work his will on the children of his foe. How sad it is that we respond so readily to the facade of strength with which he bombards our hearts. Smitten by fear, we cower from his advances, believing his every lie and needlessly succumbing to the net of helplessness and despair he casts our way. Yet it should not be so.

Years have come and gone since God first lovingly confronted me with my own lack of resistance to the advances of the evil one. Yet, much as it hurts to admit, the reproof is as current today as it was then.

> One day, late in the afternoon, I was driving down a lovely country road, smiling at the familiar sight that unfolded before me, when I heard God whisper my name.
>
> "Look, little bird, My Kanara. Look! Over there!" came His still, sweet voice, laced with the enthusiasm of delight. "Do you see it? It is you, My Love; it is you! At least, it *could* be."
>
> Looking up, my gaze was arrested by a determined little song sparrow furiously flapping its tiny wings as it flew in frenzied pursuit of the full-sized crow brazenly threatening to encroach upon her domain. Determined to protect her territory from the would-be conqueror, she fearlessly pursued the offending giant with a menacing demeanor certain to terrify the most courageous of attackers. And did that crow fly! It flew as fast and as far as its clumsy, black wings could carry it with

that spunky little sparrow tight on its tail. It flew as if its very life depended upon it.

I couldn't help but laugh at the ludicrousness of it all, yet through my mirth came the triumphant voice of my Father, "Do you see it, Kanara? Do you see? *You* are that little bird. At least, you *could* be. Though you may be small in stature, you need not cower in fear of the giants that surround you. You need not succumb to them, My child, for you are My little bird and none other can conquer your heart. So resist the giants, My child—the giants of sin encroaching upon My domain, the giants of iniquity ever lurking at the borders of your mind just waiting to swoop in upon your heart—and be vigilant, small though you be. Stay alert and stand firm for they will flee from you even as that dastardly crow flees before the righteous ire of my cheeky little sparrow. Do not let them roost in the rafters of your heart, dear one, for they are not welcome in My dominion. They do not belong. Only when they are gone will you truly be able to fly, for only then can your heart take flight to soar on the wings of My love.

Oh, the lessons we can learn by looking to the glory of God's creation and watching his creatures at work and at play. Like that little bird, we need not give in to the bullying of the adversary, for God, true to His Word, is in control and reigns victorious over all. The chains of sin the adversary used to bind our hearts have been severed, but it is up to us whether or not we leave them behind to join the army of our Lord. Our Father calls, but He will not coerce a response. He desires that we would be His, but He will not force His will on those who are loath to embrace it. Yet to any who come, He grants the promise of victory and the assurance of His favour; He has not left us defenceless, no matter what the adversary would urge us to believe.

VICTORY IS ASSURED

The evil one may be a formidable enemy, but he is not to be feared. God is the Creator and the adversary is but His creation. The created cannot be greater than the Creator. As seen so vividly in the book of Job, the evil one is subject to our Almighty God and may only do what his sovereign allows. Time and again, God's Word reminds us that the adversary is not in control, despite how it may seem to our earth-bound eyes. God alone is the Victor, both now and forevermore. Does that sound too good to be true? Check out what the Bible has to say about it.

Deuteronomy 20:3-4: While the writer of these verses may be speaking about physical enemies (also relates to many of the passages that follow), these verses speak clearly to me of our enemy, the devil, and the demons under his command. These are the enemies *I* deal with each day. "...'Listen to me, all you men of Israel! Do not be afraid as you go out to fight your enemies today! Do not lose heart or panic or tremble before them. For the Lord your God is going with you! He will fight for you against your enemies, and he will give you victory!'"

Deuteronomy 28:7: "The Lord will conquer your enemies when they attack you. They will attack you from one direction, but they will scatter from you in seven!"

Deuteronomy 33:27: "The eternal God is your refuge, and his everlasting arms are under you. He drives out the enemy before you..."

Deuteronomy 33:29: "How blessed you are, O Israel! Who else is like you, a people saved by the Lord? He is your protecting shield and your triumphant sword! Your enemies will cringe before you and you will stomp on their backs!"

Psalm 25:15: "My eyes are always on the Lord, for he rescues me from the traps of my enemies."

Psalm 55:16-18: "But I will call on God, and the Lord will rescue me. Morning, noon, and night I cry out in my distress, and the Lord hears my voice. He ransoms me and keeps me safe from the battle waged against me, though many still oppose me."

Psalm 56:9: "My enemies will retreat when I call to you for help. This I know: God is on my side!"

Luke 10:19-20: When His disciples return, astonished and overjoyed by the fact that demons were subject to their command, Jesus says, "Look, I have given you authority over all the power of the enemy, and you can walk among snakes and scorpions and crush them. Nothing will injure you. But don't rejoice because evil spirits obey you; rejoice because your names are registered in heaven."

John 10:27-29: Likewise, He notes, "My sheep listen to my voice; I know them, and they follow me. I give them eternal life, and they will never perish. No one can snatch them away from me, for my Father has given them to me, and he is more powerful than anyone else. No one can snatch them from the Father's hand."

II Corinthians 4:8-9: Speaking to the people of Corinth, Paul notes, "We are pressed on every side by troubles, but we are not crushed. We are perplexed, but not driven to despair. We are hunted down, but never abandoned by God. We get knocked down, but we are not destroyed."

II Thessalonians 3:3: To the people of Thessalonica, he says, "But the Lord is faithful, and he will strengthen you and protect you from the evil one." (NIV)

II Timothy 4:18: To Timothy, he writes, "...and the Lord will deliver me from every evil attack and will bring me safely into his heavenly Kingdom. All glory to God forever and ever! Amen."

James 4:7: James reminds us that we are not subject to the control of the adversary. "Submit yourselves therefore to God. Resist the devil, and he will flee from you." (KJV)

Revelation 20:10: Finally, writing about the vision he is given about what is to come, John tells us about the finality of Christ's victory over the evil one. "Then the devil, who had deceived them, was thrown into the fiery lake of burning sulfur, joining the beast and the false prophet. There they will be tormented day and night forever and ever."

ARMED FOR BATTLE

chapter six

Packing for three weeks in the great outdoors is no small feat for, as every good boy scout knows, preparation is vital. It's always a juggling match between space and practicality, though. Never quite sure of what to expect, it seems a person needs to pack pretty much everything—sweatshirts and turtlenecks, long pants and heavy socks, shorts and tanks, tee-shirts and capris, swimsuits and watershoes, pj's and slippers, jackets and hats, sandals and runners—and that only covers the clothes! The list seems endless, but we all know that the very thing we leave behind is destined to become imperative, no matter how insignificant it might appear before we depart. It's Murphy's Law. We need to come armed—armed for any type of weather and circumstance that might present itself—or suffer the consequences of our folly.

Arming ourselves for battle isn't much different. We don't always know what to expect, or when to expect it, yet we must be prepared for whatever might come. No good commander sends his troops into battle unarmed. Full body armour, bullet-proof vests, camouflaged outerwear, helmets, gas masks, boots, weaponry—they all have a part to play in keeping a soldier from falling and bringing him safely home when his tour of duty comes to an end. A good commander knows that suitable armour is integral to the success of any mission, for it protects a soldier from harm.

In Ephesians chapter 6, Paul tells us of the armour the children of God have been given in the war that rages between our Father and His adversary. It is a familiar passage, often quoted and empowering, but not always easy to grasp.

> *A final word: Be strong in the Lord and in his mighty power. Put on all of God's armor so that you will be able to stand firm against all strategies of the devil. For we are not fighting against flesh-and-blood enemies, but against evil rulers and authorities of the unseen world, against mighty powers in this dark world, and against evil spirits in the heavenly places.*
>
> *Therefore, put on every piece of God's armor so you will be able to resist the enemy in the time of evil. Then after the battle you will still be standing firm. Stand your ground, putting on the belt of truth and the body armor of God's righteousness. For shoes, put on the peace that comes from the Good News so that you will be fully prepared. In addition to all of these, hold up the shield of faith to stop the fiery arrows of the devil. Put on salvation as your helmet and take the sword of the Spirit, which is the word of God.*
> (Ephesians 6:10-17)

It is always a joy to teach my young, and not-so-young, students about the armour of God. Of course, there is only so much of it they can truly comprehend, but they certainly understand more than we might imagine. The image of spiritual armour is metaphorical in nature, somewhat abstract and not always easy for our concrete minds to comprehend, whether we are four years old or forty. Many would wonder at the idea that I would even try to explain it to four and five year olds, but the adversary does not wait until we are grown to mount his attacks. In fact, the more vulnerable we are, the more likely it is that his attacks will be successful. Knowing this, it is essential that we teach our children early, for they, too, whether we wish to admit it or not, are under attack. Like anything else I teach my students, it is particularly gratifying to find that, in the act of simplifying the subject matter for their young minds, I inevitably find a growing understanding blossoming within my own heart. This is, in essence, how I explain the armour of God to them.

The first piece in the Armour of God is the Belt of Truth. We need to know without question what is true and what is right. We must be able to recognize the lies of the enemy and cling to the truth, no matter how convincing the evil one's claims may be. The better we know God—the more familiar we are with His Word, the closer we are to His Son—the better equipped we will be to recognize those lies when they are presented to us. While the adversary would rather we live in blind acceptance of the falsehoods that He would feed us, our Father gives us the Belt of Truth to protect us. We must know what is right and true.

The second piece in the Armour of God is the Breastplate of Righteousness. It isn't good enough for us to simply know what is right and true, we must act upon it. "Do what's right," I implore my children. "It will protect you from much evil." And it will. I think of some of the choices I, and others I know, have made over the years and sigh, knowing the simple act of righteousness would have saved us all much grief. We need to do what is right.

The Helmet of Salvation is a little trickier to explain. We must remember that we are in the middle of a war much bigger than ourselves. We are powerless, except that our Father empowers us. We have been caught in the snare of the evil one and bound by sin, and there is nothing we can do to save ourselves. There is no way for us to make ourselves good again or make our souls worthy to stand in the presence of our holy God. We cannot argue ourselves out of our sins or plead ignorance. No defence can stand, for we are guilty and the consequence of our sin is grave. Yet Jesus has come to remove from us the stain of sin and grant us His righteousness. He has come to save us, if only we will turn to Him. That is the Helmet of Salvation—recognizing that we can do nothing to make ourselves worthy of our Father's love and accepting the gift of forgiveness that comes only through our Saviour, Jesus Christ.

Next come the Shoes of Readiness. Wearing them, we are prepared to step forth into battle. We are ready to do whatever God says, whenever

He calls, no matter how unusual or difficult or frightening the task. We are ready to share His good news, the Gospel of Peace, that our brothers and sisters in Christ might be gathered once more into the arms of our Father. But to do that, our eyes must be opened to see the opportunities He sets before us, and the ears of our hearts attuned to hear His voice that we might respond to every impulse of the Holy Spirit within us. With our feet shod with readiness, we are ready and willing to march at the command of our Lord. Whether or not we desire to do so. Whether or not it makes sense to us. Whether or not it fills our hearts with fear. We are prepared to answer His call with willing obedience to His Word. A soldier's life is not a life of ease.

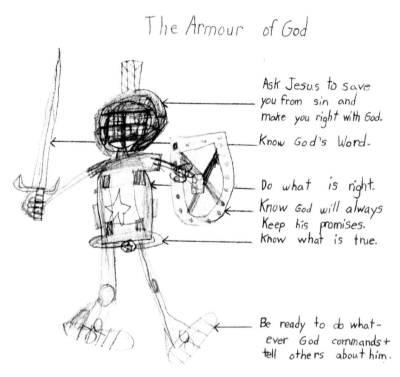

The Shield of Faith is one of my favourites. We know God is good; we know He is victorious; we know He is faithful. Our unshakable belief in who God is shields us from the fiery darts the evil one would hurl our way. Knowing God is who He claims to be, that His provision is sure, that His faithfulness endures forever, stands as a shield between us and the evil one that cannot be destroyed. In Hebrews chapter 11, we read that it is by faith the saints are deemed righteous. May God increase in us the faith to trust in Him.

The final piece of armour is the only piece of weaponry found in the armour of God. We are not meant to fight the evil one; that is not our job. We are called to stand our ground and resist, and in resisting, we are told the evil one will flee from us. We are told plainly that the Sword of the Spirit is the Word of God. Jesus gave us the perfect example of how to wield the Sword of the Spirit in His encounter in the wilderness with the adversary as described in Matthew chapter 4. Whenever Satan tempted Him, Jesus quoted Scripture to repel the attack. And it worked. The evil one cannot stand against the authority of God. To wield the Sword of the Spirit, we must not only know our Father, but we must know His Word, for against it no evil can stand.

Between the Belt of Truth, the Breastplate of Righteousness, the Helmet of Salvation, the Shoes of Readiness, the Shield of Faith and the Sword of the Spirit, we are well armed and well protected. To know truth and do right, to accept the goodness of our Saviour, and to be ready to respond to His call—these are the garments we need to survive the war. To know His Word, and to believe with all our hearts that which He has revealed to us, are the weapons we require to resist the advance of the evil one. It sounds so simple, and it is. If only simplicity and ease were synonymous. Thanks be to God that He alone is our strength and salvation.

RESTING IN THE PRESENCE OF OUR LORD

chapter seven

There is more to winning a war than being well armed and fitted for battle. Discouraged soldiers—fearful, hungry, deprived of rest—do not fight well. How can they? Similarly, no matter how carefully and conscientiously we don the armour of our Lord Jesus Christ, and no matter how often we sharpen our blades, we are vulnerable if we do not take the time to rest in the presence of our Commander and meditate upon His Word. Yet in the busyness of our lives, how easy it is for us to let the tyranny of the urgent commandeer our time.

There is nothing more integral to our daily lives than taking time away with our Lord, despite the busyness of our schedules and the obligations which vie for our attention. Unrushed periods of prayer and meditation, time in His Word, moments of worship—these are the things that strengthen us for battle and give us the courage to resist. But it's hard. We're busy; we're tired; we want to do other things. Instead of resisting the enemy, we find ourselves resisting the Lord by neglecting our relationship with Him. We try to prioritize it for we know it is essential, but too often we find it turning into just another thing to check off our list of daily accomplishments. A hurried reading, a whirlwind prayer and the job is done.

It was about this time last year that I made a decision. Disturbed by this trend in my own life, I determined that I would get up at six o'clock every weekday morning to meet with my Lord. I would set an alarm for seven so I wouldn't have to watch the time and I would open my heart to His presence. And I did—at first. For the initial two and a half months of the school year, I got up as planned. I read from my Bible and prayed, quietly meditating upon His Word. Often I wrote, sometimes I played music or sang and I enjoyed it with all my heart—despite the early hour—as I drew ever nearer to the One I love.

The change occurred slowly. Somewhere around the beginning of November, I found myself overwhelmed by the duties and obligations of bread-winning and incredibly low on sleep. Compromise began to seep into my routine as I allowed first one thing, and then another, to claim part of the time I had set aside. One day I had to clean my apartment, another, wrap a gift. Pretty soon, I was still getting up at six, but I wasn't even cracking the spine of my Bible. As much as I detested it, a quick prayer had replaced my time of renewal and I was on to the day's business. It happened so slowly, I didn't even realize what I had done until sometime in May when I noticed I was still getting up at six—to cook and eat a good breakfast, no less. It's been years since I've eaten breakfast!

That's what happens when we're under attack. The enemy's first priority is to neutralize our times of rest and renewal in the presence of our Lord and remove the opportunities we cherish that allow us to draw near to the One he abhors. The adversary does not want us to draw nearer to God, for he knows it will only fortify us with the strength and courage we need to resist his every move. He doesn't want us to spend time with our Lord because he knows that is exactly what our Father desires most.

We dare not underestimate the importance of our time alone with God. Like Mary of Bethany, we need to purposely choose the "better part" and rest at His feet, not only when our work is done, but every moment of every day. Then we will not only be armed and equipped for battle, we will also be prepared to stand firm in the face of attack. Peter's admonition is as wise today as it was when he made it: "Stay alert! Watch out for your great enemy, the devil. He prowls around like a roaring lion, looking for someone to devour. Stand firm against him, and be strong in your faith." (I Peter 5:8-9a)

THE GIFT OF THE SABBATH

"Observe the Sabbath day by keeping it holy, as the Lord your God has commanded you. You have six days each week for your ordinary work, but the seventh day is a Sabbath day of rest dedicated to the Lord your God." (Deuteronomy 5:12-14a)

God knew from the start that we would need dedicated time spent with Him if we were going to be prepared to resist the attacks of the evil one. Hence, He commanded us to set aside one full day each week to rest in His presence. And a glorious day it is! For me, it is the best day of the week—the one I look forward to all week long—when I actually celebrate it. On it, I rest from my labours, focus on developing my relationship with God and enjoy the break from the responsibilities and routines that commandeer my days.

So why does it seem so incredibly difficult to celebrate the Sabbath according to God's command? Because it is the last thing our adversary wants us to do. He knows time with our Father will strengthen us and draw us closer to the One he would destroy. He knows it will make us less susceptible to his dastardly ploys. He knows it will delight the heart of his greatest foe. If he can keep us from following that fourth commandment, he has won a valuable victory.

If you would like some practical ideas on how to spend more time with God by celebrating the Sabbath (or Lord's Day) more fully, check out Appendix A. It's odd how a command so compelling can be so difficult to follow in our everyday lives. May God give us the strength to obey when everything within us would rebel.

RESISTANCE IS NOT FUTILE
chapter eight

Resistance is futile. The passionless mantra of the dreaded Borg of the Star Trek saga could be that of the adversary himself. There is no denying it serves him well. But it isn't true. Resistance is not futile—not in the movies and not in real life. It's what we do when the enemy we face is greater than ourselves and it is the role which we have been assigned in the longstanding war between the Lord God of Hosts and the prince of this world.

God knows that, in our humanity, we do not have the power to overthrow the evil one. Hence, the call is not for us to fight the enemy, but to resist and wait for the deliverance of our Lord. There is a big difference. Notice that, in the armour God has bestowed upon us, there is only one offensive weapon—the Word of God. By standing firm in the face of opposition, by clinging to the Scriptures and by repeating the words of our Lord, we let God fight for us.

The Bible is full of examples of situations in which God fought for His people. The stories of Joseph, the exodus from Egypt, the conquering of the Promised Land, the war with the Midianites, the standoff between David and Goliath, the crucifixion. Our God is a great warrior and will stop at nothing in the fight for His people. All He asks of us is that we listen for His voice, obey His orders, and stand firm in the face of attack.

The adversary may be bigger than we are, but he is not bigger than the One who fights for us, the One who has already claimed the victory.

"Rejoice not against me, O mine enemy:" Micah says. "...when I fall, I shall arise" (Micah 7:8 KJV). "If God be for us, who can be against us?" Paul asks (Romans 8:31b KJV). "In all these things, we are more than conquerors through Him that loved us" (Romans 8:37 KJV). We are the victors, for victory has been assured through the death and resurrection of our Lord.

Resistance is not futile, though that is a secret the evil one guards well. As simple as the concept may be, though, resistance is not something that comes easily, or without cost, for any of us. It requires planning, effort, stamina and downright determination to do what is right when all the powers of hell would tempt us to do otherwise. It requires an unwavering commitment to the will of our Lord, an all-surpassing devotion to the heart of our Master, and a power far greater than ourselves to accomplish. It requires that we recognize the attacks of the evil one, not as random ambushes threatening to disarm and destroy us alone, but as calculated attacks, strategically enacted by the evil one in an attempt to wound the heart of God and win for himself the victory that none but our Lord may claim. It requires that we not be caught unaware. "Be alert!" Peter instructs, and he should know, for he, like we so often must, had to learn that lesson the hard way. We will not resist what we do not recognize as a threat. But the more fully we grasp the magnitude and nature of our position as children of the Most High, the more committed we will be to consistently and whole-heartedly resist the devil's schemes, no matter what the cost.

Recently I came upon an episode of the 1970's television show *Fantasy Island* entitled *The Capture of Tattoo*. In it, the loyal Tattoo is kidnapped by the arch-enemy of the God-like figure, O'Rourke. While O'Rourke realizes his friend is in peril, he recognizes that his nemesis holds no real power over his friend, for his enemy holds no real power over him—despite the evil one's diabolical posturing. And so O'Rourke leaves Tattoo to capably deal with the enemy while he looks protectively on, ready to step in if, and only if, it becomes necessary. He will only let the charade go so far. He knows his sidekick is well equipped to resist the ploys of the enemy; Tattoo is neither defenceless, nor alone. Meanwhile, though he is too small to actually fight his way out of the clutches of the enemy, Tattoo resists the evil one's every move until, in exasperation, the enemy gladly relinquishes him to O'Rourke and grudgingly concedes defeat.

I found it a fascinating and deeply moving story for it mirrors beautifully the story in which we find ourselves. We may, at times, feel powerless and alone, but we are not. Our Father has equipped us to resist the evil one and the promise of His presence is very real. In James 4:7b (KJV) we are told, "Resist the devil, and he will flee from you." We may not be equipped to fight the enemy, but we can resist his advances in the authority of our Lord, for the adversary has no right to rule the hearts and minds of God's holy ones, and he knows it.

RESISTANCE: THE VICTORY OF THE LOWLY KINGFISHER

Spotting a promising resting place, the glorious kingfisher glided to a stop. She had been haunted, stalked, accosted by the intruder for longer than her harried mind could tell. Exhaustion weighed upon her as she clenched her claws around the dead limb and folded her weary wings upon her back. She shivered, recalling the shadow's relentless pursuit. Would it never rest? Would it never stop harassing her? Surely it wouldn't find her here.

But she was wrong.

Fear crowded her thoughts as she watched it approach her resting spot. Her eyes narrowed as it neared and her wings tensed for flight.

"Resist, my child. Resist." A welcome voice rippled through her being, filling her with courage and hope. "It is not futile, My Love—the war has already been won. Resist the shadow and it will flee; it will flee from you and you will be free. Resist it, dear one, resist and stand firm. Do not give yourself over to its wiles, convincing though they may seem. Resist, My child, and be free."

Arrested by the intensity of the tender plea, the kingfisher cocked her head, her eyes never leaving the advancing shadow. She had a choice—a choice she alone could make. Maybe the monstrosity that stalked her every move was not as powerful as he appeared. Could it be that there was, indeed, one greater? Her thoughts bubbled in anticipation of the freedom she might enjoy should there be such a one. Did the shadow bird really hold no sway over her save that which she allowed? Was its only power truly in intimidation and posturing?

"It is, My child," came the gentle voice she so longed to hear. "It is. You always have a choice. You can play his war games as he desires or you can refuse, resting in the victory that is already yours. It's up to you, beloved. You need not succumb to his ploys. It will not be easy, for he is a powerful adversary, but it can be done. I will be your courage and strength if only you will call upon me. Look to me, beloved. Look to me and resist the power of the adversary. Look to me and live."

Nodding silent assent to the glorious presence pervading her soul, the trembling kingfisher perched on the once leafy bough, firmly refusing to give way to the deplorable creature accosting her. Stopping her ears to its hideous taunts, she wrapped her claws ever tighter around her perch and fixed her gaze upon the horizon, hardly daring to breathe.

"Did you think I wouldn't find you?" the shadow bird cackled. "You should have waited for me. You're weak; you're spineless; you're... you're... you're nothing! But you are *mine and you will never fly from me again."*

She shifted uncomfortably as his tirade grew, fury snapping his every word like a lash. Yet still she held firm, refusing to allow her tormentor to cow her into submission. With all her strength, she clung to the branch, resisting insult after insult, taunt after taunt, attack after weary attack. And, wonder of wonders, the evil one fled.

Father, grant us the courage and strength to resist the evil one that he might flee from us. Let us not be intimidated by his threats or fooled by his ploys, but instead, let us live in the freedom You created us to enjoy, for we are Yours, O Lord, and no one can tear us out of Your hand.

A PLAN OF RESISTANCE

chapter nine

Resistance is not something that happens on its own. It is something for which we must actively plan and prepare. It is something we must not only talk about, but act upon, something that requires consistent follow through. It is not easy, though practice certainly makes a difference. It is like forming a habit. When the light turns red, we stop; when the fire alarm rings, we exit the building; when the evil one attacks, we resist. Whether we want to or not. It is not something we stop to think about, it is something we simply do. Yet every habit has to start somewhere. That's where a plan comes into the picture—a plan of resistance to combat the charge and send the enemy running in the opposite direction.

But we must also acknowledge that a plan of resistance, no matter how good, cannot be static. Plans change; they have to. Consider for a moment how effortlessly the microbial world adapts itself to attack, becoming immune to the disinfectants and medications we would use to eliminate its harmful effects. Is the evil one not far greater? He knows what he's up against and he will do anything in his power to reduce our plans to the rubble of defeat. It's up to us to recognize and expect attack, even in the most unexpected places and at the most unlikely times. The adversary is a devious and unconscionable foe, intent on wreaking havoc in the lives of the saints. Fighting fair is not something for which he is known. It is impossible for us to foresee his every move, and equally impossible for us to plan specifically for each individual scenario, but we can prepare a general plan of resistance that can be modified to fit the specifics of a given attack even in the height of battle.

While your plan might differ significantly from mine, here are some of the basic tactics I find helpful as I seek to resist the advances of the evil one. Perhaps they will help you in formulating a plan for yourself. I call these my SCRAP tactics. Notice how the first letter of each, when combined, conveniently forms the word *scrap*. I know no better tools to have on hand when I find myself in a scrap.

Substitution: When temptation jumps up to bite you, be prepared with specific thoughts or actions that are incompatible with the evil one's suggestions and implement them instead. You can't do one thing if you are already doing the opposite.

Command: Don't be afraid to invoke the name of Jesus and command the evil one to leave you alone. He has no right to assault you, for you belong to Another. However, I would caution you not to enter into conversation with him; his lying lips can make anything sound like truth, and you will only open yourself up for further attack.

Recitation: Know God's Word. Find verses that countermand the dictates of the evil one and recite them whenever he strikes. Simple statements taken from verses, scriptural songs, prayers and personal revelations are your best defence. I use something I have come to call memory beads (see Appendix B) to help me remember God's Word and stand firm.

Avoidance: Learn to recognize the times, places and situations in which you are most vulnerable to attack and, as much as it is in your power, try to avoid them. If they cannot be avoided, look for ways to manipulate them in such a way that they will not be so imposing.

Prayer: Call on God to save you; He will. Daily pray for the protection of Jesus as you ask God to clothe you in the spiritual armour He has provided. Ask Him to speak His truth to your soul and bring to mind His words. Entreat Him to help you to recognize the attacks of the evil one and stand firm.

Now it's your turn.
1. Look back at the five or six areas of greatest vulnerability and most frequent means of attack you identified in Chapter Four. Choose the one you would most like to address. Be sure to pray about which one God would have you target as He knows what we do not and He sees connections where we see none. Note your choice here:

_____

_____

_____

_____

2. Think about when, where, and in what situations you experience the attack most keenly.
Times:

_____

_____

Places:

_____

_____

Situations:

_____

_____

3. Is there anything you can do to avoid or nullify these triggers?

_____

_____

_____

_____

_____

_____

4. Are there any substitute behaviours you could use to keep you from succumbing to the attack?

_____
_____
_____
_____
_____

5. List as many verses, phrases or songs as you can that you could use to resist the assault. Be sure they are entirely scriptural. God's Word is powerful because He is powerful. Memorize them or mount them in significant places so you can recite them when the attack comes. Consider preparing a set of memory beads (Appendix B) to help you focus on them in times of need.

_____
_____
_____
_____
_____
_____
_____
_____

6. Meditate on these verses and ask God to reveal to you His heart on the matter. Write a prayer here that you can use when the evil one attacks.

_____
_____
_____
_____
_____
_____
_____

Remember, habit making takes a long time and there is no secret formula for success. We will fall; we're human. But we have a High Priest who is able to keep us from falling and present us blameless before God. (Jude 24) I take such encouragement from the words of Paul in Hebrews 10:14 (NIV, italics mine), "For by one sacrifice He has made perfect forever those *who are being made holy*." Learning to resist the attacks of the evil one is one way in which we are being made holy. Imagine: Our Lord Jesus has already made us perfect, despite our shortcomings. Our perfection is not dependent upon our own holiness, but upon the righteousness of our Saviour who fought the evil one in our stead and emerged victorious that we might reign with Him forever. It is dependent upon our beloved Bridegroom who recognizes that we are but dust, yet cherishes us regardless. Hallelujah!

KEYS TO RESISTANCE

Resistance is one of those things that can only be learned through practice. These are some of the things I have found most helpful in my quest to resist the attacks of the adversary. I wish I could say I have mastered them, but that would be a lie. I do, however, think I am growing—if only, as Paul says, "from one degree of glory to another" (II Corinthians 3:18 NRSV). May God's strength be ours as we seek to resist the arrows of the evil one.

Recognition: Recognize the attack when it comes and be willing to call it what it is. Be aware of whom you are dealing with, what he desires, the lengths to which he will go and his regular patterns of attack in your life.

Preparation: Have a plan and be prepared to follow it. Avoid situations in which you know you will be tempted. Don the armour of God, cover yourself in prayer and rest in the presence of your Master, secure in the knowledge that He is in command.

Knowledge of God's Word: Know God's Word; it's the only way to keep that Sword sharp!

Consistency: Be consistent in responding to attacks. Inconsistency, as every parent knows, only leads to greater battles.

Adaptability: Expect the unexpected and be flexible. The adversary is a worthy foe; his weapons are many and varied. He is not beyond changing his approach.

Stamina: Persevere, even when there seems to be no way out. The greater the resistance, the greater will be the attack.

Determination: Determine to do what is right, despite the intensity of the opposition.

Like a discarded doll, Cosette lay sprawled across the dusty cobbles, abandoned and alone. Tears spilled from her eyes as she drew her legs to her chest, her quiet whimpers lost in the sighing of the evening breeze. Manuél was gone. Torn from her aching arms, led away by the enemy, destined to bear the weight of the evil one's ire, though he deserved it not. A groan rumbled from deep within her and she cursed beneath her breath. She shivered as the night air closed in around her. The sun had long set beyond the rim of the western wilderness and a handful of determined stars dotted the night sky. *He's going to die. In my place. Because I pledged allegiance to the wrong master.* Desperate to banish the thought, she clasped her hands to her head. *No one, but no one, crosses Nyoke and lives to tell about it.* Her fingers pulsed as she clutched handfuls of hair and pulled the strawy mass away from her scalp. The pain felt good. Fitting.

A volley of raucous laughter erupted from the open door of the tavern and she turned to see the cherry-nosed barkeep slosh mugs of golden ale on the table before his eager patrons. Cosette grimaced. Though thirst burned in her throat, a wave of nausea trembled through her belly as she watched the men gulp the sordid brew. The very thought of partaking of the inn's famous ale appalled her and she wondered how it could have once seemed so appealing.

I must do something to help Manuél. Inhaling sharply, Cosette held her breath and staggered to her feet, wondering what to do next. Her options were limited. She knew where the tyrant and his foul band of cutthroats were headed—at least, she thought she did—but what good would that do her? She could follow them and look for... *For what? A way to help Manuél escape?* She snorted at the thought. Like there was anything she could do to help him escape. If she couldn't free herself from the clutches of her jailer, what would make her think she could free Manuél? *Perhaps if I could find Jaired...*

An urgent whisper from the shadows beyond the walkway arrested her in mid-thought.

"Cosette?"

Cautiously, she peered into the darkness, hardly daring to move.

"I heard what happened and came as soon as I could."

Cosette's pulse raced as the figure of a woman, no older than herself, emerged from the bushes. She looked almost angelic in the pale light of the village inn. Her face glowed with joy and her smile radiated wonder despite the tears that bathed her cheeks.

"I came as soon as I heard. I knew you would need..." Her voice trailed into silence as her eyes met Cosette's. "You don't know who I am, do you?" Rushing forward, she scooped Cosette's hands into hers and peered into her eyes. "Cosette, it's me—Ilana—your sister! Surely you remember *me*."

"Sister?" Cosette gulped. *Again with the sister. First Jaired, now this... what did she say her name was? Ilana?* Inhaling sharply, she closed her hands around the woman's fingers. Could this be the Ilana she'd been looking for all day?

"Think, Cosette. Think! We've been waiting for you for days... weeks... months." The stranger paused for a breath, her brow furrowed. "It's true, Cosette." She nodded her head vigorously. "Really, it is. Manuél and I have been waiting for... well, forever, it seems. Ever since Jaired told us you'd be coming."

Her words tumbled out in short, excited bursts. "Jaired said we were to watch for you, and Manuél... Oh, Cosette..." Her excited prattle ceased and a look of anguish filled her eyes. "When Manuél left this morning, he implored me to find you. He told me that you would need me. That we'd both need each other." She lowered her head and shrugged. "I didn't know what he was talking about. He can be so cryptic at times, you know."

Cosette blinked rapidly. She drew her hands away from the animated woman before her and edged her way into the shadows as Ilana babbled on. Her head throbbed with the effort to follow the young woman's words. Why did this woman, whom she had never met before, seem so frighteningly and alluringly familiar?

"Don't you get it, Cosette? The time has come! The time he warned us about. I understand now." Ilana paused and stepped closer, reaching once more for Cosette's hands, her eyes sparkling with unshed tears. "It's time for us to go home."

Cosette nodded in bewilderment at Ilana's impassioned monologue, not sure how to respond. That the young woman meant her no harm was clear, but she had no idea of what the girl was talking about. "Go home?" Cosette's eyes narrowed as she fixed them on the stranger and an angry tear quivered down her cheek. "I don't have a home." She yanked back her hands and turned abruptly, prepared to flee.

"Wait! Cosette," Ilana pleaded. She slid her hand onto Cosette's shoulder and squeezed it gently.

Cosette winced at the pain that laced the young woman's voice.

"I... I..."

"You what?" Cosette snarled. She brushed Ilana's hand away and turned to glare at the forward young woman. Were all of Jaired's friends alike?

"I've missed you." Ilana sighed, obviously deflated. She reached to enfold Cosette in an awkward embrace. "I was afraid I would never see you again."

"Again?" Cosette wrenched herself out of the stranger's arms with a mirthless snort. The unaccountable familiarity of the woman frightened her. "This is the first time I've ever met you."

"Oh, I wish you could remember." Ilana blinked her eyes rapidly as she stepped back. "We need to find Manuél." Swallowing hard, she extended a hand. "Will you come with me?"

Cosette eyed the woman's hand warily, afraid to take it, yet not knowing what else to do. One thing was certain. She had to find Manuél and she couldn't do it on her own. She hesitated, frustrated by her limited options, then, jaw set, she jerked her chin in affirmation and grasped the proffered hand. If Jaired and Manuél trusted this woman, she would also.

Cosette relaxed as she felt the reassuring squeeze of her new friend. The ghost of a smile tugged at the young woman's lips and Cosette almost smiled in return. If only she could recall where she'd met this woman before.

* * *

Regal plumes of orange and magenta framed the eastern sky where the rising sun peeked above the horizon. Dawn. Jaired stifled an angry epithet and ground his teeth. It seemed so incongruous. The putrid stench of night waste wafted through the air as he neared the pits, its acrid odour stinging his throat as the walls of the compound came into view. Drawing a ragged breath, he crouched, shivering in the pre-dawn coolness of the savannah, desperate to make sense of the horrifying images that plagued his weary brain.

Iron-clad knuckles, slick with blood, pounding the face of an innocent man.

Mangled flesh, torn by the iron-tipped phalange of the enemy's whip-bearer. Ragged. Seeping. Raw.

Buckled knees.

A pale head sagging on a whip-scarred chest.

Hardened faces distorted in cruel glee...

Jaired shook his head and blinked away his mounting tears.

The time will *come when I shall lay down my life for our brothers and sisters, Jaired.*

A chill tingled up his spine at the remembered words and he moaned. How could this be happening?

When that time comes, my friend, all will seem lost. You will watch as the last breath is squeezed from my lungs and my body is surrendered to the abyss..."

Jaired pressed white-knuckled fists to his ears and choked back a sob. Yet still the words plagued him. It had happened just as Manuél had said. However could he have known?

But do not give in to despair, beloved. Though the darkness may overwhelm your spirit, remember my words. All will be well. Our father will not abandon me, Jaired; the king will not allow any of his children to be destroyed. Not now—not ever."

Jaired let out a long, uneven breath and ran a grubby hand through his tangled hair as he stood.

"All will be well," he mumbled into his beard. "All *will* be well." He blinked his throbbing eyes and trained them upon the mighty tree overhanging the great abyss.

"You had better be right, Manuél." He lifted his head to the heavens as the first piercing finger of the rising sun broke through the clouds and illuminated the tree. "You had better be right."

part iv

WE BELONG TO HIM

The unyielding ground bit mercilessly into Cosette's back. Restless, she moaned as she struggled to pull the ragged fringes of her wrap more tightly about her shivering shoulders. Who would have imagined the desert could get so cold? Her stomach lurched as a parade of horrifying images clawed their way into her consciousness, and her heart began to race. With a vicious shove, she thrust herself into a sitting position and angrily willed the offending pictures away. Yet the more vehemently she strove to banish them, the more aggressively they seemed to assert themselves.

Drawing her knees to her chin, she curled her arms around her head and rocked, bracing herself against the flood of memories that tormented her soul. She palmed a tear from her cheek as the face of Manuél filled her mind, his sun-kissed face beckoning her forward, his anguished eyes beseeching her to trust. Memories of their final meeting bombarded her and she flinched. He was so unlike anyone else she had ever met. So warm, so compassionate, so full of love. She could see it in his eyes. Though not a word had passed between them, Cosette couldn't help but feel as if she knew him, or was it that he knew her? She pressed her lips together, but couldn't suppress the smile that leapt to her eyes at the thought. *Is this what love feels like?* As quickly as it had come, the joyful thought fled as the events of the previous day prevailed upon her memory.

The sordid laughter of her adversary and the brutality of his henchmen had contrasted starkly with the quiet dignity and power of Manuél. Why, oh why, had he handed himself over to Nyoke? She rubbed a hand across her aching eyes. Why did Manuél not leave her to the fate she so undeniably deserved and save himself? *Yet, where would I be now if he had?* Her body stiffened and a sob broke from her throat as she relived those final, terrifying moments outside the inn.

His eyes met hers, so ardent and full of compassion, brimming with confidence and unspoken resolve. The intensity of love shining from their depths overwhelmed her and her breath caught in her throat.

Jolted from her reverie, Cosette's brow furrowed in recognition. She had seen those eyes before; Manuél was no stranger! She knew him well—or did she? *Perhaps he just reminds me of someone I once knew.*

Suddenly alert, she jumped to her feet and began to pace. "It isn't Padrick; it isn't Michale; it isn't Addie..." She tapped her right forefinger thoughtfully against the fingers of her left hand as she enumerated the possibilities. "Think. Think. Think," she chided herself. Dropping her hands to her sides, she blew out a long, slow breath. Why did this strange man seem so familiar?

Unbidden, the parade of images returned and her legs gave way beneath her. The insistent voice of Ilana as she hurried Cosette through the streets of the despised village, their horrifying midnight flight across the desert sands, the throbbing pain that had accompanied her every move... *No-o-o-o-o-o-o!*

* * *

Rolling onto her back, Cosette rested her arm across her forehead and sighed. The stars twinkled in the heavens above, drawing her gaze and daring her to hope, but she couldn't help but wonder what hope there could be. With a huff, she brushed away the tears that trickled into her ears and threw herself onto her belly. She had to rid herself of these memories before they consumed her entirely. Yet, try as she might, she could not keep them from surfacing.

Numb from the pain and exhaustion of their journey, Cosette limped into the bristly haven of underbrush that lined the banks of the hidden spring. The welcome gurgle of water greeted her and she quickened her pace, eager to assuage her growing thirst. Within moments, she found herself at the edge of a pool fed by a trickling stream. Its waters shone like a jewel in the moonlight, casting a gentle glow upon the shore, and she stopped mid-stride. A disquieting image of a young, curly-headed girl, her face alight with laughter, fluttered at the corners of her memory. The girl dabbled her toes in a stream, much like the one Cosette now saw, only bigger. Much, much bigger. The sun sparkled on the rippled surface of the little river and a glorious waterfall cascaded nearby. Kicking her feet in the water, the girl squealed as the splashes rained down upon her and she threw out her arms in delight.

Cosette raked a hand through her hair and let the air rush from her lungs. No sooner had the image come, than it was gone and, though she couldn't quite tell why, she felt somehow bereft. Falling to her knees, she thrust her hands into the pool and eagerly cupped the life-giving droplets to her parched lips. They tasted good. Never before had a mouthful of water seemed so wonderfully refreshing, so comfortingly cool, so undeniably alive. Heartened, Cosette drank deeply, memories of curly-headed girls and brown-eyed strangers who weren't really strangers, banished—if only for a time.

At last, thirst quenched, she sat back on her heels and dried her face with the edge of her wrap. The curtain of despair began to lift as she basked in the unusual tingling sensation that spread throughout her body. There was something deliciously unusual about that water. Almost immediately, the throbbing of her blistered feet subsided and her head began to clear.

"Ilana?" Reverence filled Cosette's voice. "What is this place?"

"Feeling better?" Ilana smiled. She settled on the bank beside Cosette and slid an arm around her friend's shoulders. "We made it, Cosette! Can you believe it? We found our way to the Spring of Vrede—the Spring of Peace. Have you ever seen anything so beautiful?"

Stunned, Cosette scanned their unexpected sanctuary. Her lips parted as the light of the fledgling day illuminated the horizon, casting a golden glow upon the desert oasis. She had heard of such places before, but she'd never truly believed they existed.

"This is where he told us to meet him." Ilana nodded exuberantly. "It's right where he said it would be."

"'*Ilana, child...*'" she whispered, cupping her free hand gently over her cheek. Her eyes misted as she gazed into the distance, repeating the comforting words of Manuél. "*'Should anything happen to me—and* dear one, you must know that it will—do not be afraid. Instead, gather our brothers and sisters and lead them to the Spring of Vrede. Wait for me there, Ilana. On the third day, I will come for you. Comfort each other with my words and drink deeply from the Fount of Peace, for all will be well.'"

As the words faded into silence, Cosette noticed, for the first time, the ragged band of strangers scattered along the banks of the bubbling pool. *Brothers and sisters? The Fount of Peace?* Surely Ilana didn't think she was that naïve. As wonderful as the fairytale sounded, it was just that—a fairytale—and she refused to succumb to its spell.

"It's only a matter of time, Ilana." She shuddered at the flatness in her own voice. "You know that as well as I do." The words pained her to say as much as they clearly pained Ilana to hear, but she thrust her shoulders back and continued. "Face it, it's over. You know he isn't coming back. No one escapes the clutches of the enemy—not even Manuél." She lowered her head, massaging her forehead with her fingertips. With a sigh, she dropped her hand and raised her eyes to meet Ilana's. "*Especially* Manuél. Nyoke hates him more vehemently than any other. There's no way he will let Manuél come here to meet with us. And furthermore, you know that when he's done with Manuél, he's not going to rest until he destroys us, too."

Cosette paused and tossed a pebble into the spring. A volley of ripples spread across its surface and she sighed. "Oh, Ilana, what are we going to do?" She lifted her hands helplessly in the air. As much as she wished things were different, if she knew Nyoke—and she most certainly did—there was no hope for them. She crossed her arms in front of her and glanced at her supposed sister.

Pressing her lips together, Ilana closed her eyes and nodded. "I know it seems hopeless, Cosette, but it's not. Manuél said he would meet us here in three days, and he will. I know he will. I don't know how, but I do know he will." Ilana's chin quivered as she let her hand fall from Cosette's shoulders. "Manuél knows things we don't, Cosette, and I've seen him do the impossible. He doesn't make promises he can't keep." Ilana's eyes held an intensity Cosette had never seen in them before. "We've just got to trust him. He's never failed us before. Why would he start now?" She stopped as if awaiting a response, but none came.

"Manuél knew exactly what he was doing when he handed himself over to Nyoke. Of that you can be certain. And if he knew what he was doing, you can be sure he has a plan. We must do as he asked and wait for him here." Ilana gave Cosette's arm a comforting squeeze and rose to stand before her. "He would want us to rest, Cosette. Rest our bodies and strengthen our hearts so we will be prepared for what is to come. But above all, he would want us to trust his word and be at peace. He said so."

Ilana's eyes bore into hers, but Cosette was not convinced. However could she believe such nonsense?

* * *

With a long, satisfying yawn, Cosette stretched her cramped legs and sat up. Heedless of the chill, she let the wrap fall from her shoulders as she surveyed the growing camp. Two days had passed since her conversation with Ilana. Two dishearteningly long circuits of the sun across the sky. Two mind-numbing, soul-searching eons.

Just one more to go. She rolled her eyes at the thought. *One more day and the truth will be known.* Rising quietly, Cosette hurried to the pool, careful not to awaken the others. She needed to think. The cool water refreshed her as she stooped to splash it on her neck and rub it across her face. Easing herself back on her heels, she marvelled anew at the healing properties of the water. With every sip, her mind became more alert, her energy increased, and her courage was renewed. It puzzled her. The fact that her bruised and battered body, so stiff and sore from the endless abuse it had endured, was now almost healed, astounded her still more. What was in that water? Cosette tossed a pebble into the pool as her thoughts turned back to the day they had arrived at the oasis.

A heavy silence fell between the two girls as Cosette struggled to accept the words of her mentor. "Wait? Rest?" Cosette pushed herself to her feet. "Come on, Ilana. Don't you get it? It's over. Manuél is gone. It's hopeless. When Nyoke finds us, he'll be livid. We're doomed."

Ilana looked to the heavens and sighed. "I wish you could remember what things used to be like—before that snake came into our lives. I know you may think we haven't known each other for long, Cosette, but you have to trust me on this. Everything is going to be fine."

Cosette stifled an angry retort and turned away.

"You'll see," Ilana persisted. I know you don't believe it, but Manuél *will* come. He promised. The adversary may think he has won, but he doesn't know Manuél." Ilana lapsed into silence as Cosette straightened her shoulders and strode away. The conversation was over.

Cosette groaned as she forced her heavy eyelids to remain open. The yearning for sleep was unbearable, yet terrified to subject herself to the nightmares she knew would follow, she fought to resist its growing demand. If only Ilana was right. If only Manuél had somehow foiled Nyoke's plan and was still alive. He couldn't have—could he? After all, whatever Nyoke wanted, Nyoke got. Still...

"Manuél..." The whimpered cry broke from deep within Cosette's heart, despite her determination to restrain it. "Manuél, please...you've got to come back. I need you." A wave of gut-wrenching sobs shuddered through her body as she dared to admit the truth. "Please, please come back."

* * *

The sun could barely have passed its zenith when Cosette awakened, confused by the unearthly darkness that enveloped the camp, startled by the wild tremors that shook the earth beneath her. She leapt to her feet, stricken by the realization that something was desperately wrong. *Where has everybody gone?* Edging toward the place where Ilana usually slept, she scanned the empty bedrolls, unnerved by the unusual stillness. Had Manuél come for them and left her behind?

"You're awake."

Cosette started at the voice of her friend. Sensing the hint of despair in Ilana's voice, she stiffened and her heart skipped a beat.

"Come. Jaired is here. He has news."

Comforted by the gentle touch of Ilana's arm around her waist, Cosette allowed herself to be led toward a small fire kindled at the centre of the camp. *So that's where everyone went.* She tensed briefly when Ilana rested her head against her shoulder, fearful of what was to come, but she couldn't help but smile at the thought of seeing Jaired again. The realization that he was near was every bit as comforting as Ilana's unexpected behaviour was alarming. Would he have news of Manuél?

Her pace quickened as she and Ilana hurried toward the agitated group of pilgrims milling about the fire pit. If there was news, she wanted to hear it. Now. Her brow furrowed as she scanned the growing crowd. Where had all these people come from and what were they doing here? There had been but a handful when she drifted off to sleep. What was going on?

Pausing on the edge of the firelight, Cosette peered around the circle of strangers. Everywhere she looked, people were gathered in groups of two or three, murmuring quietly to each other. Locked in a tearful embrace, one woman rocked another gently back and forth, crooning words of comfort in her ear, while another couple clung to each other and sobbed. Still others spoke using animated gestures, clearly discussing a plan of attack, while some stared fixedly into space, apparently heedless of the world spinning on around them. The scene seemed eerily familiar to Cosette. Even the faces seemed familiar, yet she didn't know any of the people before her—or did she? She had to find out what was going on.

"Where's Jaired?" The frantic words exploded from her mouth before she could stop them. Harsh, commanding, panic-stricken. She snapped her mouth shut when all eyes turned toward her, and tried not to squirm. Ignoring the heat in her cheeks, she surveyed the gaping faces before her. What was wrong with these people?

"Where's Jaired?" she repeated, her growing panic clipping the edges of every syllable. "I want to see Jaired."

A questioning murmur rippled through the crowd. "Jaired?"

"Jaired?"

"Who's Jair— oh wait. Jaired. I know him. He's..."

Cosette jumped at the gentle touch of a hand on her shoulder and spun to face the figure that had approached her from behind. Drawing a hand to her chest, she found herself face to face with the man who had freed her from the clutches of the enemy. "Jaired," she breathed. She released her hold on Ilana and threw herself into his arms, shifting only slightly when Ilana joined their embrace.

"Sh-h-h-h," he soothed. "Take heart, little lamb." His quiet voice calmed her. All would be well. Jaired would know what to do. Grasping Ilana's hand tightly in her own, she stepped out of Jaired's embrace, her head bowed to hide her flaming cheeks.

"Have you seen him?" The whispered words slipped from her lips before she had time to censor them.

"Yes, I've seen him." Jaired paused as his gaze flickered from Cosette to Ilana and back again. "He bade me make haste to the Spring of Vrede." A sad smile parted his lips and he inhaled deeply. "He told me he would meet us here the day after tomorrow... that it was time for him to take us home."

"You mean he escaped?" Cosette's eyes widened and she reached out a hand to grasp Jaired's forearm.

"No." He shook his head sadly and laid a comforting hand over hers. "Escape was not part of Manuél's plan. The last time I saw him, he was dangling from the hanging tree, his eyes glazed in death as Nyoke looked on and laughed."

Jaired's eyes fluttered as his words faded into silence. Cosette recognized the unmistakable glint of pain that flashed in their depths when he looked away, obviously steeling himself to continue. His hand dropped from hers and he stepped back a pace, his teeth pinching his upper lip.

Cosette stood rigid, her heart pounding in her chest. *What could possibly be worse than what he had already told them?* Reaching once more for Ilana's hand, she squeezed it convulsively, comforted by the feel of another hand in hers. "Jaired?" Her broken whisper shattered the silence that had settled over the camp.

Jaired raked his fingers through his rumpled hair before lifting his eyes to meet hers. "I wanted so much to go to him, Cosette—to free his body from the tree, to prepare his lifeless shell for the burial he deserved—but I couldn't do it." He averted his eyes as the words tumbled from his lips. "His instructions were clear. I was to leave immediately and come directly to the spring." He paused again and shrugged, his eyes pooling with unshed tears. "How could I disregard his final command?" His voice softened. "How could I deny him his dying request?"

Stepping forward, Cosette fell into Jaired's arms and sobbed. She knew how hard this must be for her friend. He and Manuél had obviously been close.

Many long minutes passed before she could bring herself to slide from his arms and look him in the eyes. "So," she announced, "he's gone." She hated herself for what she was about to say, but it couldn't be helped. Someone had to say it. With a deep breath, she plunged forward. "What's this nonsense, then, about him meeting us here and taking us home?" Cosette leaned forward and thrust her fists into her hips. The vitriol that erupted from within surprised even her. "Tell me, Jaired, how exactly is a *dead* man supposed to meet us here, let alone lead us to a home we've never even known?" She paused to swipe a tear from her eye and catch her breath. "You said he was different, Jaired; you said he wasn't like the rest. You said I could trust him."

* * *

Jaired hung his head as Cosette's tirade continued, wishing he had the answers to her questions. He knew that Manuél wouldn't fail them, but she needed answers, not assurances, and he had no answers to give her. He didn't know how a dead man was going to meet them or lead them anywhere, but he did know Manuél—and he knew the king. Nothing would stop the king from getting his children back. Nothing could. His love for them was too great. No, though Jaired didn't know how, he did know this: Manuél would come. He promised.

Jaired watched as Ilana approached Cosette and tenderly slipped her arm around her shoulders before leaning in to whisper something in her ear. A puzzled frown replaced the angry scowl wrinkling Cosette's face and the bitter accusations died on her lips as she turned to look at her comforter.

"But how?" Cosette lifted a hand and stepped away. "That's impossible."

"Not for the king," came Ilana's soft reply. "Nothing is impossible for him." Her eyes sought Jaired's and he nodded for her to continue. "It may seem an impossible feat to us, but nothing is impossible for him, Cosette. Nothing." Her voice rose and excitement lit her eyes. "Don't you see? He can do anything. He's the king!"

"Anything?" a trembling voice repeated.

Jaired looked around to see a score of pale faces leaning in, straining to hear every word.

"Anything," another voice breathed.

A growing sense of wonderment filled the air as the word was repeated over and over again.

"Anything."

"Anything."

"Anything."

"*Any*thing."

Jaired surveyed the group of weary souls pressing in upon them. Stirred by the glorious hope he saw growing on their faces, he threw back his head and raised his arms to the heavens. "ANYTHING!"

Cosette shook her head as the hushed pilgrims exploded into shouts of joy, everyone talking at once.

"So it's true? He's really coming?"

"How could we have been so blind?"

"Of course he's coming. The king won't let the enemy's plans stop him, even if they do include Manuél's death. He's the king of life!"

"King of Life!"

"King of Life!"

One by one the pilgrims joined the chant until the words echoed from the heavens above.

"King of Life! King of Life!"

"Yes, he *is* the King of Life." A lone voice rose above the rest. Cosette turned to see Ilana step toward the gathered crowd. The voices around her immediately stilled. "But, he is more than that. Far more. He's the King of Life because he's the King of Love."

Cosette watched as a chorus of heads bobbed excitedly in agreement. "It is as you say," Jaired replied. "Come, my friends, we must rest and ready ourselves to meet our king. Manuél will be here the day after tomorrow."

* * *

Cosette slid her hand gently down her leg and smiled as hundreds of tiny bubbles chased each other to the surface of the pool. It was hard to believe that a whole day had passed since Jaired's return. If he was right, that meant Manuél would arrive tomorrow. But if he was wrong... She shuddered, unable to bear the possibility that he might be mistaken. Weary of the endless battle of emotions, Cosette plunged her head beneath the sparkling waters and swam to the far shore. She marvelled at the changes that had come over her since she had left the compound. Gone were the angry contusions that had covered her body, the mottled bruising that darkened her skin. Gone, too, were the cuts, the abrasions, the blisters, the welts that had brought her tormentor such delight. And gone was the dirt and grime that had accumulated over the years, fouling her clothing and body and hair. Her pain was gone, her freedom restored. She felt like a new person. She couldn't remember the last time she had felt so alive. *If only it could last.*

Gliding across the pool, Cosette stepped from the water and donned her tunic. Immersed in the bubbly warmth of the spring, she hadn't realized how cool the air had gotten. She shivered as she gathered her wrap around her shoulders and headed for the fire. A skittering sound startled her and she snapped her head around, certain that Nyoke had tracked them down at last, but she saw only the snakelike tail of a desert rat disappearing into the undergrowth behind her. Relieved, she resumed her trek. Worse than the thought that Manuél might not come, was the certainty that Nyoke would. She squinted as she scanned the dusky horizon. He was out there. Somewhere. She could feel it. Her body may have found healing in the crystalline waters of the spring, but the wounds exacted upon her spirit were not so easily salved. Fear stalked her every move. Fear that Nyoke would find them. Fear of the torturous punishments he would visit upon them. Fear that Manuél wouldn't appear as he promised, or worse yet, fear that he would, but that he wouldn't want anything to do with her. After all, was she not the cause of his heinous death? The others might believe in a happy ending, but when had she ever seen one of those? She wanted to believe their stories of a loving king whose limitless power made the impossible possible, but she feared giving way to hope lest that hope be dashed, as she knew it most surely would, on the jagged rocks of reality.

Willing away the disturbing thoughts, Cosette hastened toward the fire pit to warm herself before its mesmerizing flames. Just one more night and the truth would be known, one more night and they would know their hope was vain. She wondered vaguely if Jaired had a backup plan, and snickered at the thought. *A backup plan? Why would he have one of those?* If only she could be as certain as he that Manuél wouldn't fail them.

* * *

Cosette yawned and stretched as the first rays of the dawning sun lit upon her brow. Wondering what the new day would bring, she rolled onto her side and savoured the few moments of peace before the bustling camp awoke. *Would he or wouldn't he?* The question drummed through her head, demanding an answer—an answer she was certain she already knew. Would Manuél transcend the bounds of death to deliver them or would Nyoke's claim on him be too strong? She had no doubt that Manuél would meet them if he could, but death had a way of interfering with the best of intentions. Could it be that Manuél had finally made a promise he could not keep?

Cosette's stomach churned with the certainty of defeat. The last thing she saw before drifting back into a fitful sleep was a vision of Nyoke, his face contorted in a grotesque grin as he pointed at her and laughed. Terrified, she clamped her hands to her ears, but not before she heard his triumphant howl. "You, *my dear*, are mine."

* * *

Startled into wakefulness, Cosette scrambled to her feet and shook the sand from her skirt. All around her, people shouted and danced as they gathered their belongings and rushed toward the eastern bank of the spring in answer to some unknown summons. Confused, she scanned the skies. The sun had barely risen above the tops of the gnarled baobabs clustered along the shores of the oasis. Did these people not realize the horror and disappointment this day held in store?

"Come on!" Ilana snagged Cosette's elbow and pulled her forward. "Look! He's almost here!" Cosette's eyes followed Ilana's pointing finger across the dismal sands to a dark mass gathering in the distance. Speechless, she turned to Ilana, her eyes wide as she drew a trembling hand to her mouth.

"What's wrong?" Ilana asked.

Struggling to keep her knees from buckling beneath her, Cosette swayed, thankful for Ilana's steadying touch. Her tongue, thick and sluggish, clung to the roof of her mouth as she desperately tried to form the words. "We're doom—"

"Doomed?" The surprise in Ilana's tone stung and Cosette pulled away, feeling more alone than ever. "Cosette, it's Manuél!"

"Manuél?" Cosette croaked. "How can you be so sure?" She craned to look over Ilana's shoulder and shuddered. "Someone is coming, yes—a whole horde of people if you ask me—but how do you know it is Manuél?" She shifted her glance nervously from Ilana to the advancing army and back again. "It looks more like Nyoke and his legions to me." Stifling a cry of despair, Cosette turned back toward the camp. "Ilana, he's found us. You might as well just accept it. It's over."

Hardly had she taken two steps when she felt the tug of Ilana's hand arresting her flight and she spun back, her will to fight evaporating like raindrops in the noonday heat.

"It's not Nyoke," Ilana cried. "Would you just listen for a minute!" Cosette averted her eyes, but made no move to leave. "Jaired set a watchman to alert us to Manuél's coming. When the watchman noticed a suspicious cloud of dust rising on the horizon, he sent a scout to investigate. The scout just returned." Ilana paused, looking expectantly at Cosette.

"And?"

"He saw Manuél! You'll never believe what has happened, Cosette. Manuél is alive and the compound has been destroyed. The people with him were Nyoke's prisoners. When the walls crumbled, their chains were loosed and they were freed!"

Cosette raised a brow at her friend, unconvinced. "How?"

"Come on, Cosette. How am I supposed to explain to you things I don't even understand myself?" With a playful poke, Ilana stepped backward and laughed. "Ask Manuél! All I know is that they're saying the moment Manuél's breath returned to him, the stronghold of the enemy collapsed and the captives were set free." She nodded knowingly. "And Nyoke—well, Nyoke just stood there gaping while Manuél led the captives away, his face as pale as the snow on Mt. Negrero."

Cosette shook her head, unable to believe her ears. Desperate to shield her heart from the pain of further disillusionment, she stomped at the seeds of hope springing to life within it. *Only a fool would fall for such an outlandish tale.*

* * *

Cosette trailed behind Ilana as they followed the others across the sandy plain. Certain as she was that they were walking into a trap, remaining at the spring was not an option. If Nyoke didn't find her with the others, the spring would be the first place he would look. There were only so many places to hide. She slowed to watch as the first of the eager pilgrims melted into the advancing throng dancing its way toward Vrede. The hearty hugs and shouts of joy that greeted them did much to still the hum of angry hornets buzzing in her belly, yet a nagging doubt remained. Nyoke could be so deceptive.

Suddenly aware of how far she had fallen behind, Cosette sprinted to catch up with Ilana as she neared the fringes of the excited crowd. How she wished she could be as trusting as her sister. Ilana had never even entertained the idea that this might not be Manuél; she, on the other hand, could barely bring herself to acknowledge that it just might be him. Her pulse raced as she drew nearer, her eyes flitting from one joyous face to the next. And then she saw him—vibrant, noble, *alive.*

"Manuél..." Her voice, tinged with awe, was swallowed up in the tumult of voices that surrounded her. Overcome, she halted, her hand leaping to her chest. He was taller than she remembered, his shoulders broader, his face less chiselled. His arms were spread to encircle two of the men she recognized from the spring as he strode across the sand, listening to their tale. Then, with a meaningful look from one to the other, a mischievous glint lit his eye and he threw back his head in a burst of merry laughter. Cosette stiffened, staring at the man she had never expected to see again. She had seen that face before—or one very much like it—laughing exactly like that in her dreams.

A palpable silence jarred her from her thoughts and she edged backward, looking furtively for a place to hide, but it was too late. His eyes firmly fixed upon hers, Manuél stepped away from his two friends and inclined his head toward her, a lopsided grin curving his lips. He was hardly a stone's throw from where she stood, alone and exposed, her heart clanging against her rib cage. Heat flooded her face and she raised her hands to her cheeks, surprised to find a river of tears streaming down the sides of her nose. *Who am I trying to fool, tagging along with Ilana and Jaired?* Cosette bit her quivering lip and forced herself to focus. *He's coming this way.* Her breath came in short, painful gasps as Manuél drew near, and her hands fluttered at her sides. *What am I going to do?*

"Cosette?"

His quiet voice only increased her turmoil.

"M-Manu..." She stopped, words failing her.

"Aren't you going to join us?"

She glanced up at his face, her eyes arrested by the angry red scar that slashed his neck. With a strangled cry, she fell before him and wept, her tears bathing his feet as she choked out a frantic confession. "I'm so sorry, Manuél! I didn't mean for him to take you. It's all my fault. All my fault..." Burying her face in her hands, she lapsed into silence, interrupted only by the small hiccupping sobs of a soul spent in grief. How could he ever forgive her?

The moments stretched into minutes as her sobs gave way to quivering breaths. With a final sniff, Cosette wiped her face with her wrap and pushed herself onto her knees. Hoping to make a hasty retreat, she froze at the sight of Manuél crouching on the sand before her, and a fresh set of tears blinded her eyes. She resisted at first when he reached to draw her into his arms, but soon surrendered herself to his embrace.

Cradling her head to his bosom, he ran his fingers through her hair and softly hushed her. "Dear Cosette. Dear, dear Cosette. You are worried and upset about so many things. How I wish it were not so. You are such a delight to me, beloved."

Daring to look up, Cosette gasped, astounded to see Manuél gazing into her eyes, a solitary tear sliding into his beard as he lifted her face toward his. "Oh, my beloved one," he soothed, "I love you and I always will." He lifted his hand to her cheek and brushed away a tear with his thumb. "No matter what," he finished.

Once more, he pressed her head to his chest and rocked her in his arms as he hummed the refrain from Jaired's ballad. Comforted, Cosette lifted her head and rested it upon his shoulder. Her eyes widened when she saw the rest of the entourage kneeling in a circle around them, their arms encircling each other as they raised their voices in song. Never could she remember feeling so loved.

"So, will you join us, Cosette?" His voice was eager, intense, pitched so only she could hear. "Will you let me take you home?"

Locked in the safety of his embrace, she squeezed her eyes shut and held her breath, considering all that she had to gain and lose. She would be foolish to refuse, and she knew it, but... *No. There are no buts!* Exhaling sharply, Cosette opened her eyes to gaze upon her saviour. Silence surrounded them as she pursed her lips and nodded. "I will."

* * *

Manuél was on his feet the moment the whispered words left her lips. Drawing her up beside him, he whirled her around in his arms, tossing his head back as gales of glorious laughter tumbled from his throat.

Cosette swayed when he finally set her down and reached out a hand to steady herself. One after another, vivid memories, only hinted at in her dreams, crashed upon the shores of her heart: Happy children frolicking in the oakwood, swimming in the River of Delights, chasing feather-winged butterflies in the meadow, dancing with the king. She fingered a tear from her eye and rubbed it wonderingly between her fingertips as the haze of forgetfulness began to lift. She remembered spinning in the arms of the king as they laughed together, falling to the ground in exhaustion, rolling onto her belly to gaze upon her beloved daddy. Tears had rolled down his face when their eyes met. She had been confused at the sight, for she had never seen eyes cry before. Yet, more puzzling than his tears, was her daddy's repeated assertion: *"I love you, Cosette, and I always will—no matter what."*

Cosette smiled as she recognized the words so often repeated by Jaired and Manuél. Yet there had been more: *"If you remember nothing else, remember that,"* the king had said. She remembered thinking, "Of course you love me. I love you, too," and skipping off to play, ignorant of the trials his cryptic words implied.

Cosette lowered her head. The events that followed had haunted her nightmares since she was a child: Her flight with her brothers and sisters to the edge of the Oaken Hills and the dizzying leap into the forbidden lands beyond. The great earthquake and the terrifying abyss that had opened at her feet. The horrifying realization that there was no way home and that she would never see her daddy again.

The comforting arms of Manuél enfolded her as the memories rushed on: The stranger who had befriended them only to enslave them in the Mines of Despair and turn them against each other. How foolish they had been to trust him. He had been at the root of it all—the greed and the selfishness, the cruelty, the lies, and worst of all, the forgetfulness that had descended upon them. She recalled her eagerness to accept Nyoke's sinister offer to free her from the mines if she would become his mistress, and she shuddered.

"Cosette." The word was gentle, yet demanded a response. Slowly blinking her eyes, she looked up.

Manuél raised an eyebrow and leaned in until his lips nearly touched her ear. "You remember." It was a statement, not a question.

Cosette lowered her head and nodded, unable to meet his gaze.

"Our daddy misses you, you know."

Cosette's head snapped up at the unexpected words and her eyes locked on Manuél's. "You wouldn't say that if you knew," she whispered, shaking her head.

"Knew what?" came his tender reply. "Knew that you'd prostituted yourself to the enemy, broken every law it is possible to break, forgotten our father even exists?"

Cosette's jaw dropped further with each pronouncement.

"I know all about it, Cosette, and so does Father. But that doesn't change a thing. We both still love you—no matter what."

The way he stressed those last three words sent tingles up her spine. Cosette clamped her mouth shut and sighed as glorious memories of Manuél bubbled to the surface. How she had loved the times when he had walked through the garden with their daddy. She had loved Manuél from the moment she had first seen him—delighted in racing him up the twin oak trees at the edge of the Oaken Hills, revelled in chasing him across the stepping stones at the base of Glory Falls, exulted in following him wherever he went and hiding when he turned to look. However could she have forgotten him?

"So, are you ready to go home?" Manuél's words startled her. Confused, she opened her mouth to speak, then snapped it shut again without saying a word.

"Well?" he laughed.

Cosette cocked her head to one side and lifted a shoulder. "If you're sure you still want me."

He raised an eyebrow in her direction and shook his head, a smile lighting his eyes. "Come on, everybody," he bellowed, his smile broadening as he reached for her hand. "Today we must rest and gather our strength for the journey before us. We're a long way from home."

* * *

The rest of the day drifted by as they rested on the shores of the spring and bathed in its healing pools, quenching their thirst with draughts drawn from its sparkling waters. "Drink deeply," Manuél had instructed them soon after they arrived. "It will strengthen you for the journey ahead. This was once, like the River of Delights you remember from home, a teeming tributary of the great River of Life, known as the Channel of Peace."

A chorus of oohs and aahs filled the glen as the pilgrims recalled their days in the garden.

"While this is all that remains of that glorious channel on this side of the abyss," Manuél continued, "its source can yet be traced to the River of Life."

"The River of Life..." a trembling voice echoed. "Yes, I remember that." It spoke slowly, reverently. "That was the great channel from which flowed the River of Delights. I used to spend hours exploring its hollows, collecting stones along its shores..."

Tiny smiles flitted across the faces of those around him and dozens of heads bobbed as memories of those long forgotten days began to surface.

Hanging on Manuél's every word, Cosette smiled as he told story after story of their early years together, laughing at the delightful memories they evoked. But when he broached the story of their disobedience, every muscle in her body tensed. That was not a story she wanted to hear.

"Father was devastated as he watched you, drawn by curiosity and the lure of the enemy, gradually reject his love to wander in the land of the adversary," Manuél began. "He had known the time would come, but that didn't lessen the sorrow as he watched his beloved children abandon him."

Cosette's shoulders sank. She remembered following behind the others on that fateful day, struggling with the desire to explore the unknown, yet torn by her yearning to be at her daddy's side.

"Father wept that day like I'd never seen him weep before, not only for *his* loss, but even more so, for the horrors he knew *you* would be forced to endure as a result of your disobedience."

Cosette stifled a sob, remembering the tear she had wiped from her daddy's face that day so long ago. She hadn't understood it then, but she did now, and her heart groaned in shame.

"And so the time had come," Manuél continued. "I knew what I had to do. "Just inside the gate of the garden hung a rope. It was narrow, but strong, fashioned from the long, steel-like filaments of the bloodbriar vine." Manuél scanned the faces before him. "My heart was pierced with sorrow as I recalled the long, arduous days in which Father had applied himself to the task of painstakingly gathering the knife-like filaments and intricately braiding the strands to form a rope no sword, save his own, could sever. His hands were bloody and raw by the time he was done, but the finished rope was sturdy and supple, light in weight, and long enough to span a distance far beyond measure."

Cosette leaned forward, eager to hear more. She remembered seeing the unusual rope at the entrance to the garden and wondering about it, though it had never crossed her mind to ask what it was for.

"I went to fetch the rope as soon as Addie and Evie here stepped onto the sands of the desert." Manuél reached to squeeze the hands of the man and woman who sat next to him and the corners of his mouth lifted in an affectionate smile. "Slowly, Father and I followed, waiting at the edge of the Oaken Hills until every last one of you had crossed the border into the forbidden lands. Time was short and we both knew what had to be done. With a final, tearful embrace, I slung the rope over my shoulder and stepped to the edge of the grassy sward."

Manuél paused, exhaling sharply as he recalled his final moments with the king. "Father's eyes glistened as he took my head in his hands and touched his forehead to my own. '*Go, my son,*' he whispered. His voice was husky with emotion. '*Go to them Manuél; be with my children. Comfort them in their time of distress and bring them home.*'

"My heart broke as I took his calloused hands in mine and brought them to my lips. 'I will, Father,' I vowed, fully aware of all that promise would entail. 'Neither tribulation nor trial, death nor defeat, the adversary himself, nor all the legions under his command shall be able to prevent me from completing the task you have set before me.'"

Breathless, the children waited for Manuél to continue, their eyes following his every move.

"He nodded at me then, his eyes dark and solemn, for he, too, knew the price that would have to be paid, perhaps even better than I. '*Then go, my son. Bring my children home.*'"

The faraway look slipped from Manuél's eyes like a lonely cloud on a summer's day and he looked fondly around at the group of enraptured pilgrims sitting at his feet. "And so, as the rumbling of the earth began, I turned and leapt across the widening chasm, Father's final words echoing in my ears. *'I love you, Manuél, even as I know you love me—and we both know how much we love them. Don't let them forget, Manuél... Please don't let them forget.'*"

* * *

Cosette sat motionless, her eyes fixed upon Manuél as the story unfolded. Her mind reeled with questions. Standing, she stepped toward him to kneel at his feet. "But why?" she choked. Hot tears filled her eyes as she gazed beseechingly into his. "Why didn't we see you? Why didn't you take us home right away?" She paused, struggling to contain the waves of rising bitterness that threatened to overwhelm her. "Why weren't you there when Nyoke came along?"

"Oh Cosette," he soothed. He ran his hand down the back of her head and let it come to rest upon her shoulder. Pain glinted in his eyes. "I was there, beloved, but in the chaos of the moment, as the great abyss opened at your feet, I slipped into the undergrowth, knowing the adversary was near." He hesitated and looked down, letting his hand drop from her shoulder. "I could have taken you home then, Cosette, but you weren't ready."

Manuél's eyes burned with compassion as he lifted them once more to hers. "You would have been relieved to be home and grateful to be freed of the consequences of your actions, but in time, not truly grasping the glory that was yours, you would have once more found yourselves hugging the borders of the kingdom and longing for the forbidden lands beyond."

Silence fell between them and Cosette hung her head. She yearned to claim that he was wrong, to assure him that she would have been ready, but she dared not, for in her heart, she knew that he was right. She stifled a groan as the waves of bitterness began to recede and Manuél's voice once more broke the silence.

"When Nyoke came, I watched him enchant you with his lies and lead you into his traps. Over and over, he tried to ensnare me also, but to no avail. I knew with whom I was dealing and I knew whom I could trust—and it wasn't him. Many were the attacks he waged against me in those days. Time after time, he strove to divert me from my mission, but in the power of our father, I stood firm. And, one by one, I sought you, breaking the chains that bound you to the will of the adversary and sending you out to seek for our long lost brothers and sisters that they, too, might be freed."

Cosette's eyes wandered about the little band of travellers and came to rest on Jaired and Ilana. A knowing smile lit their faces as they met her gaze and she mouthed the words, "Thank you."

"Yet sadly," Manuél continued, "not all were willing to see." Cosette turned to face him once more and, laying her arm upon his knee, she lowered her head to rest it in the crook of her elbow. His voice grew pensive. "Preferring enslavement to the truth, they rejected the very idea of a loving father, and a king who adored them, and refused to bow their knees to any but themselves. They could not see that their true allegiance was not to themselves, but to the great deceiver of the king's children, Nyoke himself."

Manuél's face brightened and he stretched out his arms to include them all. "But be not downcast, my beloved ones, for in us our father takes great delight. We must make all speed and go to him."

A ripple of affirmation stirred his eager listeners and they began to rise. "Just before dusk, let us gather here, prepared to travel. It will be a long and arduous journey, but in the strength of our father, we will prevail."

Cosette lifted her head. "But you didn't tell us the rest of the story."

"That, my dear one, is a story for another time." Manuél winked and gently removed her arm from his knee before he stood. "For now, you must rest. Dusk will be here sooner than you think."

* * *

Manuél roused them shortly before they were to leave and urged them to make haste as they prepared to begin their journey. "Bring nothing but the clothes you wear," he had insisted, though few had anything else to bring. By the time the final rays of the sun descended below the horizon, they were off, hurrying through the cooling sands with a song of joy bubbling from their lips and the thought of home lightening their steps.

At first, Cosette didn't pay much attention to the direction in which they were travelling, but as the rising moon began to cast shadows upon their way and she started to sense a certain familiarity with the land, a surge of panic rose within her. An unexpected burst of energy catapulted her forward and she pushed her way through the weary throng until she walked right behind Manuél. Breathless, she grabbed his hand in both of hers and pulled him around to face her.

"Ma-nu-él," she stammered, "do you know where we are?"

"Yes." His voice was steady, even calm.

"But..." She stepped back a pace and dropped his hand.

Closing the space between them, Manuél slid his arm around her waist and urged her forward. She trembled, as much from his presence as from her fear, and stared straight ahead. At least she wouldn't have to face her fate alone.

They walked in silence for a time until her breathing slowed and her body relaxed into his. "Cosette?" he whispered.

"Yes?" Their eyes met in the darkness.

"Do you love me?"

"Do I love you?" she repeated, incredulous. "Of course I love you. I loved you in the garden before Nyoke claimed me. I loved you, though I couldn't even remember you, when you surrendered yourself to the enemy in my stead. I loved you when you met me by the spring and comforted me despite the wicked things I had done." She stopped to blow out a long, uneven breath. "Yes, I love you. I loved you then and I love you now. How could you even ask such a thing?" Hurt, she turned her face from his and averted her eyes, hoping to hide her burning cheeks.

"Oh, my Cosette..." Catching her chin with his forefinger, he turned her face once more toward his and gazed intently into her eyes. His voice was tender, gentle, beseeching. "I need you to trust me, beloved. I have not rescued you only to turn you over to the enemy. There are many things you do not know, many things you cannot yet understand. You must trust me."

The intensity of his gaze made her legs feel wobbly.

"Will you trust me, Cosette?" His eyes searched hers, demanding an answer. "Though the pathway is hard and failure seems assured, will you trust me?" He combed a tendril of hair from her face and twirled it around his finger. "Though the consequences are grave and your every sense forbids that you follow, will you trust me?" His eyes bore into hers. "Though I lead you into the very heart of the enemy's stronghold and ask you to do the impossible, will you trust me?" Stepping away, he lowered his gaze and let his hand fall to his side. "Do you love me enough to trust me, Cosette?"

Hardly daring to breathe, Cosette stood in silence, wanting more than anything to respond with the affirmation he desired, but torn by the shards of fear that still gripped her heart. A host of conflicting thoughts muddied her brain as she contemplated the alternatives. On the one hand, entrusting herself to another had caused her untold grief in the past. Manuél, on the other hand, had never failed her or misled her, so why should he do so now? Besides, where would she be if he hadn't intervened on her behalf? And what would become of her if she chose not to follow? Was he not the only one she could truly trust?

Trembling, Cosette flung herself into Manuél's arms and buried her face in his chest. "I trust you," she murmured. "I trust you." Her pounding heart stilled as he drew her closer and her arms encircled his waist. "Wherever you lead, I will follow. Whatever you ask, I will do. No matter how difficult or absurd it may seem, no matter what the consequences may be, whatever the cost, I will endure." She lifted her eyes to seek his, "Only, Manuél? I'm so scared! Help me to do as I've promised."

His responding chuckle was one of delight as he gave her shoulders a reassuring squeeze. "Walk with me, beloved," he whispered into her hair. "Just walk with me. Our destination draws near."

* * *

The purple rays of dawn were just beginning to streak the sky when they arrived at the gate through which Cosette had fled the compound less than a fortnight earlier. Knocked off its hinges, the gate hung askew, its posts twisted and torn from their moorings. As Manuél gathered her brothers and sisters around him, Cosette stared at the gate, confused. That the stronghold of the adversary had been destroyed, she knew, but the reality of its destruction had not registered until she saw the remnants of the gate lying broken at her feet.

The sudden quietness that surrounded her jarred Cosette and she turned to find the eyes of her new-found family watching her. She tried to laugh, pretending all was well, but the sympathetic glances of the others assured her she wasn't fooling anyone. They were all scared—every last one of them—and there was no use pretending otherwise. With a squeeze of her hand, Manuél pulled Cosette near, silencing her fumbled apology as he enfolded her in his arms. "Trust me, little lamb," he whispered into her ear. "Remember—you promised." He released her and winked. Face flaming, she nodded, her eyes never leaving his as she settled herself at his feet.

"We are about to enter the Compound of Defilement in which Nyoke has committed so many unspeakable atrocities." A chill shivered up Cosette's back at Manuél's words and she glanced toward the imposing structure looming ahead of them.

"You've all been here before, and I know it is not a place to which you wish to return." Manuél's voice rose as a moan shuddered through the sombre crowd. "I know what you suffered within these walls," he assured. I know, for I was here. I wept as you groaned beneath the veil of the adversary's vile intentions and mourned as you struggled to break the shackles of his will." He gestured toward the compound and waited for their eyes to follow. "I know you do not wish to pass through this gate, but it is the only way home."

Rising, Manuel took a step toward the forbidding entrance, then turned to face them once more. "Do not be alarmed when you see Nyoke and his henchmen," he warned, "for they can no longer harm you." His voice softened. "You must remember that you are no longer his to command, no matter how vehemently he may try to convince you otherwise." He lifted his hands. "Now listen: They will mock you and try to cow you into abandoning the journey, but do not be deceived. They have no power over you now. None. Nyoke's dominion has been destroyed and the king reigns victorious. We, my friends, are the king's children. What have the king's children to fear?"

Cosette gulped as a fresh wave of terror threatened to undo her. *What have the king's children to fear? What have the king's children to fear?* Her racing pulse slowed as she repeated the words over and over in her mind. *What have the king's children to fear?* All would be well, it had to be. She would trust Manuél, just as she'd promised.

* * *

No one spoke as they gathered at the gate, steeling their hearts for the trials that were sure to come. Frantically, they fought the ghosts of a past they wished they could banish from their minds forever, their hearts set upon the home they wished they had never abandoned. If only they had listened to their daddy. Fear hounded them as, one by one, they followed Manuél through the dreaded gate and into the ruined compound, his final instructions still echoing in their ears: *As soon as you come through the gate, join hands and keep together. Stay close to me and help each other along. Above all, remember that we are the children of the king. The adversary wields no power over us. None.*

The sun climbed higher in the sky with each passing moment as the wary party made its way into the compound, the children's spirits buoyed by Manuél's final words: *We must go; Father is waiting.*

Cosette stumbled along between Jaired and Ilana, her shoulders bent beneath a burden of fear and shame. Among the last to make their way through the gate, they quickened their pace to catch up with the stalwart band of pilgrims that trudged on ahead. Still, by the time they reached the centre of the courtyard, the sun had nearly reached its apex.

Cosette gaped at the destruction that greeted her. On every side lay the ruins of the once mighty fortress, its impenetrable walls crumbled, its grisly towers levelled. Scores of leaden-eyed slaves scowled as they worked amid the ruins, clearing the rubble and reinforcing what little remained of the inglorious structure. Cosette could hardly believe her eyes as her friends tugged her forward. Not a stone remained of the despised cell she had once called her own. Not one.

The opposition to their presence grew slowly. An angry scowl here, a scornful laugh there, a scathing sneer, a mocking snort. "Look at you hypocrites! Following that no-good troubadour of yours like he could save you or something. You think you're better than us, eh? Well you're not. You're just a bunch of gullible, sissy-hearted—"

"Heed them not, my friends." Manuél's voice calmed Cosette as she sidestepped the growing insults. "They have not the power to harm you." She took a long, deep breath and willed herself to put one foot in front of the other.

"They have not the power to harm you," a sing-songy voice parroted. She looked up to see a gaunt stonemason looking her way. "Ha! Who's he trying to kid? Not the power to harm you!" He smirked, obviously amused, and went back to work, but not before tossing a handful of debris her way. He laughed when she jumped to one side to avoid the shower of broken sticks and stones, then picked up his trowel. "Fools," he muttered, shaking his head. "Some people'll believe anything."

The taunts and insults escalated as the weary travellers made their way across the courtyard. Dire threats accompanied their every move and rock after rock hurtled toward them, but not one of the fist-sized projectiles touched the little band. With each step, Cosette sensed a growing courage taking root in her soul. Perhaps, as Manuél said, these people really were powerless to hurt the king's children. Even so, it surprised her, when time after time, Manuél stopped to invite their tormentors to join his little company. Of course, they boldly refused his offers, choosing instead to laugh in his face and spit at his feet, yet curiously, they did not hinder his passage, or that of the weary ones who followed. It seemed Manuél was right. Again.

* * *

As they neared the tumbled remains of the courtyard's eastern wall, Cosette glanced up, dismayed to see the gnarled branches of the Tree of Execution overhanging the ruins. The thought that it, of all things, had survived the quake irked her, yet despite the rubble that surrounded it, the detestable tree stood firm, its roots burrowed deep in the sandy soil just beyond the gate. Cosette swallowed hard as she surveyed the tree of death and realized for the first time where their weary trek was taking them. "Not here, Manuél—please... " Her lips barely moved as she whispered the words. "Not the hanging tree."

"Ha! And you thought you could trust him!"

The infuriatingly familiar voice of her adversary rang in Cosette's ears and she turned to see his smiling face coming toward her. Every muscle in her body seized and she came to an abrupt stop, only vaguely aware of the determined urging of her friends as they strove to prod her onward, their urgent voices entreating Manuél to release her from the enemy's spell.

Nyoke was almost upon her now, his obsidian eyes begging her to join him, his bejewelled hand beckoning her forward. "Come with me, Cosette." He reached for her hand. "You can trust me. I've only ever wanted the very best for you."

Suddenly faint, Cosette swayed as dizzying images of her life with Nyoke spiralled across her mind. As if in a dream, she saw herself huddled in the corner of a fetid cell, uselessly trying to shield herself from his angry blows; grovelling piteously at his feet in an attempt to curry his favour and placate his wrath; forever looking over her shoulder, waiting for the next attack, never certain from whence it would come.

Chilled by the potent images, Cosette shuddered at his beguiling smile. A slight movement caught the corner of her eye and she blinked. Gradually she became aware of the circle of friends that surrounded her, placing themselves strategically between her and the enemy. Like a gentle summer breeze, their quiet murmuring washed over her.

"Manuél, come help her."

"She needs you, Manuél; she is afraid."

"Come quickly, Manuél, she is weak and cannot withstand the attack."

"Manuél…"
"Manuél…"
"Manuél…"

With a start, she awoke from her stupor and thrust her arms forward as if to ward herself from harm. "Manuél!"

Nyoke paled and took a step backward.

"Manuél, come save me!" Her voice was stronger now and she took a calming breath, relieved to feel a familiar hand light upon her shoulder.

"It is over, Nyoke." Manuél spoke slowly, quietly, but there was no mistaking the power behind his words. "Be gone from here, oh ancient enemy of the king. You hold no power over the children of the Most High." With each phrase, the adversary shrank further from the little band, his eyes darkening with fury as his impotence became clear. "You are welcome here no longer, Nyoke; your glory days are past. Take your legions and depart at once."

Cosette gasped as the one whom she had once thought invincible shrieked his displeasure and turned to summon his troops. Wide-eyed, she watched as the fearsome tyrant stalked from the courtyard, trailed by his ribald group of followers. Never before had she witnessed such unbridled hatred as that which emanated from the eyes of the adversary as he cast a final glance over his shoulder at Manuél. He never had taken kindly to loss.

* * *

Alone in the courtyard at last, the weary travellers erupted in shouts of triumph, pumping eager arms in the air and slapping each other on the back. But when Cosette opened her mouth and began to sing, all eyes came to rest upon her. Not since their days in the garden had they heard anything like it. Piercingly beautiful, her voice filled the courtyard. It started softly, and grew until it echoed from the crumbled walls, bolstering their hearts with courage and awakening their souls to the yearning they had so long forgotten.

"Come away, come away—"
Don't you hear his tender call?
"Come away," hear him whisper,
"Come away.
For you are mine, my beloved—
You are mine, my love so fair.
Come away, for you I'm waiting,
Come away.
Oh, come away, for you I'm waiting,
Come away. Come away."

As the final notes faded, Cosette raised her arms to the heavens and let her longing spill from her heart in a rain of healing tears. She didn't know where the song had come from, but the spirit within her rejoiced as its words wound their way into her heart. "Manuél—take us home," she whispered, turning to find him at her side.

In answer to her plea, Manuél extended his hand and closed his fingers around hers as he led her toward the gate. Jostling for a place by his side, the others followed, a reverent silence surrounding them as they marched ever closer to the dreaded Tree of Execution.

* * *

Though the distance was short, the little company was hot and sweaty by the time Manuél called an end to their march at the foot of the Hanging Tree. As they sat in its shade, far from the yawning abyss that opened at its base, Manuél handed around a flask of water, drawn from the Spring of Vrede, that their hearts might be strengthened for the final leg of the journey.

"So where do we go from here?" Evie asked, mindlessly sifting handfuls of gritty sand between her fingers.

Manuél capped the flask and slung it over his shoulder. "We cross the abyss."

A murmur of consternation rippled through the distraught company.

"The abyss?"

"Now we have to cross the abyss?"

"How are we supposed to do that?"

"You know…" Manuél knelt to join them on the sand. "I never did finish telling you the story I started back at the spring. Perhaps it is time you heard the rest of it."

Cosette inhaled sharply, curious, yet afraid. But when Manuél beckoned her forward, she went to him and rested her head against his shoulder, comforted by the security of his presence.

"The time came," he began, "when the last of our daddy's children—save for those who would join us when the compound collapsed—had been released from the bonds of the enemy." His eyes swept the weary crowd before coming to rest upon Cosette. "I had waited long for that hour to arrive, though I knew it would bring for me the greatest trial I would ever face. Yet, while the cost would be high, so too, would be the joys—the utter annihilation of Nyoke's dominion and the return of my father's children to his side."

Cosette closed her eyes and tried to shut out his voice. She didn't want to hear what came next, didn't want to know the price he had to pay, didn't want to face the agony she knew she had cost the one she loved more than life itself. But it was no use.

"When the time had come," he continued, "I offered my life in exchange for another's." His voice softened and he paused.

Cosette felt the gentle caress of his hand upon her arm and squeezed her eyes shut yet again, willing herself not to cry.

"Nyoke, of course, was elated by the unexpected offer and had me taken directly to the whipping post in the courtyard. There I was flogged until my body hung limply from the post as Nyoke stood by, filling my ears with his sadistic laughter and sinister threats."

Cosette stiffened, her fist clenched to her mouth, as the scene unfolded in her mind. She wanted to yell, "No! Stop! No more!" but the words stuck in her throat.

"When Nyoke finally tired of his game, he slashed the ropes holding me to the whipping post and I fell to my knees, my back shredded by the metal-tipped phalange of the flogger's lash."

Gasps of horror hiccupped through the little group with each new revelation.

"My legs barely held me as he hauled me to my feet and shoved me toward the Hanging Tree. I stumbled, and he cursed. Snatching the whip, Nyoke jerked me to my feet and drove me forward, my ankles burning like fire where his whip licked my heels."

Manuél stopped as the weeping of his brothers and sisters crescendoed. He knew it was hard for them to hear, but it was a story they had to know if they were ever to truly grasp the depth of his love for them. The moments turned to minutes and their tears began to subside, yet still he waited. They needed time. Time to process. Time to think. Time to mourn. When the final sobs had, at last, given way to sniffles, and the sniffles to quiet sighs, he cleared his throat and resumed his tale.

"Now, Nyoke was amused by the rope I carried, presuming in his depravity, that I had brought it in a bid to escape. It occurred to him, therefore, that it would be great sport to use my own rope as the instrument of my death. But I understood what Nyoke did not. The rope I had carried with me for so many years had been fashioned for that very moment."

"I forgot about the rope!" Jaired's eyes widened. "You never went anywhere without it."

Ilana nodded. "I always wondered what it was for."

Manuél took a deep breath. "Nyoke thrust me to my knees at the foot of the Hanging Tree and tossed me the rope Father had made so long ago. The tip of the tyrant's sword pierced my side as he demanded that I tie one end of the rope around the base of the tree and form the other end into a noose."

Cosette winced. *Nyoke.* Even his name repulsed her. Spiteful, manipulative, masochistic, depraved. He was all the things Manuél was not. Even now, she could imagine the laughter in his eyes as he pressed the tip of his sword further and further into the side of her beloved, all the while relishing the pain of his prey.

"Though Nyoke thought he was baiting me, my soul sang as my fingers knotted the narrow rope and tied it securely around the base of the tree. The colour of the rope blended with the colour of the ancient tree's bark and I could barely see it in the dim light of the coming dawn, but I knew it would hold. Nyoke laughed when I tugged on the rope to test the knot, and he jabbed me once more with his sword. 'The noose?' he snarled."

Cosette reached over to take Manuél's hand in hers, twining her fingers through his. She didn't want to hear the rest of this story. Though she was curious to hear how it ended, the details were almost more than she could bear.

With an understanding nod, Manuél squeezed Cosette's hand. "I formed the noose quickly, though my fingers throbbed with the effort. Nyoke scowled as I tossed it over the branch of the Hanging Tree then slipped it expertly over my head and around my neck. That I would willingly accept my fate, chafed at his long held delusions of power and aroused in him an anger unlike any other. He snatched the rope from my hands not far from the noose and pointed to a long board that overhung the chasm. Once more, he used his sword to nudge me forward, paying out more and more rope until I stood at the end of the board.

"A sudden breeze rustled in the leaves and I glanced upward. The noose hung from the branch directly above me, its rope wound securely around a post near the edge of the abyss before leading back to the base of the tree. Nyoke controlled the rope himself, relishing the torture it would visit upon me as it stole my final breath. Already I could feel the noose pressing against my throat and I swallowed hard. Without warning, Nyoke tipped the plank into the abyss."

The pilgrims leaned in closer, hardly daring to breathe as his tale continued.

"My feet flailed in mid-air as my hands struggled to ease the crush of the rope, my lungs craving one last breath. Nyoke's grim laughter taunted me as my body writhed at the end of the rope and the pressure in my head built. With every movement, the rope cut more deeply into my flesh and I willed my body to be still. At last, though I could not stop my lungs from trying to fill, my final breath was spent. Darkness closed in upon me and I knew no more."

A gasp rippled through the little group as the king's children sat back, stunned. They knew in their heads that he had died, but the reality of his presence had denied the truth to their hearts. Until now.

Slowly Jaired rose from the group and made his way to Manuél's side. His hand shook as he placed it upon his friend's shoulder, for he knew the part of the story at which Manuél could only guess. In a soft voice, Jaired took up the tale. "Nyoke watched Manuél's lifeless body hang limply from the rope and crowed with delight. He stood there for many minutes, wanting to be sure his nemesis was truly dead, I suppose, then, with a regal flourish, he took his sword and slashed at the rope that held Manuél's body in place. But his blade did not sever the rope. Over and over he slashed at it, but to no avail. With an enraged howl, Nyoke released the rope from the post and watched as, one by one, its coils trailed Manuél's body into the chasm.

"The rope was longer, I think, than he had anticipated," Jaired continued, "but at last it came to an end with a thunderous crack as the limb from which it hung tore from the tree and crashed into the pit. Only the end of the rope tied to the trunk remained, but try as Nyoke might, it could neither be severed nor untied."

Jaired cleared his throat and looked toward Manuél. "There's really not much to tell. Nyoke scowled and cursed as he gave one final, violent tug on the rope and headed back to the compound. I expect he figured his work would be easier now with no more troubadours, for as he reached the gate, he laughed." Jaired stiffened, reliving the moment. "His sinister chortle sent shivers up my spine."

Manuél slid a hand up to squeeze Jaired's forearm.

"Thank you, my friend. Thank you for standing by me to the end, for not abandoning me in my time of trouble."

A sheen of moisture misted his eyes as he stood to embrace the one who had shared in so much of his sorrow. For many minutes they held each other, openly sharing their grief, until at last Manuél broke away and wiped his eyes, his arm still firmly wrapped around Jaired's shoulders.

* * *

"There's more that I must tell you," Manuél announced solemnly, "for the story does not end there." He took a deep breath and smiled as he settled himself once more on the sand. "Down, down, my body plunged into the horrifying abyss, though I remember it not, for death had, indeed, claimed me. It wasn't until later that I knew—when I opened my eyes to see the most beautiful sight imaginable, the face of our daddy gazing into mine.

"'Well done, my son,' he whispered. His voice sent shivers of joy racing up my spine. It had been so long since I had seen him. I raised my hands to my neck and felt for the rope, finding only a scar where once it had cut off my breath."

Gasps of wonder filled the air as the children eyed the telltale scar that slashed his neck.

"I dropped my hands to my sides, suddenly aware that I felt no pain, and looked down, surprised to find my wounds had been replaced by scars. Father laughed as I sprang to my feet and capered about, revelling in the new-found strength that infused my being. Grasping his hands in mine, I swung him around and around before finally falling into his waiting embrace. The plan had, at last, been accomplished. The greatest struggles were behind; the most glorious joys yet to come. With a contented sigh, we parted. There was just one more thing that had to be done."

Manuél paused to smile at the awestruck faces glued to his. "He had come for me, just as he promised." His eyes sparkled. "He had removed the noose that bound my neck, and healed the wounds inflicted on me by the enemy with a single touch of his hands. He had breathed into my lungs the breath of life and the chains of death that bound me had been destroyed. I was alive! More alive than I had ever been before—at least, that's how it felt." He trailed off, a gentle chuckle rolling from his lips.

"Father wrapped me in his mantle and tied the rope to my waist, for I would need both of my hands for the ascent, then we headed toward the opposite side of the abyss. It wasn't long before we came upon a narrow rope ladder hanging over the edge of the great chasm. I recognized it, for I remembered our daddy weaving it from a length of the rope that now trailed in the sand behind me."

"Oh-h-h-h!" Cosette's eyes danced in excitement. "I always wondered what that ladder was for."

"Me, too," someone said, and they all laughed.

"Rung after rung we climbed toward the top of the chasm." Manuél's eyes wandered to the edge of the abyss. "It was a long and difficult climb, but at last we emerged at the top where we were greeted by exuberant shouts of joy from the many servants in our father's house. With great ceremony, Father untied the ladder and tossed it over the edge of the abyss as a deafening cheer erupted from the mouths of our loyal countrymen."

Hardly able to contain his joy, Manuél stood and began to pace. "As the cheers subsided, Father removed a knife from his belt and cut the rope from my waist. 'My children, Manuél... how are my children?' He cast a hopeful eye my way as he placed the end of the rope in my hand and curled my fingers tightly around it.

"'They're ready to come home, Father.' I opened my hand to reveal the rope. 'I must go to them.'

"He nodded, his eyes closing as he lowered his head. When he opened them again, he could not hide the glow of anticipation that burned within their depths."

Manuél stopped his excited pacing to glance at the brothers and sisters he so adored. "He's been waiting for you for a long time, you know." Touched by the befuddled looks they exchanged, he knelt once more in their midst. "There's not much more to tell. I took the rope and secured it to the Tree of Provision..."

Heads bobbed as the wayfarers recalled the mysterious tree that stood, ancient and alone, at the edge of the Oaken Hills. There was no other tree like it in all of the garden and it had often puzzled them.

"I pulled the rope taut, forming a narrow bridge across the chasm, and knotted it with care. Then, unwilling to wait any longer, I bid our father goodbye once more and stepped out boldly. The rope felt solid beneath my feet and I held my head erect as I took the first step, my toes clinging to the narrow line as I moved forward, my eyes focused on the mission before me. I was half way across the chasm before I realized what I was doing, but the strength of our father rested upon me and I went on, my feet never faltering.

"The Hanging Tree loomed above me as I set foot upon the shores of the forbidden lands and the earth trembled beneath me, yet I knew I was in no danger. I had a job to do, the job I had longed to do since I first arrived in this accursed wilderness."

Manuél stopped. Everyone knew what happened next: the quake that decimated the compound, the march to the Spring of Vrede, the journey back to the Hanging Tree.

"So what do we do now?" someone asked. All eyes looked to Manuél.

He spread his arms wide as if to embrace them all. "I take you home to Father!"

* * *

Now that she knew what to look for, Cosette could see the slender rope stretching from the base of the Hanging Tree far across the abyss. But while Manuél might be able to cross it, she knew that she could not. Who among them could? Shivers of dread tingled down her spine at the thought. *I knew this was too good to be true.* She glanced at her new-found brothers and sisters, relieved to see that she was not alone. Swallowing hard, she looked at Manuél, her eyes burning with unshed tears.

"You look at this rope and tremble," he said, inclining his head toward her.

His eyes were soft and full of compassion, but she could not hold his gaze. Fidgeting with her wrap, Cosette sniffed softly and looked away, unable to bear his pity.

"You know you are unable to cross it," he continued quietly. "And you are right."

A collective gasp shook the little group and everyone began to talk at once.

"We aren't able to cross it?"

"What do you mean, we aren't able to cross it?"

"Then, what are we going to do?"

"Do not despair, my friends, our father is anxious to see you." Manuél's voice, calm and triumphant, rose above their terrified lament and descended upon their hearts like a salve. "It is true that you cannot cross the abyss without falling, but I cannot fall as I cross the abyss," he declared, "so I shall carry you." Flinging an arm toward the gaping chasm, Manuél rushed on. "Who wants to go first?"

Cosette didn't know what to think as she watched her fellow travellers disappear one by one across the chasm in the arms of Manuél. So slender was the rope, it looked as if he walked on air, yet not once did his footsteps falter, nor did he sway along the way. Twice she noticed Nyoke furtively slip from the shadows to saw at the rope with his sword, fouling the air with obscenities when the rope failed to give way, but not once did he deign to touch the king's children and her alarm gave way to relief.

Little by little their numbers dwindled until Cosette stood alone beneath the Hanging Tree, chewing her thumbnail as she watched the last of her friends disappear across the Chasm of Death. A worn path soon formed where her pacing feet trod as the minutes crawled by. Nyoke emerged from the undergrowth to hack once more at the rope, and she covered her ears to block the villain's enraged screech when its strands remained unblemished. Emboldened by his failure, Cosette studied her foe and scowled.

When his frenzied attacks bore nothing but frustration, Nyoke straightened and returned his sword to its sheath. His chest still heaving, he fixed his eyes on Cosette. "Left behind, are we?" His lip curled. "You really thought he'd come back for you, didn't you?" His eyes narrowed as he stepped menacingly toward her.

Planting her fists on her hips, Cosette returned his stare. Enough was enough. "Be gone, Nyoke. You have no business here. I am no longer yours." She stiffened when he froze, stifling the urge to look behind her. His face was pale, his eyes wide with fear. *Could it really be that easy?* With a derisive snort, Cosette whirled around and ran headlong into Manuél.

"Are you ready?" he grinned, extending his hand toward her. The shadow of fear that wrestled within her fled as she gazed into his sparkling eyes and she nodded.

"Then come. It is time for us to go."

His breath was warm against her ear as he scooped her into his arms and stepped to the edge of the great abyss. Cosette hid her face in his chest and tried not to think of the journey that lay ahead. Overwhelmed by his strength and passion, she closed her eyes and raised her arms to encircle his neck as he stepped onto the rope. "I love you, Manuél," she whispered. "Thank you for taking me home."

* * *

It seemed as if they had barely left the Hanging Tree when her daddy's booming voice hailed them. "Cosette! My beloved—my little pet lamb!"

The exuberance in his voice made her heart race. *He was coming. For them... for her.* Oblivious to the void beneath her, Cosette scrambled from Manuél's grasp and into the outstretched arms of her daddy. She felt like a little girl again—cherished, treasured, loved—and she giggled for the first time since the day she had left the garden. The familiar answering rumble deep within her daddy's breast released a flood of welcome memories and she raised dancing eyes, to peer over her shoulder at Manuél. He, too, was smiling. As they turned, Cosette reached to take his hand in hers and squeezed it excitedly as they took the final steps toward home.

As soon as they set foot on home soil, the king set Cosette on her feet and drew his sword. Confused, she stepped back as a triumphal cry leapt from the king's lips and he swept the sword across the rope an arm's length from the edge of the abyss. The answering cheer that echoed from the happy throng rang in her ears and she looked around her in surprise. Speechless, she marvelled as the severed rope snapped back toward the forbidden lands. Suddenly her life in exile seemed very far away.

Cosette stood for a time, staring across the chasm, hardly daring to believe that she was home. Yet there could be no doubt. She pressed a palm to her chest to still the flutter of her heart and took a long, cleansing breath. The nightmare was finally over.

Peals of friendly laughter jolted her from her thoughts and Cosette gave herself a shake. Turning toward the happy sound, she noticed a crowd of strangers hovering at the edge of the oakwood, their eyes trained on her. A shy smile flickered across her face when she realized she had been caught pinching herself, and her face warmed. The king winked at her as he turned to greet Manuél, and she blushed even more, recalling the days when she had loved nothing better than to sit on his knee and snuggle in his arms. A great longing to be near him seized her but, she stifled it, aghast. *Look at me.* She glanced down at the front of her dress. Teeth clenched, she wet her thumb and rubbed it over a patch of dirt on her arm, but it only smudged the silty smear and made it worse. *I'm filthy, my dress is torn, my hair's a mess. What was I thinking?* Her eyes downcast, she backed away from the king, hoping to lose herself in the crowd, but she didn't get far before a vivacious young woman hurried toward her and flung her arms around her neck.

"Cosette? Oh, Cosette!" She cupped her hands around Cosette's face and gazed at her adoringly. "Now you're a sight for sore eyes!" Her words tumbled over each other as she jabbered on, barely stopping to breathe. "It's so good to finally meet you. Why, the king has told me so much about you." She stopped, her gaze drifting fondly from the tips of Cosette's toes to the tousled mop of straw-coloured hair crowning her head.

"I've waited so long for this day to come, and now that it's here, I can hardly believe it! She planted an exuberant kiss on each of Cosette's cheeks and enveloped her in another hearty embrace.

"Forgive me," Cosette stammered, "but, do I know you?" She pasted a polite smile on her face as she stepped back a pace, putting some much needed space between them.

"Not nearly so well as I know you, I expect." The young woman chuckled merrily. "But that won't last for long. I'm your—what did he call it? Your helper? Your attendant? Your... companion. Yes, that's it. Your companion."

Cosette glanced over her shoulder as a familiar hand came to rest on her lower back. A surge of relief washed over her, followed swiftly by a wave of consternation when she remembered the filth that clung to her clothes and hair.

"I see you've met Gretta." The king raised an eyebrow, suppressing a smile. "She's been very eager to meet you."

"I–I– can see that." Cosette glanced from the king to Gretta and back again. She tried to think of something else to say, but no words came and her stuttered reply melted into silence. Embarrassed, she lowered her eyes.

"The two of you are bound to become very good friends." The king placed a hand upon each of their shoulders. "I chose you especially for each other. But I digress." He leaned toward the young woman. "Our Cosette has endured a long and difficult journey, Gretta. She is weary and needs nourishment. It is time you saw her home."

His eyes crinkled as he turned to eye Cosette. Gently cupping her chin in his hand, he lifted her face toward his and waited for her to meet his gaze. "Be at rest, my beloved. We shall meet again soon." With that, the king pressed a gentle kiss to Cosette's cheek and disappeared into the crowd.

Cosette stood motionless, staring after the king, her fingers resting lightly upon the cheek he had just kissed. "How could he, in his glory, stoop to lay his lips upon a filthy wretch like me?" She spoke quietly, wonderingly, not realizing she had spoken aloud.

She jumped when Gretta placed a hand on her shoulder and bent to whisper in her ear. "It's because he loves you, Cosette. He never did stop loving you, you know—not for a moment. Even when he was consumed by grief, knowing you had forgotten him. Even when his heart was rent, knowing you spent your nights in the arms of his ancient foe..."

Cosette's chin quivered as memories of her life in Nyoke's dominion churned within her.

"Though he yearned for you and wept for you every moment of every day, he never did stop loving you. To do so would have been to deny his own heart."

Cosette sighed as the river of tears she had tried so hard to restrain burst forth and coursed down her face. With a watery smile, she turned to embrace her new friend. "I'm tired," she murmured.

"Then let's go home so you can rest."

* * *

Cosette followed Gretta through the thinning crowd and into the woods. Happy memories engulfed her as she padded along the ancient footpath behind her companion and excitement lightened her heart. "It's so good to be home, Gretta. How could I ever have forgotten this place?" She bunched her hair behind her head and gazed into the leafy branches.

Gretta stopped and reached for Cosette's hand. "Strange things happen when a person's far from home, I guess." She pressed her forefinger to her bottom lip and shrugged. "That's what the king says, anyway." Urging Cosette forward, she hurried down the path. "I do suppose he's right. He always is, you know."

Cosette's brow wrinkled as she thought about her companion's observation and she grimaced. "I wish I had remembered that."

The girls lapsed into silence as they scurried along the trail. Cosette stumbled a time or two over the worn and knotted roots that crisscrossed the pathway, but Gretta was never far ahead and always seemed to appear at her side exactly when Cosette needed her most.

In time, Cosette's energy ebbed and her feet began to slow, but determined to keep up, she pushed herself forward in anticipation of the long, satisfying rest she knew awaited her at the end of her journey. With Gretta to steady her and encourage her onward, she trudged down the path toward the home she had unwittingly yearned for throughout her life in the forbidden lands. And the closer she came, the lighter her steps grew until she could have sworn she actually flew.

The trees thinned as they approached the edge of the towering oakwood. Cosette smiled wistfully as her eyes surveyed the meadow before her, strewn with wildflowers and alive with the fluttering wings of colourful butterflies.

"It's beautiful, isn't it?" Gretta's hushed voice broke the stillness.

Cosette nodded.

"Don't worry, we'll come back to enjoy it again later." Gretta held out her hand. "After you've eaten and slept—if you want to, that is."

Cosette slid her hand into Gretta's. Her head whirled as she tried to process the wonders that bombarded her in this land she once called home. Everything seemed so much grander than she remembered. Grander, more majestic, more thrilling. With a gentle tug, her companion drew her forward and led her along the tree line toward a great, golden gate, flung open to the lands beyond. Cosette recalled the gate from her childhood, although she had never before known it to be open, and she stopped, wary of where her guide was leading her.

"Gretta..." she paused, her mouth suddenly dry. "Where are we going?" Suspicion laced her voice as she drew her hand back to her side.

Gretta cocked her head, her forehead wrinkling. "Home."

"I thought my home was that way." Cosette pointed across the meadow and into the heart of the garden where the River of Delights glinted in the afternoon sun.

"Oh." Gretta nodded, her shoulders relaxing. "Of course. It's true that was once your home, Cosette, but your home no longer lies within the walls of the garden. A new home has been prepared especially for the children of the king within the gates of the city. It's more wonderful than you could possibly imagine."

Cosette squinted, trying to catch a glimpse of the city's shining turrets and gilded domes through the open gate. Enraptured by the sight before her, she didn't notice that Manuél had joined them until his hushed voice fell like a gentle breeze upon her ear.

"On the day that our daddy made you and gave you a home in the garden, I presented him with the plans for this great city so there would be a place where we could live together forever." A soft chuckle rippled the air. "He didn't stop working on that city until every last board had been pounded and every last brick laid."

Cosette turned to him. She could hear the reverence and pride in his voice when he spoke of their daddy. "Will the glory never end?" she sighed.

With a smile that beamed brighter than the midday sun, Manuél opened his arms to her and she fell into his embrace. "Not for as long as our daddy lives, beloved. Not for as long as our daddy lives." He drew back to look her in the eye and gently swept a lock of hair from her face. "And he's going to live forever!"

* * *

Cosette pressed a trembling hand to her mouth as they walked through the golden gate and into the city. Magnificence and grandeur surrounded her on every side. Dwarfed by the spiralling towers and enthralled by the floating gardens that lined the main thoroughfare, she followed Gretta along the golden-hued streets, her eyes roving from one glorious sight to the next. Before long, they stopped at a beautiful stone cottage situated on the grassy bank of the River of Delights.

When Cosette's eyes fell upon Ilana standing in the doorway of the cottage, she couldn't contain the squeal of joy that welled up within her. Sprinting up the cobbled pathway, she threw herself into Ilana's waiting embrace and laughed as they clung to each other and swayed.

With a final squeeze, Cosette stepped back, her hands coming to rest on Ilana's shoulders. "What are you doing here?" She gave Ilana a playful shove and eyed her expectantly.

"Why, I live here, my dear." Ilana affected a regal pose and drew an open palm to her chest in feigned surprise. "With Yaletta, my companion." She gestured expansively toward the grinning young woman by her side.

A fit of giggles seized them as their bemused companions herded them through the door and into the cozy sitting room of the quaint little cottage prepared for them by the king.

"Wow..." Cosette's hand leapt to her mouth as she stared around her at the wood-panelled walls and intricately woven carpet.

"You can say that again." Ilana grinned.

"Wow," Cosette repeated, and they both began to laugh.

The two girls spoke little as they sat side by side on the padded birch-wood rockers scattered around the stone fireplace in the corner of the sitting room. Lulled by the dance of the flickering embers, Cosette fell into a deep and dreamless sleep, waking only briefly when Gretta led her to a room and tucked her into the softest, most luxurious bed she had ever known.

"I love you, Manuél," she murmured as she rolled onto her belly and pulled the covers up around her ears. "I'm so glad to be home."

* * *

"Are you awake?" Ilana shook Cosette's shoulder insistently, her voice rising. "It's morning!"

Cosette threw off the velvety blanket that had warmed her through the night, and leapt to her feet. Sunlight streamed through the open window of their chamber, filling the room with warmth and light.

"So, what do you think we should do tod—"

The door opened behind them and they turned as one to see Gretta setting a tray of steaming oatmeal on a little table in the centre of the room. "Cosette... Ilana..." Her eyes twinkled as she nodded at each of them in turn. "What a beautiful morning! I'm so glad to see you are up. I do hope you slept well." She pulled a chair out from the table.

The girls looked at each other and grinned.

"Come now. Sit and eat, then we'll see to baths and get you dressed for your audience with the king," Gretta continued. She bobbed her head comically as she spoke. "It wouldn't do to keep him waiting now, would it?"

The girls obediently took their places at the little tea table. Cosette added sugar and cream to her oatmeal and stirred it absently, her brows drawn in thought. Ilana, obviously less interested in the fare before her than she was in the cryptic words of Cosette's companion, pelted Gretta with a barrage of questions. Cosette smiled as she raised her spoon to her mouth, her eyes fixed on Gretta; she, too, was curious.

"What do you mean, an audience?" Ilana questioned. Not waiting for a reply, she rushed on, "What is an audience anyway? What do you do at an audience? Will anyone else be there? Who all has been called to attend?"

All three looked up, questions forgotten, as Yaletta bustled through the door bearing two long gowns woven from the finest white silk and intricately embroidered with strands of red, blue and gold. The necklines were studded with the most lustrous pearls any of them had ever seen and a thin double chain of purest gold lay draped between glittering sapphire clasps pinned to each shoulder. The gowns were sleeveless and flowing, each accompanied by a soft, scarlet under blouse and cinched at the waist with a long, tasselled sash.

Ilana gasped. "Are those for us?" She stood and walked slowly toward the magnificent robes. Her jaw dropped as she reached out to touch one of the dresses, but before her hand could touch the lustrous fabric, she stopped, her eyes flickering toward the woman still holding the glorious garments.

Yaletta smiled and offered the larger of the two robes to Ilana. "Yes, they are for you. Manuél brought them by this morning." She smiled as Ilana rubbed the satiny fabric between her thumb and forefinger. "This one is yours and the other belongs to Cosette."

Yaletta took the gowns and arranged them carefully in the closet. "But you really ought to hurry, dear." She placed the two sets of soft linen undergarments she had tucked under her arm on the bureau. "The king is expecting you."

As if a gong had been struck, the room erupted in a flurry of activity. Ilana hurried to the table to eat her breakfast. Baths were drawn and Gretta and Yaletta skillfully arranged the girls' hair, adorning their curls with fine silk ribbons and strings of pearls before helping them into their glorious new robes. Ready at last, Cosette and Ilana slipped their feet into the soft, silken slippers Manuél had provided and stood before the oval mirror in the corner of their bedroom.

The transformation was radical. Cosette stared at her reflection in the glass, a slow smile lighting her eyes as she lifted a hand to touch her chest, her hair, her lips.

"Beautiful!" Gretta exclaimed. Giggling, Cosette enveloped her companion in a fierce hug. Though they hadn't known her for long, she and Ilana had already become accustomed to Gretta's endless prattle and had not expected her succinct declaration.

Gretta cleared her throat as she stepped out of Cosette's embrace, clearly moved by her new friend's show of affection. "Come now, we must go." She smoothed a wrinkle from Cosette's sleeve and straightened the tassels on her sash. "You are, indeed, glorious, my dear ones." She let her gaze rest upon them for a long moment before nodding with satisfaction. "You so remind me of him."

"Of him?" Cosette smiled and Ilana nudged her when they realized they had spoken in unison.

"Why of the king, of course," Gretta babbled, astonished that they should even need to ask. "You are, after all, his children—and of Manuél, too, I might add. The two of them are so alike."

Ilana and Cosette looked at each other in awe, then turned back to peer at themselves in the mirror.

Gretta stepped up behind them and slipped her arms around their waists. "Yes, you remind me of both the king and Manuél. Two peas in a pod are those two, always thinking and acting as one. The resemblance is striking, actually. It's a wonder I didn't notice it before."

"Are you three coming?" Yaletta rushed into the room, stopping mid-step as soon as she saw the girls. "My, my! Aren't you the very picture of the king himself." She shook her head and sighed. "Why there's no question whose children you are."

The girls lowered their eyes, humbled by the praise. The thought that they might resemble their daddy raised goosebumps on Cosette's arms and a rush of heat warmed her face.

"Come, my friends, we must go." Yaletta shooed the girls toward the door. "The king awaits you, and the others have already begun to assemble in the Hall of Judgement."

"The Hall of Judgement?" Cosette gulped. Her face slackened and she swayed.

Gretta reached gentle hands to steady her and guided her to a chair. "Don't be afraid, Cosette." She pressed a hand to each of Cosette's cheeks and bent to look her in the eyes. "Let your heart rest in peace and trust Manuél. He has not returned you to the arms of your father only to let you be destroyed."

Cosette squeezed her eyes shut, recalling her promise to Manuél. Gretta was right; she must not give in to her fear. *I will trust Manuél.* She repeated the words like a mantra, her mouth carefully forming each, though she whispered them deep within her heart. *I will trust Manuél. I will trust Manuél.*

* * *

Cosette clutched Ilana's hand as they joined the cluster of frightened children approaching the great Hall of Judgement. The pounding of her heart echoed in her ears and her breath tightened in her chest. *This is it.* She sniffled softly and offered a quavering smile at the answering squeeze of Ilana's hand in hers, though it did little to comfort her. The great marble edifice loomed above them as they drew nearer and Cosette's courage failed her. *What are we going to do?*

Inside the Hall of Judgement, all heads were bowed as Cosette and Ilana followed a stone-faced giant toward the seats prepared for them. All was quiet save for the music of a lone flautist filling the hall with the heart-rending lament Jaired had first sung to Cosette as she lay, near death, back in Nyoke's compound. Yet, instead of infusing her spirit with hope as it had then, the music crushed her heart with the agony of grief. She staggered to a hardwood bench and fell to her knees in front of it, her breath coming in great wracking gasps. Kneeling on the cold, marble floor, she wept into her hands, overwhelmed by the sorrow that engulfed her, overcome by the shame that descended upon her heart.

Cocooned in her own private world of pain, Cosette hardly noticed the stilling of the crowd as the king stepped onto the dais. Yet she couldn't miss the gasp of awe that rushed through the room when he took his place on the magnificent sapphire throne overlooking the gallery. His iridescent robes glowed in the dim light of the hall and his royal sceptre glinted in the early morning rays filtering through the stained glass windows. Splendour crowned his head as he perused his trembling subjects.

She pushed herself back onto the bench, straining to see as Manuél entered the hall and seated himself on the magnificent throne at the king's right hand. Clad in robes of purest white, his resemblance to his father was more poignant than ever. Could it really be true that she resembled them both?

Manuél swept his eyes over the beleaguered group of pilgrims fidgeting in the seats before him. They looked so beautiful arrayed in the regal robes he had prepared for them. If only they could see themselves as he saw them. Compassion filled him as he gazed upon each face. They were frightened, penitent, ashamed. Far from the joyful pilgrims he had carried home. While their choices had ensured for them a difficult path, their hearts yet beat in rhythm with his own, even as his heart beat in rhythm with that of their father. How desperately they wanted to please, yet how often they found themselves vexed by trouble of their own making. He knew they were curious, willful, impulsive; they couldn't help themselves. Yet, wanderers though they be, he loved them. Who was it that once said that the good that he would, he did not and the evil he abhorred, that he did? It described his beloved ones perfectly. But no longer. Though they but saw it in part, they had been changed, renewed, transformed by their trust in him and their love for the king. They were not the same as they once were. Through their suffering, their pain, their betrayal, they had been made perfect, and they belonged to him.

Sensitive to the turmoil he knew writhed within each heart, Manuél looked to the king and nodded, signalling his readiness to begin.

* * *

A trumpet call rent the air and Cosette jumped, furiously wiping her eyes with her sleeve as she scrambled to stand. Her heart galloped against her ribs and her breath came in short, shallow puffs as she stared at the kingly duo seated upon the dais. With a lift of his brow, Manuél caught her eye and his lips curved in a reassuring smile.

"Breathe," she instructed herself. "Breathe." Her eyes never leaving his, she blew out a long, uneven breath and tried to smile, but she couldn't keep her chin from quivering. His eyes warmed with understanding and a love she could not comprehend pulsed through them. Cosette forced herself to focus on the king as the final notes of the trumpet faded and he raised his sceptre to the heavens.

"Let us proceed." His solemn pronouncement echoed in the great hall, ricocheting around the room as it rose to reach the furthermost corners. "Be seated."

A sudden flurry of activity riffled through the hall as the children of the king hastened to obey his command. Cosette lowered herself to the bench, her back stiff, her shoulders tense. A sinking feeling burned beneath her ribs and she shifted self-consciously in her seat, absently smoothing her robe before forcing her twitching hands to rest on her lap.

"Let him who would accuse the children of the king come forward." The king's voice intoned.

A movement near the corner of the dais caught Cosette's eye and she slid forward on the bench, her knuckles white as she grasped the back of the seat in front of her. *Nyoke!* "How did he get here?" she hissed, her whisper barely audible among the rising voices of the crowd. It seemed everyone was asking the same question.

Cosette's hands grew clammy and she shrank back in her seat, frantically fighting to avoid his arrogant gaze. A sinister grin cracked the face of the one she abhorred and she wondered if he had already seen her. Every second seemed an eternity as silence once more enveloped them and a great heaviness filled the hall.

"Ahem." Nyoke cleared his throat grandly. "With whom shall I begin? Let me see..." His voice trailed off as he slowly swept the room, looking for his first victim.

Cosette sucked in a breath when his eyes came to rest upon her.

"Why Cosette," his honeyed voice purred, "how lovely it is to see you here, my *dear*." His emphasis on the word *dear* chilled her and she shuddered, bracing herself for what was to come. Abruptly, his voice changed and he looked to the king. "The prosecution calls Cosette Theophilus to the stand."

Cosette felt, more than heard, the sudden rush of air whistle past her ear as Ilana gasped and the room began to spin. A shiver of foreboding tingled up her spine and she looked to the king, sensing the gravity of her plight in his tight smile. He was nodding at her now, his sceptre extended, inviting—nay, commanding—her to come forward.

Certain she would be unable to bear the weight of the chastisement to come, Cosette shifted her pleading gaze to Manuél. Tears sprang to her eyes as he slowly blinked and nodded, a gentle smile tipping the corners of his lips. He mouthed something, but she couldn't quite make out what it was. It looked like *trust me*, but she couldn't be sure and she dropped her eyes.

Alternatives exhausted, Cosette stood and edged her way to the aisle, steadying herself on the backs of the seats before her as distraught faces looked on. As she neared the end of the row, a familiar hand squeezed hers and she glanced up to see Jaired. Their eyes met and he dipped his head reassuringly, but she couldn't muster a smile in response. She paused before slipping into the aisle and took a deep breath, then stumbled toward the box-like riser before the dais on which she was directed to stand. Alone and exposed, she wobbled up the steps, her cheeks burning, her shoulders slumped. Her legs quaked with the effort and she lurched forward. With a final sway, she fell to her knees as the accuser began his tirade.

"Now this is a woman I know all too well," he intoned. "She is a wanton and unscrupulous woman, a woman who has lived a life of unquestionable wickedness and thrived on the perversity of others. Listen as I list for you but a sampling of her sins: First, she disregarded the will of her sovereign and selfishly chose to disobey his commands." He looked pointedly at Cosette as he spoke, barely suppressing a smirk at her hiccupping sobs.

"She repeatedly betrayed the heart of her king and turned to his enemies for solace. She *rewarded* every man who promised her pleasure and harboured bitterness and resentment toward each in her heart when he did not deliver. She has seethed with anger and boiled with hatred to the point where she has threatened murder. She even took the life of the defenceless child growing within her womb." His voice increased in volume as he turned to face the king.

"She is a liar... a deceiver... a cheater... a thief... and she honours not those who have been put in authority over her. If there is a law to be broken, this woman has broken it, and it is time that she be held accountable."

Cosette rocked convulsively upon the platform, her face buried in her hands, her shoulders shuddering with the force of the great, wailing sobs that escaped her soul as Nyoke pummelled her with his accusations. They were true—every last one of them—and her heart reeled at the thought. He knew it; she knew it; the king knew it; everyone knew it. She was all that he had said and more.

"How do you plead?"

Cosette gulped for air as the king's voice replaced the vitriolic tirade of the accuser. How *did* she plead? She considered for a moment the alternatives, though she knew they were few. How could she plead anything but guilty? That was exactly what she was: guilty of betraying the love her father had lavished upon her, guilty of disobeying his command, guilty of consorting with the enemy and letting evil consume her. Guilty, guilty, guilty! How could she deny what they all knew to be true?

"Guilty," came her whimpered reply. "Guilty. Guilty. Guilty." Her rising wails filled the hall and she fell prostrate before the king, her hopes dashed on the shores of her past. "Gui-i-il-ty..."

* * *

Unable to bear her pain any longer, Manuél rose from his seat on the dais and stepped toward Cosette, placing himself directly between her and the king. Glancing at the accuser, he turned toward his father and approached the throne. Boldly. Confidently. His head held high. Cosette's wailing diminished as his powerful voice echoed through the auditorium.

"It is true that this woman stands accused of many evils." Not a breath could be heard in the great Hall of Judgement as his sonorous voice rang through the room. "Yet I hereby absolve her of all guilt, for she is mine."

A hopeful gasp rippled through the assembly as every eye turned to witness the response of the king. With no need for further testimony, the king nodded his head and extended to Cosette the Sceptre of Mercy. "The court finds the defendant, Cosette Theophilus, not guilty."

A roar of approval erupted from the crowd.

"Case dismissed."

Cosette raised her head, dazed. *That's it?* Her eyes wandered from the king to his sceptre and back before coming to rest on Manuél, and her heart swelled within her. He had rescued her. Again. He had placed himself between her and the judgement seat and had claimed her, defiled though she be, as his own. She studied his hand as he reached for her, then raised her eyes to see his radiant smile shining upon her and the plumbless depths of his eyes overflowing with joy. Overwhelmed, she pressed her head to his feet and clung to him as a fresh flood of tears swept over her.

The murmuring of the crowd intensified as Manuél bent to lift Cosette's face in his hands, urging her to stand. Gentle and soft, they smoothed the tears from beneath her eyes and traced the shape of her cheek. "You are mine, Cosette." His voice was pitched so only she could hear. "You always have been. I'm not going to let anyone tear you from my grasp."

Cosette swallowed hard and covered his hands with hers.

"You are dearer to me than you could possibly know, little lamb. No matter where you have been, no matter what you have done, no matter what anyone else says, I love you."

Hardly daring to breathe, Cosette let his words settle in her heart, trying to grasp all that he was offering.

"Arise, beloved. Arise and fear not." He slid his hands down her arms and drew her upward as he spoke. Cosette lowered her eyes as the joy of her newfound freedom fought with the remnants of her shame and she groaned.

"Look at me, Cosette." His voice was firm, yet inviting, and she lifted her head once more. "You are not the woman you once were. The life of evil you once called your own is no longer yours, for you are mine." She sniffed back a sob as the reality of his claim took root in her heart. "I have released you from the guilt of your transgressions and removed from you the chains of sin that bound you to the one who would see you destroyed."

Manuél's eyes twinkled as he bent to place a lingering kiss upon her forehead, his whispered words meant only for her. "I told you that you could trust me."

He stepped back and winked at her, a teasing smile twitching at the corner of his lips, and a bubble of laughter burst within her. Forgetting all else, she threw herself into his arms and surrendered herself to his embrace. "I love you, Manuél. I love you *and* I trust you." She stepped back to look him in the eyes. "Never again will I doubt your word."

A nod from the king caught Cosette's eye and she looked up to see his radiant smile beaming upon her. "Come, daughter, and sit with me upon my throne." His voice rumbled like thunder. "Our job is not yet done for we still must decide what to do with your brothers and sisters."

Cosette's brow puckered as she looked to Manuél, but his answering smile heartened her and, head held high, she stepped onto the dais. She felt like a child again as she hurried toward the king. A shy smile parted her lips as she remembered that final day on the green and she was struck by how much, and yet how little, had actually changed since then. Though much had transpired since that life-changing day, the king had remained constant. She had changed. Her brothers and sisters had changed. The landscape had changed. But the king had not changed. A thrill of joy tingled through her at the thought.

Closing the space between them, Cosette reached for the hand her father extended and allowed him to draw her near. Goosebumps rippled down her arms when he encircled her waist with his arm, drawing her to sit on the edge of his throne. It felt good. Very good. She was home with her daddy. At last. The certainty that all would be well engraved itself upon her heart and she let out a long, slow breath. Recalling the last time she had sat like this in his arms, Cosette leaned in close to whisper, "Daddy, why are your eyes wet?" She cocked her head to one side, just as she had so many years before and raised an eyebrow as she waited for his response.

Sharing a secret smile, he winked at her and thumbed a tear from her cheek then turned once more to face the accuser. "Let's get on with this," he bellowed. "Call the next defendant."

* * *

Incensed by the inconceivable events unfolding before him, the accuser scowled in silent rebellion. The futility of his task now clear, he straightened, welcoming the rage that bubbled up from within; it gave him strength. "I may not be able to destroy them," he seethed, his words quiet and clipped as they hissed from between his tightly clenched teeth, "but I can make them quake."

Glowering at the accused, his slitted eyes surveyed the congregants, searching for signs of fear, but the mood in the throne room had changed.

The relentless terror that had permeated the room but moments before was gone, replaced by a solemn, yet growing jubilance as the hearts of the accused turned to their defender, gratefully certain of their standing in him. Bereft of power, the accuser ground his teeth as he stepped to the podium to continue his senseless barrage, his anger growing with each foiled indictment as defendant after defendant took the stand. The prince had won.

* * *

It was long after sunset when the king pronounced his verdict on the final defendant and welcomed him into Manuél's happy throng. The adversary seethed as he squinted at the prince, appalled by the transformation of the king's children. Hatred emanating from his eyes, he charged toward the king, spewing accusations at the great monarch. "How dare you rob me of what is rightfully mine. They're only going to betray you again, you know. You don't really think they're going to change, do you?"

The king rose to his feet. "Enough." The command echoed through the cavernous room and Nyoke's mouth snapped shut. "Guards, bind him and take him to the abyss."

No sooner had the words left the king's mouth, than four burly guards swept onto the dais and set upon the enraged accuser, pinning him to the floor. The piercing shrieks of the enemy rose above the metallic clanking of the heavy iron chains they used to bind him as he thrashed about in defiance of the king's command. Yet, faithful to the will of the king, the guards refused to let him go.

Overwhelmed by the stunning turn of events, Cosette watched her tormentor in disbelief, gnawing her knuckle as she fought to restrain the alternating waves of horror and relief that warred within her. Would the strength of the guards be sufficient to uphold the command of the king or would the will of Nyoke prevail?

She cringed when the evil one's shrieks rose in intensity, and squeezed her eyes shut to block out the horrifying scene as she pressed her hands to her ears in a futile attempt to silence his screams. How she heard the quiet voice of her daddy above the screeching of the enemy, she could not say, yet like a gentle breeze in the midst of a hurricane, it fell upon her ears, soft, resonant, commanding. "It's over, Nyoke. Be still."

Cosette snapped her head up at the sudden silence that filled the room.

"You knew it could end no other way." A hint of sadness tinged the king's voice. "You knew you would one day be forced to concede defeat."

Not a sound could be heard as the king paused, his eyes trained upon his foe. "This is that day."

The string of snarled curses that followed, though no doubt intended as a show of strength, was as pitiful as it was acerbic. Confused, Cosette looked up in time to catch a solemn glance pass between the king and his son and wondered at the compassion she saw reflected in their eyes. But there was little time to speculate. At a nod from the king, Manuél stepped forward and, motioning the guards aside, gripped Nyoke's arm to propel him from the dais. The adversary flinched at the touch of her beloved and yanked his arm away in an attempt to dislodge the hand of the prince, but to no avail. With captive firmly in hand, Manuél stepped regally from the dais, herding the struggling prisoner before him as easily as he might a squalling child.

The four guards fell into place behind them as the prince led Nyoke across the front of the room toward a rough-hewn door over which were carved the words, *Door of Damnation*. The stone-faced guards slowed as they approached the door, forming a vanguard behind the prince, their swords drawn in readiness should the prisoner attempt to bolt.

As they approached the door, the awareness that the end was upon him both terrified and infuriated the once-powerful adversary. His voice caught in his throat, silencing the incessant shrieks that filled the air, and his temples throbbed as he stepped ever closer to the abyss before him. Time slowed, each second lasting an eternity as the truth became clear. The king was right; it could have ended no other way.

Suddenly cognizant of the silence that filled the Hall of Judgement, he turned his squinty-eyed glare on the king, daring him to give the final command—the command that would end the war for all eternity. His lips lifted in a final smirk as he leered at his foe. The king might think this was the end, but it wasn't. Not if he had anything to say about it.

His face set, the adversary watched as the king's head lowered in the slightest of nods. Nyoke's eyes narrowed as he followed the king's gaze, noting the answering nod of Manuél as he spoke the word that would clinch the evil one's fate forever. Stunned, he watched the prince's mouth open, distinctly forming each individual sound, before it actually penetrated his consciousness. "N-n-n-n-ow-ow-ow-ow-w-w-w-w." It was a command. From his sovereign. Whether he claimed him as such or not, he had to obey. There was no other choice.

The Door of the Damned loomed before him as the steely grip of the prince propelled him forward. *This is it. It's really going to happen.* His heart hammered in his chest and he gulped for air. *I cannot let the king win. I will not. I* won't. In one final act of defiance, the accursed snake cursed the king he could not defy and leapt into the darkness beyond.

* * *

Not a muscle moved in the throne room as the adversary's horrifying shriek faded into silence. Nyoke was gone. The enemy had been defeated. They were free. It took but a moment for the realization to hit before the room erupted in deafening shouts of victory and joyful songs of praise.

Cosette gaped at the empty doorway, only dimly aware of the celebration whirling on around her. She squeezed her eyes shut and opened them again, but the chilling arch remained as dark and empty as it had been before. He was gone. For good. He would not be coming back.

Biting her lower lip, she watched, wide-eyed, as Manuél stepped toward the door and struck the lintel three ringing blows with the flat of the king's sword. Without warning, an ear-splitting rumble rattled through the hall and she fell to the floor, clasping her hands to her ears as the great rock wall in which the door had stood tumbled into the abyss.

As the dust began to settle and the falling debris came to rest, Cosette wobbled to her feet, coughing and rubbing her eyes. The startled looks on the faces of her brothers and sisters matched the uneasy feeling growing in the pit of her stomach. What was happening?

Blinking rapidly, Cosette scanned the room, intent on finding Manuél. "Manu..."

Her impassioned cry died on her lips as her eyes came to rest on a sight more glorious than any Cosette ever could have imagined. Just beyond the crumbled stone wall of the Hall of Judgement lay a grand banqueting hall, separated from them by a flower-bedecked wall of glass-like tanzanite down which cascaded a veil of sparkling water.

"Look!" someone shouted. "Over there!"

Cosette stared in amazement at the enormity of the room before her, all thoughts of the day's events forgotten. Longer than Glory Falls was high and as wide as the entire oakwood, the great hall stretched almost further than her eyes could see. Its domed ceiling reached far into the heavens, studded with an array of twinkling gemstones that reminded her of stars sparkling in the midnight sky. Light shimmered through the skylight that crowned the great dome to dance on a floor wrought of finest crystal and bounce off walls of iridescent pearl.

"Ilana?" she cried, searching the room for her friend, only to find her already by her side. She reached out to squeeze Ilana's hand. "Do you see?"

Ilana bobbed her head as they pressed closer to the wall to peer through the delicate curtain of falling water.

Cosette gazed in wonder at the long, rectangular table, draped in fine, white linen and embroidered with threads of scarlet and gold. It ran the length of the room and was festooned with garlands of delicate blue freesia and golden-hued starflower entwined with bouquets of the most beautiful red roses imaginable. The table was set for a great feast and she wondered at the sight. Transfixed, Cosette edged closer to the tanzanite wall and pressed her palms against its lustrous surface. What she wouldn't give to sit at that table.

* * *

"Come, my children!" The booming voice of the king jarred Cosette from her thoughts and she whirled around to see him making his way through the crowd of enraptured pilgrims pressing their noses against the glassy wall. "Your bridegroom awaits."

"Bridegroom?" Cosette echoed, much louder than she had intended. She cringed at the obvious incredulity that tinged her voice. Turning to look at Ilana, she shrugged, recognizing her own confusion mirrored in the eyes of her friend.

"I think that's what he said." Ilana folded her hands behind her back. "I'm pretty sure..."

"Of course it is, my friends!" Cosette's mouth fell open as the king joined them, throwing an arm around each of their shoulders. "And we wouldn't want to keep him waiting now, would we?" Heat rose to stain her cheeks as he winked at her playfully and gave her shoulder an affectionate squeeze.

"Come, my children," he boomed once more, turning to include the rest in his invitation. "It is time." His deep voice thrummed through Cosette's body and she looked at him in wonder. "The witnesses have gathered and the bridegroom has arrived. Let us go forth to meet him."

As her brothers and sisters scurried to gather behind the unlikely trio, Cosette scanned the room, expecting to see the austere, stone-hewn edifice of the judgement hall they had entered that morning. Bewildered, her heart began to race, her mind awhirl as she surveyed the room before her.

"Cosette. Cosette!"

Cosette jerked her head toward the urgent whisper, embarrassed by her momentary lapse. Ilana leaned toward her. "Do you see what I see?"

"You mean, the Hall of Judgement?"

"I don't think there is a Hall of Judgement anymore." Ilana's eyes gleamed with excitement. "Look at it, Cosette!" she exclaimed, waving her arm in front of her. "Look!"

Cosette passed a hand over her eyes and blinked. The impenetrable rock walls now rippled with vivid tapestries, and golden candelabrum, wreathed with rings of milky white roses and gauzy purple bows, lined the dais. The riser upon which she had so recently stood in shame had been removed, replaced by an elegant set of marble stairs leading to the stage above. And the flowers! Everywhere there were flowers—

fragrant and bursting with life. Birds of Paradise presiding over clustered anthurium and bountiful bouquets of purple hibiscus graced the ends of each row of seats.

Cosette's hand fluttered to her chest. "Is someone getting married?"

"They certainly are."

Both girls started at the conspiratorial voice of the king as he leaned forward to join their whispered conversation. A nervous giggle escaped Cosette and she straightened to gaze again on the palatial cathedral before her.

"Look at all those people," Ilana breathed. She shook her head slowly. "I've never seen so many people in all my life."

"Wait, Ilana, look! Isn't that Gretta? And there's Yaletta, I'm sure of it. Over there, on the dais, behind..."

"Manuél?" The girls gasped simultaneously, their eyes turning to lock on the king. His twinkling eyes danced and a bemused smile played at the corners of his mouth as he gazed into their questioning eyes.

"Have you not guessed, dear ones?"

"Guessed what?" Cosette tilted her head.

"There *is* going to be a wedding. Right now. Today!" he crowed. "See? Even now, the bridegroom awaits the arrival of his bride." He gestured toward the dais where Manuél paced, his hands steepled before him.

Cosette glanced at Ilana and lifted a shoulder.

"But who's getting married?" Ilana demanded, looking back at the king.

"Do you not see him, surrounded by a multitude of beaming witnesses, pacing like a tiger yearning for the chase, hardly able to contain his passion?"

"Manuél?" The girls' incredulous voices exploded as one. "But who will be his bride?"

"You, of course."

It took a moment for the king's response to register.

"Me?" Cosette blinked.

"Yes." The king swept his hand over the pressing crowd. "You, and Ilana, and Jaired... All the children my son has brought forth from the land of sorrow." His voice increased in volume with each proclamation until every eye rested upon him.

The king gave the girls a playful wink and turned to address his astounded children. "Come, my beloved, your bridegroom is loath to wait any longer."

Triumphant music filled the hall as he extended his arms to Cosette and Ilana, and strode eagerly toward the dais.

* * *

Cosette breathed deeply of the alluring fragrance perfuming the cathedral as she made her way down the aisle past row after row of happy, yet unfamiliar faces, her hand resting lightly on top of the king's. Her stomach fluttered as they climbed the stairs of the dais until she looked up and saw the eyes of Manuél upon her. Dark and lustrous, they radiated unimaginable love and consumed her every fear. She was his. She always had been. That was what he had said, and this was what he had meant. A shiver quivered up her spine and she drew her hand slowly to her chest. This was a fairytale come true.

Separating himself from his awestruck little flock, the king strode across the stage toward Manuél and his entourage. He clapped his hand upon his son's shoulder and gave him a squeeze, a knowing smile passing between them.

"Behold, my son—your bride."

A chorus of cheers rose from the crowd of witnesses pressing in behind Manuél as the king's triumphant cry reverberated throughout the room, and Cosette couldn't help but join the chorus with her own shout of joy.

"Do you, Manuél, take these, my children, to be your bride?" An expectant hush fell over the assembly. "Will you love her, Manuél? Will you treasure her and care for her and take her for your own?"

Cosette looked from father to son and back again. Never had she seen either of them so excited.

"I will!" Manuél threw back his head and crowed. Without waiting for their father's blessing, he bounded toward his bride, his arms flung wide to enfold them as one. "Forever and ever and ever—I will!"

* * *

Excited voices thrummed around Cosette as Gretta ushered her into the royal banqueting hall. She slowed to gaze at the exotic gardens lining the outer walls, entranced by the glorious profusion of colour and the heady fragrance of the floral menagerie. No amount of tugging on Gretta's part could lure Cosette forward as she stared around her in delight. The wall of water she had glimpsed before the ceremony fascinated her and she stepped toward it, longing to plunge her hand into the cascading rivulets. Pure as crystal, the water tumbled from heights unknown to gather into a sparkling pool of swirling water at its base, surrounded by lilies of every hue imaginable. Was this the source of the River of Life—the river from which the dazzling River of Delights flowed, the well from which the healing Spring of Vrede drew its waters? Cosette couldn't help but wonder as she stared into its depths and watched it bubble away beneath the glassy floor of the hall.

"Cosette!"

The urgent whisper startled her and she jerked toward the voice.

"Hurry, Cosette," Gretta pleaded, tugging insistently on her arm. "You must be seated. Manuél is on his way."

Cosette glanced around the room, suddenly aware of the stillness. On either side of the oblong banqueting table, her brothers and sisters sat, glowing with expectancy as they gazed toward a great latticed archway on the wall opposite the waterfall. Behind each stood a faithful companion, hands resting lightly upon the shoulders of his or her charge, face alight with unspeakable joy.

Cosette allowed herself to be led toward an empty seat near the centre of the table, directly across from Ilana and two seats down from Jaired. She cringed at the sound of her chair scraping across the floor as Gretta rushed to seat her, but when no one seemed to notice, she relaxed, thankful for the steadying hands of her companion on her shoulders. Manuél was on his way!

Moments later, a regal fanfare split the air. The children bounded to their feet as two trumpeters appeared, their long golden horns, bedecked with flowing ribbons of purple and scarlet, loosing a chorus of dancing light to spiral around the hall. Gradually the majestic air grew in volume, filling the room with its music and heightening the anticipation of the waiting bride.

"They're coming! They're coming!" someone shouted above the music.

"I can see them!" came a second voice. Excitement buzzed through the happy throng.

"They're almost here!"

Suddenly everyone was talking at once, their jubilant exclamations joining the trumpets in a glorious cacophony of praise. Cosette stood on tiptoe, shifting from foot to foot, straining to catch a glimpse of Manuél as he came through the door. "Manuél!" she shouted, as if her summons would quicken his pace. "Come quickly, Manu…" her voice fell away as the final notes of the fanfare melted into silence and the voices around her stilled.

The king had arrived, and with him, the prince.

Not a breath stirred the air as, side by side, they stepped across the threshold and into the room.

"His majesty, the king and his royal son, Prince Manuél," a sonorous voice intoned.

Lusty cheers erupted from the guests as the two smiling figures stepped toward the table. Cosette clasped her hands against her galloping heart, her eyes fixed upon her beloved as he headed toward his seat at the end of the table. He stopped often along the way to whisper a word of endearment or squeeze an outstretched hand. As he passed, he caught Cosette's eye and winked, mouthing the unmistakable words, "I love you."

"I love you, too," she mouthed back, desperate that he should know. And he smiled—a big, beaming smile that fluttered to her heart and made her spirit take wing.

When Manuél and his father at last took their seats, the feast began. Succulent vegetables of every colour were set upon the table along with savoury dishes of all kinds. An array of exotic compotes drew Cosette's eye and tantalized her nose, though she didn't quite know what they were. Curious, she looked from dish to dish, licking her lips in anticipation.

"May I have some of that?" Cosette pointed to an airy pink concoction at Ilana's elbow.

"The blueberry-pomegranate soufflé?" Gretta asked innocently.

"Why of course, Gretta," she responded in kind. "However could I have forgotten?"

They were still giggling when a white-jacketed steward approached, offering them goblets of sparkling red wine. Cosette watched, wide-eyed, as a second steward poured the wine from a ewer she had seen him fill earlier with water drawn from the pool at the base of the falls. Accepting the proffered cup, she smiled her thanks, her eyes darting from jug to cup and back again before coming to rest on the aromatic liquid swirling within. Was there no limit to the wonders of this place?

Wine glass in hand, Cosette settled contentedly in her chair. She was home; she belonged; she was with Manuél. Satisfied at last, her eyes grew heavy and her breathing slowed as strains of heavenly music floated through the air.

Roused by a sudden movement at the far end of the table, Cosette turned to see the king rising to his feet, his brimming glass raised and a delighted smile framing his regal features. Straightening, she leaned into the table, anxious to hear his every word.

"I'd like to propose a toast," he began.

All eyes turned to meet his as his voice rose to fill the room.

"To my beloved son, the delight of my heart, and to his beloved bride, his glory and joy. You have only just begun to discover the depths of love he holds in trust for you, dear ones. Rejoice in his presence, beloved, and delight in his love for you. For you are his and he is yours—and you both belong to me!"

The king's exultation grew with each pronouncement, accompanied by a chorus of rising affirmations from around the table. Hardly had his words come to an end when the assembly rose to its feet as one with a hearty, "Hear! Hear!"

The clinking and clanking of glasses ceased abruptly when the prince stepped forward, his goblet raised high in the air, his gaze locked intently on the king's. Cosette's eyes darted from father to son and back again, uncertain of which way to look.

"And to our father—the king of glory—whose reign shall last forever and ever. The gracious and merciful, faithful and true, mighty, incorruptible ruler of all. To you we bow with grateful hearts, for we are yours alone."

Happy tears filled Cosette's eyes as glasses tinkled around her and the party began anew. As if from nowhere, servants appeared to clear the tables and the dancing began.

Stepping away from the dance floor, she gazed at Manuél as he twirled among the dancers in graceful time to the music. And then he was there, his hand extended toward her, his eyes alight with desire. "Come, my Cosette—my little pet lamb—let us at last be one."

Cosette's heart skipped a beat at the sound of her beloved's voice, and oblivious to all else, she flew into his arms. As he had done when she was a child, he spun her around and around until she collapsed against his chest, overflowing with a laughter and joy she knew, at last, would never end. With a deep breath, she stepped back to behold once more the one she adored. She could hardly wait to see what would happen next.

> *Eye hath not seen, nor ear heard, neither have entered into the heart of man, the things which God hath prepared for them that love him.* (I Corinthians 2:9, KJV)

A SONG OF JOY

Sing aloud, O daughter Zion; shout, O Israel!
Rejoice and exult with all your heart, O daughter Jerusalem!
The Lord has taken away the judgments against you,
  he has turned away your enemies.
The king of Israel, the LORD is in your midst;
  you shall fear disaster no more.
On that day it shall be said to Jerusalem: Do not fear, O Zion;
  do not let your hands grow weak.
The LORD, your God, is in your midst,
  a warrior who gives victory;
  he will rejoice over you with gladness,
  he will renew you in his love;
he will exult over you with loud singing as on a day of festival.
  I will remove disaster from you,
  so that you will not bear reproach for it.
I will deal with all your oppressors at that time.
And I will save the lame and gather the outcast,
  and I will change their shame into praise
  and renown in all the earth.
  At that time I will bring you home,
  at the time when I gather you;
  for I will make you renowned and praised
among all the peoples of the earth, when I restore your
  fortunes before your eyes, says the LORD.

(Zephaniah 3:14-20, NRSV)

APPENDICES

appendix A
PRACTICAL IDEAS FOR CELEBRATING THE SABBATH

1. DECIDE WHETHER YOU WILL CELEBRATE A SATURDAY OR SUNDAY SABBATH.

I am convinced that the issue is not so much *when* we celebrate the Sabbath as the fact that we *do* celebrate it. Since there are compelling reasons to choose either Saturday *or* Sunday as our day of rest, I would urge you to prayerfully ask God to reveal to you when *He* wants you to celebrate. Then commit to guarding that day from all else, regardless of the sacrifice. It won't always be easy. In fact, the temptation to let it pass will be tremendous at times and has often been my undoing, but there is no day I appreciate more, no day I protect with such ardour. The following list shows the reasons I celebrate a Saturday Sabbath.

- First, God rested on the seventh day. He blessed the Sabbath Day and made it holy. (Exodus 20:11)
- The fourth commandment tells us to remember the Sabbath day and keep it holy. Jesus, Himself, celebrated the Sabbath. We are not told that He instructed His disciples to change the day of celebration.
- My body's rhythm naturally cries for rest from Friday night through Saturday.
- I need Sunday to prepare for the week ahead. Preparing then resting, then expecting to be properly prepared for Monday's classes does not work well for me.
- My personality is such that I do not rest well on the day I go to church as I have to get up too early and I rest best in solitude. My Sabbath celebration does extend somewhat to include the worship service on Sunday morning, though, after which I ease into the work week with breakfast out and planner in hand.

2. CHOOSE APPROPRIATE ACTIVITIES FOR THE SABBATH.

There are many special things I *do* on the Sabbath and some that I *do not*, but in all, I scrupulously avoid reducing the day to a simple list of do's and don'ts. That's what the Pharisees did, turning a day of rich celebration into a day merely to be observed. My list of rules is short and relates directly to what we are told in the Scriptures.

- No Work: Work tends to be different for all of us. I won't turn on my computer, do school work, work around the house, exercise, do a Bible study or plan, but I *will* write, sew, do crafts, go walking, play musical instruments, read, watch movies and enjoy family activities. What you will and won't do will depend very much upon that which you define as work. Sometimes the differentiation between work and non-work is subtle, though. Like this: I love to write. It is not work for me. Writing on the Sabbath is, for me, an act of worship and delight. Yet not all of my writing would pass the toil test (see below). Suppose I have an article to write for our school newsletter or a blurb to write for the local newspaper—something that just has to be done. Then it becomes work. So do I write on the Sabbath? Yes. Do I take it as license to get caught up on my writing backlog? No. Things that pass the toil test for me might not for you or your children or your spouse. That's one of the reasons the pharisaical laws were so excessive and constrictive. In their desire to obey every letter of the law, the rule makers tried to enact laws that would account for every individual in every possible situation. It's also why, I believe, God stuck to the directive, "rest from all toil."
- No Buying or Selling: Strangely enough, I won't refuse to wander through a store or marketplace on the Sabbath, although I do try to avoid it. But if I find myself building up a wish list for later purchase, it's time for me to go. I shop on Friday night for the Sabbath and Sunday morning for the rest of the week. Anything I don't have on the Sabbath I do without, unless, of course, it is essential.

- Go to Church: This can be tricky if you, like me, celebrate the Sabbath from Friday night until Saturday night. That is the reason I extend my Sabbath celebration to include the Sunday morning worship service. That and, of course, the fact that there is no more fitting end to a restful Sabbath than the joy of communion at the Lord's Table.
- Communion with God: One can rest from his/her labours, but unless, in that rest, one's heart is turned to bask in the presence of God, it is nothing but a pause in the chaos of life, not a Sabbath celebration. The Sabbath is unto the Lord and is a time of deep communion, of consciously resting in the glory of His presence, of building our relationship with Him by purposefully spending time with Him. It isn't just time away; it's time away with Him.

3. WORK OUT THE LOGISTICS.

The most important thing I have found is to establish a routine. Marva Dawn was the first to introduce me to the concept of a Sabbath routine in her book *Keeping the Sabbath Wholly* (Wm. B. Eerdmans Publishing Co., Grand Rapids, Michigan, 1989). This is a purely practical matter, not a spiritual directive. Thanks to Marva, I have discovered that as long as I follow a routine for welcoming the Sabbath, I celebrate the Sabbath. When I fail to follow that routine, I inevitably fail to engage in the celebration and succumb to the temptation to maintain my daily chores. Hence, while I am not *bound* by the routine, I do *need* the routine to help me obey God's Word (see below for a sample routine).

4. BE PREPARED, ESPECIALLY IF YOU HAVE CHILDREN TO CONSIDER.

The ideas are endless, but here are a few to get you started. Please note that many of them, including the idea of a Sabbath box, have been derived from Marva Dawn's book (*Keeping the Sabbath Wholly, 1989).*

- Have a Sabbath box filled with special toys or activities your children enjoy only on the Sabbath, but remember to change the

items in the box periodically. Older children, with your guidance, might start to build their own Sabbath boxes.
- Go on a family outing: canoe down a river; walk in a park; visit a museum or a zoo.
- Play a game of soccer, go swimming or skiing, unless of course, like me, those things don't pass the toil test for you.
- Go star gazing late at night and marvel at the beauty of God's creation.
- Read, sing, listen to music, create music together, watch a movie, tell stories, play games.
- Eat your favourite foods.
- Make it a fun day filled with all the things you and your children like best. It should be your favourite day of the week.
- Add variety to your day; don't always do exactly the same thing.
- Don't bother with the laundry or dishes or anything else; make it a true day of rest.
- Let the kids have fun making the meal and enjoy what they make, even if it is a little unusual.
- Turn off the lights and read, or play games by candlelight.
- Turn on the sprinkler and let the kids play while you recline on the sidelines listening to music, reading a book or resting solely in the presence of God.
- Try using a slow cooker to prepare in advance for meals. Just turn it on in the morning and *voila!* instant supper at six.
- When making the kids' lunches on Friday, make an extra set, adding a special treat to each bag, then stash them in the fridge for Sabbath lunch.
- Bake muffins the day before or let the baker of the family make them for breakfast if that passes the toil test for him/her.

A SAMPLE PRE AND POST SABBATH ROUTINE:
Everyone's routine will be different. This is the routine I follow most often:

Friday: Before work, I tidy my apartment and put all work away. Before coming home from work, I go to the gym, get a light supper, shop for the Sabbath and run any final errands. Upon my arrival at home, I put everything away, check and reply to any correspondence, set up the slow cooker and do any final school work.

Friday Evening: Around 9-10 pm, I'm ready to begin. I turn on some quiet and relaxing music, then I turn out the lights and go around lighting a multitude of electric tea lights. Then I enjoy a long, relaxing shower, praying that God will cleanse my heart and mind and soul from sin and renew me by His grace. I dress in special nightwear reserved solely for the Sabbath and settle in my Sabbath chair to bask in the quietness and pray. I begin reading a full book of the Bible, stopping only to meditate upon the words as God directs and going on until I am ready to sleep, then I go to bed without setting an alarm. That is my Sabbath welcome routine.

Sunday Morning: I get up early to go to our morning worship service, after which I go out for breakfast with planner in hand and the week begins anew.

THE TOIL TEST:

Answer each question honestly with a specific activity in mind. If your answers are all in capitals, it's a pass. If even one answer is in lowercase, it is a fail. If you have to reason your way into the uppercase answer, you're working already!

Do I truly enjoy it?
YES   no

Do I *have* to do it/get it done?
yes   NO

Is it edifying?
YES   no

Does it *feel* like work?
yes   NO

Katherine J. Le Gresley

Is it a break from my daily routine?
YES   no

Does anything in Scripture forbid it?
yes   NO

MEMORY BEADS

Memory Beads are related to traditional prayer beads, but differ in that the individual beads do not correspond to specific or repeated prayers. Instead, each bead represents a fluid cache of scriptural truths, Bible verses or revelations interspersed with clear affirmations of trust. I have found them to be a most helpful tool in my quest to resist the devil and combat the attacks of his minions.

HOW TO MAKE A SET OF MEMORY BEADS:
You'll need beading wire or string (length of choice plus 2.5 cm/1"), two crimping beads and a crimping tool (if using wire), a clasp (or key ring), 6 large beads, 5 smaller beads and 28 spacer beads of your choice. To make a necklace, attach one end of the clasp to the beading wire using a crimping bead (or tie it on if using beading string). String the first two spacer beads, then continue with the following pattern: 2 spacers, 1 large bead, 2 spacers, 1 small bead, 2 spacers, 1 large bead, 2 spacers, 1 small bead until 5 beads remain. End with 1 large bead and 4 spacers. Attach the other end of the clasp with the second crimping bead to complete the set of memory beads. Feel free to adjust the number of beads as desired. Beads may also be strung into bracelets or key rings according to personal taste. Alternatively, purchase a short pre-strung set of beads from a craft store and keep it in your pocket. It isn't the form that is important; the important thing is that it is handy and easy to access.

HOW TO USE A SET OF MEMORY BEADS:
When temptation assaults you:
1. Try to specifically identify the attack.
2. Pray that God would remind you of His words for the situation and fill you with his strength and peace.

3. Starting with the first large bead, repeat a Bible verse or truth that He brings to mind that speaks directly to the temptation.
4. Going to the next bead, the smaller one, respond with an affirmation of belief such as, "I will trust in You and not be afraid" or "You are able to keep me from falling." Alternatively, respond with a cry for help such as, "Help me, O Lord! I am weak."
5. Repeat steps 3 and 4 until the adversary abandons the attack.
6. Pray, thanking God for His presence, His promises, His protection, His peace; ask Him to be your strength and help you to rest in Him.
7. When temptation strikes again, be it two minutes later or two days, start at number one all over again.

SAMPLE AFFIRMATIONS AND TRUTHS:
- Surely it is God who saves me. (John 3:16-17)
- I will trust in Him and not be afraid. (Isaiah 12:2, NLT)
- Be still and know that I am God. (Psalm 46:10, NLT)
- My peace I leave with you. (John 14:27, NIV)
- Be strong and of good courage. Do not be dismayed and do not be afraid. I am with you wherever you go. (Joshua 1:9)
- You are able to keep me from falling. (Jude 24)
- His eye is on the sparrow. (Matthew 10:29-31)
- You are my refuge and strength. (Psalm 46:1)
- You will never abandon me. (Hebrews 13:5, NLT)
- You always provide a way out. (I Corinthians 10:13)
- You began a good work in me; You will complete it. (Philippians 1:6)
- Full, perfect and sufficient. (Hebrews 10:14)
- Infinitely more. (Ephesians 3:20)
- Save me, O God! I belong to You. (Joel 2:32)
- You are my hiding place. (Psalm 32:7, NLT)

A SAMPLE PRAYER USING MEMORY BEADS:
(L stands for Large Bead; S stands for Small Bead)
    L1: Fear not! I am with you. (Matthew 28:20) I will not abandon you. You are not alone.

S1: I will trust in You and not be afraid.
L2: Cast all your cares upon me for I care for you. (I Peter 5:7) If I so care for the sparrows, will I not also care for you?
S2: I will trust in You and not be afraid.
L3: I have called you by name; you are Mine. (Isaiah 43:1) No one can snatch you out of My hands. (John 17:27-29)
S3: I will trust in You and not be afraid.
L4: In this world you will have trouble, but take heart, I have overcome the world. (John 16:33, NIV) Nothing is impossible when you put your trust in me. (Matthew 19:26) I will make a way.
S4: I will trust in You and not be afraid.
L5: I am able to keep you from falling. I will allow no trial to come your way that will be more than you can bear. I began a good work in you and I will be faithful to complete it.
S5: I will trust in You and not be afraid.
L6: I alone am your refuge and strength... your hiding place... your high tower. (Psalm 144:2) I long to cover you with My feathers that under My wings you might be at rest. (Psalm 91:4)

appendix C
COME AWAY